IN AN EVIL TIME

Also by Bill Pronzini

✦

BLUE LONESOME
A WASTELAND OF STRANGERS
NOTHING BUT THE NIGHT

IN AN EVIL TIME

Bill Pronzini

Walker & Company ✵ New York

First published in the United States of America in 2001 by
Walker Publishing Company, Inc.
Published simultaneously in Canada by Fitzhenry and Whiteside
Markham, Ontario L3R 4T8

Library of Congress Cataloging-in-Publication Data

Pronzini, Bill
In an evil time / Bill Pronzini.
p. cm.
ISBN 0-8027-3353-0
I. Title.

PS3566.R67 I5 2001
813'.54—dc21   00-049996

Series design by M. J. DiMassi

Printed in the United States of America
2 4 6 8 10 9 7 5 3 1

For Mark Terry

Friend, fellow bookhound,
and cyberspace guide

*For man also knoweth not his time:
as the fishes that are taken in an
evil net, and as the birds that are
caught in the snare; so are the sons
of men snared in an evil time, when
it falleth suddenly upon them.*

—ECCLESIASTES 9:12

PART I

Early to Mid May: Rakubian

1

Wednesday Night

HE sat in the dark Lexus, on the dark street, waiting dry-mouthed for the man he was going to kill.

It was twenty of eleven by the radium dial of his watch; he'd been here an hour and still no sign of Rakubian. Habitual, every minute of the bastard's time jealously budgeted, his weeknight regimen as strict as an army recruit's . . . he should have been home long ago.

Hollis shifted position to ease cramped muscles, the pressure in his bladder. In the cold darkness he could hear the beat of his heart, or imagined he could. Steady. Accelerated but steady. One hand lay quiet in his lap, the other resting on the Colt Woodsman on the seat beside him. Palms and underarms sweat-free. Yet the dryness threatened to close his throat, and he could feel his nerves squirming inside him like a nest of night crawlers.

Across the curving, mist-choked street Rakubian's house loomed black and fuzzy-edged behind its front tangle of yew trees and shrubbery. Small place by St. Francis Wood standards, Spanish style, set well back from the street and well apart from its neighbors. A line of eucalyptus ran along the west side, their elongated shadows thick as unstirred ink. One advantage there. The fog was another. It was dense enough to blur lights and distort shapes, hide him when he crossed to the house and back almost as effectively as it hid him now behind the opaque film of wetness it had laid over the windshield.

The house and property were familiar enough; he and Cassie had visited Angela a few times in the early months, when her marriage had still been tolerable and she'd hidden the truth about Rakubian out of loyalty instead of fear. But at the same time it was an alien place. It had never been hers, was never allowed to be hers, in any way. Furnishings, decor, landscaping, everything Rakubian's, all carefully selected and rigidly governed. As he'd selected and was still trying to govern her even though her divorce had been granted. Rakubian, the control freak. Rakubian, the psychotic abuser.

Once more Hollis let himself remember the night six weeks ago, when she'd finally had enough and the whole ugly truth came out. The details were etched as if with acid on the walls of his mind: Angela standing on the dark porch, Kenny beside her crying and clutching her hand, her face pale and her body hunched, saying in a hurt little girl's voice, "Daddy, can we come home, can we please come home?" Her shamed unveiling of the bruises, welts, scabbed cuts and scratches, old marks as well as new ones. Her confession about the beatings, most of them done with Rakubian's fists but that night with an antique walking stick, and his threats to do worse to her if she didn't obey him. "Discipline," he'd called it—punishment for imagined flirtations, for violating one of his other strict rules of wifely conduct. And the abject, hammered-down misery in her voice when she begged their forgiveness for letting it go on so long, saying, "I would've left him sooner if he'd hurt Kenny, but he didn't . . . terrorized him but never hit him. Kenny doesn't really exist for David because he's another man's son. It's me he's obsessed with, me he wants to hurt."

Hollis held on to the memory, using it like a bellows to stoke the fire of his hate and resolve. It was what would let him get out of the car when Rakubian finally came home, and walk over there and ring the bell, and put a bullet point-blank into his brain when he opened the door.

No words, no hesitation.

Look him in the eye and kill him.

Take a human life, even one as sick and worthless as David Rakubian's. Him, Jack Hollis, law-abiding citizen, staunch believer in the Judeo-Christian ethic and the sanctity of life. Commit cold-blooded, premeditated murder.

But there was simply no other option. He'd been through the alternatives so many times and none of them were any good. If there was one thing the experts agreed on, it was that nothing short of a death—not a divorce decree, not the antistalking laws, not restraining orders, not support groups or round-the-clock bodyguards or the victims moving away and changing their names or even hiring a couple of thugs to break bones—would stop the committed stalker. And that was exactly what Rakubian was, committed and lethal. All the letters and phone calls, the thinly veiled and escalating threats, said so. So did the incident last week: showing up when Angela was at Long's Drugs, trying to force her and Kenny into his car in front of witnesses, punching her when she resisted. They'd had him arrested, and a few hours later he was out on bail. A judge had finally granted a temporary restraining order, and already he'd found ways, sly lawyer's tricks, to circumvent it.

Hollis conjured up another memory—the conversation

in Rakubian's office the day he'd made the mistake of going there to confront him, not long after her return home.

"You have no right to interfere in my personal affairs, Hollis. Angela isn't yours any longer, she's mine."

"The hell she is. She's filed for divorce, she wants nothing more to do with you."

"I don't believe in divorce. I won't accept it. Angela will never be free of me, why can't you and she understand that? She'll always be my wife. I'll always love her more than life itself."

"You beat her like a dog!"

"I disciplined her. A wife needs discipline to learn to cleave unto her husband."

"You're a goddamn sadist, Rakubian."

"Hardly. What I am is an old-fashioned realist. The world would be better off if there were more men like me. I take my marriage vows and duties seriously and I believe in them to the letter. For better or for worse, till death do us part."

"I won't let you hurt her any more than you already have."

"You have no say in the matter. What I do or don't do is between my wife and me."

"Stay away from her! Stay away from my grandson!"

"I suggest you remember what I've told you, that you tell Angela to remember it. For better or for worse, till death do us part."

The implication, the promise had been crystal clear: If I can't have her, no one else will. Oh, yes, no mistake—Rakubian was the classic profile of a homicidal stalker. Inflexible as stone, egotistical, delusional, sociopathic. A ticking time bomb. Allow him to live, and before too much longer he would explode in the deadliest way imaginable.

Taking his life first wasn't murder; it was self-defense, an act of survival. Either David Rakubian died or Angela would die. Kenny, too, most likely. Cassie, Eric, himself . . . anyone Rakubian perceived as standing in his way was at risk. Hollis would not let that happen. His family meant more to him than anything else, including his own life.

Yet the enormity of the act still frightened and sickened him. Determination on the one hand, revulsion on the other. As if he were existing on two overlapping planes, half on one and half on the second, a schizoid state that would end only when he squeezed the Woodsman's trigger.

If he squeezed it.

If he could go through with it.

He kept telling himself he would, but how could any man with his background, his moral code, be absolutely sure until the moment came? Decide to take a life, be convinced it was morally justified, even crave the relief it would bring . . . conceptual abstracts, like one of the buildings he designed in its embryonic stage. An edifice of the mind. Drawings, blueprints didn't make a building a reality; steel, stone, wood, brick, physical labor created the actual structure. Same principle here. Rakubian's death and his family's safety could not become a reality until the trigger was squeezed, a bullet tore through flesh, bone, brain tissue.

An image came into his mind: Rakubian sprawled on the terra-cotta floor of his foyer. Blackened hole in his face, blood, twitching limbs, eyes glazed and sightless. Another image: himself standing on the porch, smoking gun in hand, the knowledge of his responsibility swelling and distorting his features until they were no longer recognizable.

Another image: the buck, thirty-five years ago.

His child self inside the bright red hunting jacket, the hiking boots pinching his toes, the rifle cold-hot in his hands, his eyes staring down at the bloody spasming body of the deer and watching it die. Pop's arm tight around his shoulders, the stillness of the woods and the lingering after-echoes of the shot and the animal's last gurgling, dying breaths. And Pop saying, "Good clean lung shot, son, I'm proud of you," Pop saying, "Just take it easy, the first kill is always the hardest," Pop saying, "Be a man, now, wipe the puke off your mouth and get hold of yourself," Pop saying, "It's your buck, Jack, you killed it and by God you're going to gut and dress it."

Eleven years old. First kill. Only kill. Went hunting twice more with the old man, froze up and couldn't fire at the only other deer that came his way, Pop saying disgustedly that time, "Buck fever, after you already lost your cherry. I'm ashamed of you, boy." And Pop red-faced and angry the second year, when he learned his son had left camp with an unloaded rifle; stomping around in the chill mountain air and shouting, "This is the last time you come out with me, the goddamn *last* time. You haven't got the guts for a man's sport."

Wrong, Pop. It wasn't a matter of courage at all. An outdoorsman, the old man, all rough edges and surface feelings and lack of imagination. He'd mistaken sensitivity, empathy for cowardice. His son had guts, all right; a man knows if he does or doesn't, proves it to himself in a hundred different ways as he matures, and Jack Hollis refusing to shoot another deer—or to hook a fish in Tomales Bay, or to play contact sports, or to do any of the other things Bud Hollis considered manly—had nothing to do with the stuff he was made of. Neither was being able or unable to kill a hated enemy a test of his courage. Of his humanity, yes. Of the essence of him, yes. But not of his manhood.

Come on, Rakubian, he thought.

Damn you, come on!

Growing edgier by the minute, and nothing to he done about it. Normally he was a patient man, but an hour of sitting like this in the cold car had frayed him raw inside. The longer the wait went on, the harder it would be to use the .22. No denying that. He could call it off, go home, return tomorrow night, but it would be twice as hard to nerve himself to it a second time. Stick it out another twenty or thirty minutes, at least. He could stand that much more.

Maybe, he thought then, he ought to do this a little differently. Go over there right now, hide in the shadows near the attached garage where he could empty his bladder. When Rakubian drove in, drift inside behind the car and use the gun in there. The garage walls were thick and would muffle the shot, even with the door open. Another factor: It would be too dark in the garage for anyone happening by to see in from the street. On the porch, he'd be in clear view because Rakubian would almost certainly put on the outside light before opening the door. . . .

No. Bad idea. Suppose it was another hour or more before Rakubian showed? With the blowing fog, the night was bitter cold; waiting outside, even bundled in his overcoat, he would numb and cramp before long. He didn't have his gloves and he couldn't fire the .22 with stiffened fingers. Nor was there any guarantee he'd be able to enter the garage without Rakubian seeing him and taking some kind of counteraction. Or that he'd be able to get close enough, or see clearly enough, to put him down with a single shot.

The original plan was still the best. Stay put, wait it out here. Wait five minutes after Rakubian got home, then walk over, ring the bell, shoot him as soon as he opened up. A quick glance to make sure he was dead, then walk, not run, to the car and drive away.

Chances were no one would hear the shot; a .22 Woodsman makes a pop not much louder than a released champagne cork. And with any luck no one would see him, notice or be able to identify the car's make or color. He would be suspected, of course, because of that stupid outburst in

Rakubian's office, but Gabe Mannix would alibi him for tonight if necessary—all he'd have to do was ask. Two other
things in his favor: a man like Rakubian, a ruthless personal-injury attorney, must have plenty of other enemies.
And the Woodsman had been Pop's, an old target pistol he'd
never bothered to register.

He might just get away with it, at least in this life. If he
didn't, well, it might not matter much in the long run. Even
if a good criminal attorney pled extenuating circumstances,
got a murder charge reduced to manslaughter, he still had
the goddamn cancer to contend with. Maybe he'd get lucky
and beat the odds there, too . . . and maybe he wouldn't. No
point in worrying about it now. The important thing, the
only important thing, was to keep his family safe.

Hollis ran a hand over his face, felt and heard the heel of
his palm scrape on patchy beard stubble. Poor job of shaving
this morning. Too keyed up, his hand not quite steady.
Missed a few spots, nicked himself in three or four places.
Cassie had noticed the bad shave and the edginess both,
commented on them. After twenty-six years of marriage they
were sensitive to each other's moods. The look on her face
when he'd told her he would be home late, he had an important meeting with a prospective client. Her afternoon call to
the office, the questions, the unease in her voice. If he
hadn't cut her off short, she might have tried to bring it out
into the open. He hated lying to her, but it was better than
an open confrontation. Nothing she could say would have
changed his mind anyway.

Headlights appeared at the intersection two blocks
down, threw a wash of diffused yellow-white against the fog
as the car turned upstreet toward him. He slid lower beneath
the wheel, as he had the other times headlights approached,
his hand closing around the hard rubber handle of the .22.
The beams speared closer, moving slowly, making a blinding

oblong of the mist-streaked windshield. And flicked past, the car's tires hissing on the pavement. Not Rakubian. The car kept on going and vanished around the curve behind him.

The pound of his heart seemed drum-loud. He willed himself to relax, working his shoulder muscles as he sat up. The side window was lowered enough so that he could look over the top of the glass; he put it down the rest of the way to clear off condensation, took deep drafts of the chill night air. The wind, moist and salt-flavored, made his skin tingle clammily. He rolled the window partway up again, held his watch close to his eyes.

11:05.

What if Rakubian stayed out all night? He'd been alone six weeks now . . . another woman? No. Not the way he felt about Angela. His appetites, sexual and otherwise, were too obsessively centered on her.

Long business meeting or dinner? Some kind of social function? Where the hell was he?

Hollis's saliva glands seemed to have dried up; swallowing had become painful. His breathing was off, the pressure in his bladder acute, and now his lower back and hips ached. One of the symptoms that prostate cancer is spreading: nagging pain in the back, hips, or pelvis. Symptom of stress, too, he told himself. Don't start imagining things.

Another set of headlights appeared, smeared by fog and the wet window glass into one long misshapen fan, approaching from the direction of West Portal. The lights swept past the little hillside park where St. Francis ended, and when they turned into Monterey and came uphill toward him, he sank low on the seat again so his eye level was just above the window frame. The windshield once more became a dazzling oblong—and a moment later the beams swung sharply away, into the driveway across the street.

Rakubian.

He let out a ragged breath, caught up the Woodsman and held it on his lap. With his left hand he rubbed moisture off the side glass. Taillights burned crimson through the fog; the automatic garage door began to glide up, revealing the lighted interior in slow segments. He could hear the throaty idle of the car—a silver BMW, less than a year old, hallmark of the bugger's success. He watched it roll inside, the driver's door swing open as the overhead door started to come down. He had a brief glimpse of Rakubian in a dark overcoat, then the door was all the way down and he was looking at darkness again.

He sat waiting, staring at the house. He felt . . . okay. A little queasy, the crawling sensation more pronounced and close under the skin, but otherwise calm. His hands? Steady enough, the palms still dry.

Light bloomed behind one of the shaded front windows.

All right. No point in waiting any longer.

Get out, walk over there.

Ring the bell.

Raise the gun, and when Rakubian opens the door, shoot him. Don't hesitate, don't think, just shoot him.

Rid the world of a monster.

For Angela. Kenny. Cassie. Eric. Himself.

He sat there.

Do it. What's the matter with you? Do it!

He sat there. He couldn't move.

Could not will himself to move.

Buck fever, after you already lost your cherry. I'm ashamed of you, boy.

Now the sweat came. And the shakes, and a shortness of breath, and an awareness that he was dribbling droplets of piss like a scared old man. He cursed himself, bitterly and savagely; and when the reaction ended after a minute, two minutes, it left him feeling weak and ill. He knew he could move then. He might even be able to make it across the street and up to Rakubian's door. But beyond that . . . no.

Couldn't go through with it after all.

Not tonight. Not this way.

But it wasn't finished; *he* wasn't finished. Something had to be done about Rakubian and it was still up to him to do it. All that had changed was the time, the place, perhaps the method. Whatever steps he eventually took to protect his family, they would not be as simple or as cowardly as ringing a doorbell and squeezing a trigger.

2

Early Thursday Morning

A s late as it was when he got back to Los Alegres, most of the lights in the big two-story house were on. The instant he saw that, he knew something was wrong.

He went tight on the outside, hollow on the inside. He jerked the Lexus into the driveway and left it there instead of putting it away in the garage. The Doberman, Fritz, began barking inside as soon as he ran up the stairs to the front porch. The door opened before he reached it and Cassie stood there. The wrongness was in her face, her eyes, the fact that she was still dressed, her voice when she said, "My God, where have you been? I've been frantic. I called your cell phone half a dozen times and kept getting an out-of-service message—"

He'd turned it off, like a damn fool. "Never mind that now. What happened? Why are all the lights on?"

"Come inside."

"Angela? Kenny?"

"They're all right." She tugged at his arm. "We can't talk out here."

He went past her, into the empty living room. Liquor on her breath, a half-full glass of Irish whiskey on the table beside her chair—she almost never drank anything alcoholic this late. The dog was still making a racket; she must have locked it in the kitchen or on the back porch. He turned to face her again.

"Tell me what happened."

"He was here again. Rakubian."

"Here? At the house?"

"No, in town, McLear Park. Angela took Kenny down there before supper for a few minutes. I tried to talk her out of it, but she thought it'd be all right with Fritz along. He showed up there. He must have been lurking somewhere in the neighborhood and seen her leave the house."

"Goddamn it! What happened to the neighborhood watch?"

"I don't know. People not home yet, not paying attention . . ."

"He didn't try to force them into his car again?"

"No. Kept his distance because of the dog. She said he was calm this time, didn't raise his voice."

"What'd he say to her?"

"He came right out with it, Jack. Said he'd kill her if she didn't go back to him. Her, Kenny, anybody who tried to stop him, and then himself."

Hollis ground his teeth, hard enough to bring a flash of pain along his jaw. "You or she call the police?"

"No. I wanted to—it's a clear violation of the restraining order, we could've had him arrested again. But she said it would only provoke him, make him worse."

"She's probably right."

"How could he get any worse?" Cassie said. "He's totally

irrational. He wouldn't be openly violating the TRO and making outright threats if he wasn't."

"I know that. I know."

"God, I feel so helpless."

"So do I," he lied. He crossed to the wet bar, poured a double shot of Bushmills, and drank it in one long swallow. It went down like fire, but it might have been water for all the effect it had on him.

Cassie came over beside him. "There's more," she said. "He followed them back here, parked down the street for almost an hour. Then he drove away and we thought he was gone, but a while later he was back. He drove by the house a few times, parked, left and came back again—twice more."

Down there in the city waiting for him, and all the while he was up here playing his sick games. I should've known this is where he was, should've called to find out. Stupid. Stupid!

"Jack?"

". . . Yes. What else?"

"He kept calling up," Cassie said. "Six or seven times. I know we decided not to talk to him anymore after last night, but I was so upset the first time I lost it and picked up and screamed at him. I don't even remember what I said. He told me to calm down. Can you believe that?"

"What else did he say?"

"The same garbage. All the threats thinly veiled again, to me and in the other calls I let go on the machine."

"He knows we're taping his calls. At least he's still rational enough not to want a record of his death threats."

"That's no consolation."

"I didn't mean it that way. Where's Angela?"

"She was pretty upset after the park incident. I made her lie down in her room with Kenny. Last time I looked in, they were both asleep."

"Good."

"She's not strong enough to stand up to this kind of madness indefinitely. None of us are. What're we going to do?"

Round and round, round and round. He shook his head. "I can't think right now. That dog . . . quiet him down, will you, before he wakes up half the neighborhood."

Cassie nodded and went away. She was much better with the Doberman than he was; Fritz was well trained but trusted her more than anybody else. Her veterinary training. Animals responded to her instinctively. He swung around to pour another drink; felt his stomach quiver and changed his mind. At the back of the house, the barking stopped. Pretty soon Cassie returned.

Her first words then "Where were you tonight?"

"A business meeting, I told you that."

"Don't lie to me."

"What makes you think I'm lying?"

"Your cell phone. Why was it switched off?"

"I didn't know it was. Must've pushed the button by accident."

"Dammit," she said, "you're up to something."

"No."

"Something drastic. I can feel it."

"No."

"You'd better tell me. I have a right to know."

"Cass, for God's sake."

"Whatever we do, any of us, it has to be legal. It has to make sense."

"Make sense," he said bitterly. "Get a restraining order, buy a guard dog, take a self-defense class, alert the neighborhood watch, keep a log of drive-bys, save all correspondence, record all phone calls, keep your cell phone handy at all times, join a support group. Has any of that made sense? It hasn't stopped him and it won't stop him."

"Angela is talking again about going away," Cassie said.

"Changing her name, starting a new life. She's serious this time."

"Does *that* make sense? He'll hunt her down wherever she goes if it takes him the rest of his miserable life—"

"It's the only choice I have left, Daddy."

Angela had come downstairs and into the living room so quietly they hadn't realized she was there until she spoke. Robe, slippers, her short hair lank and uncombed, her face scrubbed and colorless. Movements slow, listless. Twenty-five years old, pretty, she'd always been so pretty, the slender, wheat-blond image of Cassie at that age. Now she looked haggard, less youthful than her mother at forty-six —sharper lines around the mouth and eyes, the eyes themselves, once so full of life, faded and glassy from the constant strain. Rakubian's marks, deeper and more permanent than the cuts and bruises she'd worn like a badge of shame when she first came home.

Angela. His little girl. The ideal daughter—he'd said that to people while she was growing up, with pride and in all seriousness. Such a happy child, always laughing, full of questions, interested in everything. Never rebellious or troublesome, as Eric had been as a teenager. Never any problems until the summer after her high school graduation, when she'd taken up with Ryan Pierce and lost her head and her virginity and ended up pregnant with Kenny. And even that hadn't been so bad; the kid had married her voluntarily, and if he'd been too immature to hold down a steady job and care for a family, then been a deadbeat father for more than a year after the divorce, at least he was neither abusive nor crazy. She'd have been all right if she'd gone on to college after the split with Pierce, let Cassie and him raise her son until she got her degree and found a teaching position. But no. Trying so hard to be independent, insisting on paying her own way, working days and going to school nights . . . that damn secretarial job in San Francisco, Rakubian and his superficial charm and lavish attention, the quick and impulsive rebound marriage. One huge mistake that had put her life, Kenny's life in jeopardy. . . .

"Daddy, don't look at me that way."

He realized he'd been staring. He went to her, hugged her, stroked her hair. "Dog wake you, baby?"

"No. I wasn't asleep. I heard you drive in." She stepped out of his embrace, gave him a wan smile. "You look like you've had a pretty rough night too."

"Never mind about me. Think about yourself."

"That's all I have been thinking about. Kenny and myself. This isn't a spur-of-the-moment decision. I pretty much made up my mind yesterday. We can't go on living like this, terrified all the time, never knowing what David will do next. I have to do what's best for both of us."

"Running away isn't the answer."

"It might be. It's a hope, anyway. If we stay here . . . David meant what he said tonight. He'll kill us, and nobody can stop him."

I can stop him, Hollis thought. I *will* stop him.

Cassie said, "He'll find you, no matter where you go."

"Not with help from NOVA and Stalking Victims Sanctuary. They can arrange a new identity for us, a place to live, and a job for me. He won't find us. I have to believe that."

"But you can't ever be sure he won't. You know he'd never give up, and he has plenty of money, resources. . . ."

"At least we'll have a halfway normal life again."

"You say that now," Hollis said, "but it won't be normal or anything like normal. Looking over your shoulder every time you go out on the street, jumping every time the phone or doorbell rings or you hear a strange noise. You'd never be free of fear."

"*This* kind of fear is worse. I can't breathe, I feel like I'm suffocating right now."

She moved to the couch, slumped down on it with her knees together, her hands palms up in her lap. So young, sitting there like that. And so old. He felt as though he were choking, too. On love and rage as well as anxiety.

"We'd never see you again," Cassie said. "Either of you. I couldn't stand that."

"You will see us. We'll find a way to keep in touch, get together when we're sure it's safe."

"It'll never be safe enough. And you wouldn't dare phone or write—"

"You're forgetting e-mail. The support organizations have access to secure sites for message forwarding. *Please* don't keep trying to change my mind, it's only going to make things more difficult for all of us."

Cassie glanced at Hollis, then went to sit beside her. "Where would you go? You can't just pack up your car and start driving without a destination in mind."

"I have a destination in mind."

"Aunt Celia's?"

"Mom, we've been over and over that. Aunt Celia and I don't get along, you know she doesn't approve of me. I don't care if she is your sister, she can be a bitch sometimes, and Uncle Frank lets her walk all over him. Besides, David knows about them, knows they live in Cedar Rapids. It's the first place he'd look."

"Just for a few days . . ."

"Only as a last resort."

"Where, then? What destination?"

"Well . . . Boston."

"For heaven's sake, why Boston?"

Angela hesitated before she said, "It's about as far from Los Alegres as you can get. And a big city, a place to get lost in until I can make arrangements for someplace even more secure."

Hollis said, "You're hiding something."

She started to deny it, hesitated again, and then sighed and said, "It was Eric's idea."

"Eric?"

"He knows somebody at Cal Poly, another student whose folks have an apartment they don't use very often near downtown Boston. He's trying to set it up so Kenny and I can stay there two or three weeks."

"I thought we agreed to keep your brother out of this as much as possible."

"I couldn't help it, Daddy. I didn't go to him. He called yesterday, while I was here alone. I tried to downplay how bad things are, but he kept probing. I couldn't lie to him even if I wanted to. He knows me too well."

"And he offered up this Boston idea."

"Yes."

"How upset was he?"

"He wasn't, not the way you mean. He really isn't as hotheaded as he was before he went away to college."

Hollis wished he could be certain of that. Eric had inherited his grandfather's brooding temper, and he had a penchant for using poor judgment. Bright kid, IQ higher than anyone in the family, plenty of good qualities, but difficult to understand sometimes. They'd never been as close as Hollis wanted them to be, no matter how hard he tried to establish a tighter bond. That rebellious streak had gotten Eric in trouble a few times—suspended from high school twice for fighting, busted for smoking marijuana in a public place. And he'd disregarded family rules too many times to count. Yet he'd managed to keep up his grades, maintained a high enough GPA and scored well enough on his SAT to get into Cal Poly, Hollis's alma mater; and now in his junior year, majoring in engineering, he was in the top 10 percent of his class. Good kid at heart, who would someday be a good man—Hollis was sure of that. But that dark streak still worried him.

"When is he supposed to let you know about this apartment?"

"He thought he'd know today, but I haven't heard from him. If he doesn't call by noon tomorrow, I'll get in touch with him—"

"No, let me do it. I want to talk to him."

"Dad, you won't try to—"

"No, don't worry." His facial muscles felt bunched and tight. A tic seemed to want to start under his right eye; he made an effort to keep it still, his expression neutral. "I won't argue with him or lecture him."

"Please don't."

Cassie asked, "If it works out, this Boston apartment . . . when will you go?"

"As soon as possible. This weekend."

"That soon? All right, don't say anything, I'm not going to try to talk you out of it. But suppose the apartment doesn't work out?"

"I don't know yet. There's one other possible arrangement I can make. No matter what, though, we're leaving by the first of next week, before it's too late."

There were more words between the two, but Hollis was no longer listening. He moved to the couch, bent to kiss the top of his daughter's head. "I'm going up to check on Kenny," he said.

Much of Angela's old room had been preserved as it was when she was growing up—the stuffed animals on their shelves, the movie- and rock-star posters decorating the walls, her collection of Nancy Drew and Judy Bolton books neatly displayed. Sentiment on Cassie's part as well as on

Angela's. Kenny was asleep in the daybed next to her old twin, sprawled on his back, one hand fisted against his cheek, the other arm outflung, most of the bedclothes kicked off as usual. The night-light and the pale glow from the hall made his small face seem radiant. Sweet face, like his mother's. He resembled Angela, though he'd inherited Pierce's dark hair and complexion.

Hollis tiptoed in, lifted part of the tangled sheet, and covered the boy to his waist. He touched his lips gently to the smooth forehead, straightened, and stood looking down at his grandson in the shadow-edged light.

Nothing is going to happen to you or your mom, he promised silently. I swear it. I swear it on my own life.

In the darkness of their bedroom, no sleep again for either of them, they lay side by side without touching. Cassie had asked him to hold her, and for a time he had, but he was afraid she'd try to stir up more in the way of comfort; he knew he couldn't oblige. Sexual dysfunction, the inability to sustain an erection—that was another symptom of escalating prostate cancer. He'd pretended his recent impotence was stress-related because he did not want her to know the truth yet. The early diagnosis, the hope that the cancer was slow-growing enough to maintain a lengthy wait-and-see monitoring . . . meaningless now. It was escalating, all right. The symptoms and the last battery of tests made that plain enough. Stan Otaki was going to insist, the next time he saw him, that they begin aggressive treatment—surgery, radiation therapy. Which was why he'd canceled two appointments in a row. The way things were now with Angela and Rakubian, he could not put up with strength-sapping doses of radiation, or pressure from Cassie to allow himself to be cut open. When Rakubian was no longer a threat, then he'd see the doctor, then he'd tell her, then he'd give his full attention to fighting the cancer.

". . . you were tonight."

"What?"

"I said, you still haven't told me where you were tonight."

"Leave it alone, Cass."

"I can't. I won't. Where were you?"

The wind made noises in the Japanese elm outside the window. He listened, concentrating on the sounds. He had to pee again and he didn't want to get up and go to the bathroom so soon after the last time.

"Answer me, Jack."

"I drove down to the city," he said.

"I knew it. You went after Rakubian."

"You're jumping to conclusions."

"Am I? What did you intend to do?"

"He wasn't home, he was up here terrorizing Angela."

"That's not an answer. What did you intend to do?"

He shifted position to ease the hurt in his bladder.

"Talk to me," she said.

He couldn't go there with her. Could not make her understand, and above all would not make her an accessory. "Talk to him again, that's all. Plead with him. I knew it wouldn't do any good, but I felt I had to try one more time."

"Why didn't you tell me, if that's all it was?"

"Pride, I guess. And I didn't want you to worry."

A little silence. "That isn't all," she said. "You had something else in mind."

"Like what? What're you thinking?"

"I was scared to death all day you'd do something crazy."

"I'm not crazy," he said.

"We're all a little crazy right now. But we're not desperate enough to resort to murder."

The word seemed to hang in the heavy blackness. He

could almost hear it like an echo above the skirling of the wind.

"It's what's in your head, isn't it?" Cassie said. "I don't care about Rakubian, I despise him as much as you do—it's you I'm concerned about. I couldn't stand to lose you too."

"You're not going to lose me."

"What else would you call sacrificing yourself for Angela?"

"Come on, now—"

"No, you come on. That's exactly what it would be, a sacrifice. Even if you got away with it, it would destroy you."

"Not if it made her and Kenny safe."

"No matter what. You couldn't live with a thing like that on your conscience. I know you, Jack Hollis."

"Nobody knows another person that well." But she was right, and no use in denying it. His conscience *would* tear him up. Not that he was about to let that stop him.

Something banged outside, far off but still loud enough to carry. Ordinary sound, bump in the night, but they both lay quiet for a time, listening.

Cassie said, "The one hope I have is that you're not able to go through with it. Take a human life, even a life like David Rakubian's."

Sitting in the cold car with the .22 on his lap, frozen in place, crippled. Not able to go through with it.

"Don't try to find out," she said. "I'm begging you. Don't do it."

The darkness had begun to feel thick and oppressive, wool-like, as if it were contracting around him. "I won't let that son of a bitch hurt the kids. Or you. Or me. That's the bottom line."

"It isn't up to you. The problem is Angela's, and whether we like it or not the decision of what to do about it is hers too. *That's* the bottom line."

"Run away, live in fear somewhere else. Some solution."

"If she can stand it, so can we. I hate the idea as much as you do, but we've got to stand by her."

"What about Rakubian?"

"There must be some other way. . . ."

"To keep him from hunting her down? He's relentless. He's not going to give up, vanish from her life or ours."

"Lord, how I wish he would."

Suppose he did? Hollis thought.

Suppose he *does*?

"Promise me you'll be rational about this," Cassie said. "That you won't do anything we'll all regret."

"Rational. Yes."

"Promise me."

"I promise."

It was not another lie. Rational was exactly what he would be from now on. He needed a plan, one that eliminated the threat of potential witnesses, the necessity for a bogus alibi. One in which there was no body and no evidence linking him to any crime. A rational, detailed plan, drawn with the same care as he drew one of his building designs. Could he go through with it then?

Yes, because he had to.

"You're right," he said, "we have to let Angela do what she believes is best. Give her as much support as we can."

"You mean that?"

"I mean it. But this Boston idea . . . I don't care for it at all. It's one thing to have people in support groups helping her; they know what they're doing. But trusting complete strangers three thousand miles away? Even if Eric can arrange it, I think it's a mistake."

"So do I. I'll talk to her again, try to persuade her not to rush into anything. If she won't listen, we'll just have to let her go. But at least get some information from Eric about his friend's family when you talk to him."

"I will."

"The only other thing we can do is pray," she said. "Trust in God to keep them safe."

God, he thought, God created David Rakubian, didn't He? God isn't the answer.

The answer is me.

3

Thursday Morning

NGELA and Kenny were still in bed when he left the house. Cassie usually got up when he did, even though she wasn't due at Animal Care until ten, but not today; she was inwardly focused, uninterested in both coffee and conversation. He understood her reticence and was grateful for it. His head ached from tension and lack of sleep; he had no more patience than she did for a replowing of last night's hard and bitter ground. They'd talk later, after he spoke to Eric and she had another go-round with Angela.

On the way downtown he tried calling Eric's private number at his Cal Poly dorm. Busy signal. And another at the number of his roommate, Larry Sherwood. Dorm life was a lot different now than when he'd gone to college; there were private phone lines in each room, to accommodate computers as well as telephones. Constant computer use made getting through difficult sometimes. He'd just have to keep trying.

The building Mannix & Hollis, Architects, shared with

two other small businesses was a converted and refurbished
Victorian, once someone's elegant home, on the bank of the
Los Alegres River near the boat basin. An attractive location,
with a view of part of the historic downtown district across
the waterway. And a barometer of how well he and Gabe
were doing, how far they'd come since pooling their talents
and starting the firm in the old, cramped quarters on North
Main fourteen years ago.

He parked in the adjacent lot, next to Gloria's noisy—
"farty," she called it—little Nissan. Gloria Rodriguez, the
firm's occasionally irascible, often foulmouthed (in both
English and Spanish) and indispensable jack-of-all-trades:
computer draftsperson, bookkeeper and accountant, recep-
tionist, secretary. Most mornings she was in and working
before he arrived; Gabe, a habitual slow starter, seldom
showed up until after nine-thirty. Gloria's computer work-
station was a neat island in the office's chaotic sea of angled
drafting tables and flat-topped tables cluttered with designs,
specs, U.S. and California code books, supply catalogs that
hadn't been shelved with the others covering one wall. She
swiveled away from her Mac as he entered, hoisted her
plump body out of her chair, and scowled at him. He knew
that scowl. Knew even before she pushed three business-size
envelopes at him that David Rakubian was its source.

"These were shoved under the door when I got here," she
said. "Looks like that *verga* has taken to hand-delivering his
crap now."

Hollis took the envelopes. Same as the others, plain
white, except that the only computer-generated typing on
these was his full name, Jackson M. Hollis. Gloria wasn't
reticent about opening anyone's mail; the fact that the envelopes were still sealed meant that she didn't care to view the
contents any more than he did. She knew all about
Rakubian. He could not have kept the situation from her

and Gabe if he'd wanted to, not after the phone calls and mailings began coming here as well as to the house.

"I'll bet he showed up at your place last night too," Gloria said. "He didn't go after Angela and Kenny again?"

"No. Phone calls and drive-bys, mostly."

"Jesus, Jack, how much more of this can she take?"

"Not much more. She's made up her mind to go into hiding with the boy."

"Oh, shit. When?"

"Soon. I doubt we'll be able to talk her out of it this time."

Gloria scowled and heaved a sigh. "I hate to say it, but maybe it's the best way. I mean, guys like Rakubian, stalkers, psychos . . ." She crossed herself and added, "I don't understand how God can let people like him walk this earth."

Hollis didn't respond to that. He said, "I'll be in my office," and crossed to enter his private cubicle at the rear.

He threw the envelopes on his desk, cocked a hip against the edge, and tried again to call Eric. Still busy, both lines. He resisted an urge to bang the receiver down, went to open the blinds.

The early fog was beginning to burn off; pale sunlight sparkled on the muddy brown water below. For a time he stood looking downriver, watching a small launch glide beneath the D Street drawbridge. Pleasure craft and dredgers were all you saw on the river these days. Not so long ago, when Los Alegres had been an agricultural center mostly undiscovered by day-trippers, San Francisco commuters, Silicon Valley dot-commers, and voracious suburban developers, there had been barges loaded with feed and grain from the old mills that had once flourished here; and until the mid-sixties, barges and small cargo ships had carried chickens, eggs, produce, and other goods to and from the San Francisco Bay markets.

Everything changes, he thought. For good reason, bad

reason, no reason at all. Blink your eyes and familiar things, things you've taken for granted all or most of your life, are suddenly different. Blink your eyes and everything you've built, the whole perfectly designed, rock-solid structure of your existence, is so unstable it might collapse at any time.

He turned from the window, sat at his desk. The thick file with Rakubian's name on it was in the locked bottom drawer; he took it out, set it beside the three envelopes. Looked at them, looked away at the framed blueprints of two of his AIA award-winning home designs on the wall. Out front he could hear Gloria running the big copy machine. He was aware of the faint, not unpleasant ammonia smell of blueprints that seems always to linger in architects' offices, that was overpowering for a time after the blueprint service made delivery of a new batch. Familiar, comfortable. One more part of his life on the brink of irrevocable change because of a tiny malfunctioning gland and one man's psychotic obsession.

Three or four minutes passed before he finally stirred and picked up one of the envelopes, tore it open. Single sheet of white bond paper, black computer printing in its exact middle. Two words in oversize capital letters.

SHE'S MINE!

He laid the sheet aside, ripped open a second envelope. Several lines on this one's single sheet, also neatly centered.

> But our love it was stronger by far than the love
>   Of those who were older than we—
>   Of many far wiser than we;
> And neither the angels in heaven above,
>   Nor the demons down under the sea,
> Can ever dissever my soul from the soul
>   of the beautiful Angela B.

Hollis tasted bile in the back of his throat. Poe again. Rakubian and Poe, one madman fascinated by another. "Annabel Lee." He knew that was the source of the stanza because Rakubian had sent others to Angela, each of them, like this one, with her name—Angela B. for Angela Beth— substituted for Annabel Lee.

The third envelope. And still another stanza from the same poem, the intent behind this one as clear as it was sickening.

> For the moon never beams, without bringing me dreams
>> Of the beautiful Angela B.
> And the stars never rise, but I feel the bright eyes
>> Of the beautiful Angela B.
> And so, all the night-tide, I lie down by the side
> Of my darling—my darling—my life and my bride,
>> In her sepulchre there by the sea.
>> In her tomb by the sounding sea.

Tight-lipped, he opened the file, lifted the thick sheaf of papers inside and slipped the three new sheets onto the bottom. Keep all correspondence in chronological order . . . as if that would do any good in stopping a homicidal stalker. He let the file remain open in front of him, picked up the phone again.

This time Eric's line was free, but it was Larry Sherwood who answered. "You just missed him, Mr. Hollis. He left about five minutes ago for his ten o'clock."

"Can you try to catch up? Or get word to him in class? It's important we talk as soon as possible."

"Something wrong? I mean—"

"No, it's not serious. But there is some urgency."

"I'll let him know. Where should he call you?"

"My office."

Hollis put the phone down, looked again at the file. The

top papers were a dossier on David Rakubian that he'd compiled from conversations with Angela and a San Francisco attorney who knew him, and some research on his own. It was fairly complete: Know your enemy. He read through the facts and figures once more—looking, this time, for something he might be able to use in the new plan he was forming.

David Thomas Rakubian. Born in Fresno thirty-five years ago, only child of second-generation Armenian parents. Father a raisin grower, mother a librarian, both now deceased. Loner as a child, no interest in sports or other activities, preferred the company of books. Didn't date much as a teenager or as an adult—told Angela he'd been a virgin until he was twenty-four and seemed proud of the fact. High IQ, high enough to qualify for membership in MENSA, and an intense student—straight A's, valedictorian of his high school graduating class. Studied law at UCLA, high marks there, too; LLB degree and immediate placement after graduation with a respected L.A. firm. Moved to San Francisco after passing the state bar exam, to accept a better-paying position with an old-line Montgomery Street firm. After three years, decided corporate work was too limiting and opened his own practice specializing in aggressively handled, high-yield personal-injury cases. Successful from the first, won two big settlements in two years, the second allowing him to buy St. Francis Wood real estate before his thirtieth birthday. Refused to expand his operation since, because taking in partners meant relinquishing some control. Still maintained a small suite of offices with only two employees—a paralegal, Valerie Burke, who'd been with him for five years, and Janet Yee, the latest in a string of secretaries.

Political conservative. Strong antiabortion beliefs and an advocate of family values, but without any right-wing religious bias. Claimed to believe in God but seemed to consider organized religion beneath him. Staunch supporter of the

Second Amendment, but no ties to the NRA or any other pro-gun group. Didn't own a weapon of any kind as far as Angela knew. Which meant nothing, of course. If he wanted one, he wouldn't have any trouble getting it.

Outwardly charming, cold and inflexible on the inside. Tenacious, often ruthless in his legal methods. Uncompromising. Unforgiving.

Massive ego—center-of-the-universe type. Angela: "He's close to being a solipsist. You know, a person who believes he's the only reality and everything and everybody else are self-creations."

Control freak. His way or no way. Never admits to being wrong, to any fault or deficiency. Fearless. Believes he's smarter than anyone else and therefore indestructible.

Violent tendencies. No record of arrest for any crime before the attempted kidnapping, or of abuse against women before Angela. Had one other serious relationship, he'd told her, but wouldn't say when or identify the woman. No one else knew or would say who she was, so there was no way of finding out if he'd abused her, too.

Living relatives: none. Friends: none. During the eleven months Angela lived with him, they never once entertained at home (except for the handful of times Hollis and Cassie were allowed in the house) and saw no one socially except an occasional business acquaintance.

Hobbies and interests: books on the law, and gloomy prose and poetry by Poe, Hawthorne, Henry James, Blake. Poe in particular: collected rare editions of his work and books about it and his life. Collected artwork of the same Gothic sort; his house was strewn with nineteenth-century paintings, statuettes of brooding ravens and gargoyles, a life-size bust of Poe. Referred to himself as a "neo anti-quary." Liked the symphony and heavy Russian classical music. Didn't like opera, plays, modern music, or films of any kind. Refused to own a TV set. Wouldn't permit Angela to use her personal computer at home. Nor allow her to continue working, spend time with her friends and family, talk to another man in his presence, do much of anything at all that interfered with his concept of the subservient, dutiful wife.

Rakubian in odious and bitter sum.

The rest of the papers in the file were evidence, clear if not legally conclusive, that he was a ticking time bomb. Letters, notes, one-line messages to Angela, to Hollis, to Cassie, professing his love, his imagined ownership, his rage and frustration, his demands and implied threats. Quotations about love and death from Poe and others. Listings of all his phone calls, drop-bys, drive-bys, and confrontations. Uncashed checks made out to Angela, one for $500 and another for $750. Records of deliveries of expensive clothing, exotic perfume, bouquets of flowers—and the other items, disguised as presents in beribboned and fancy-papered boxes, such as lace underthings scissored into strips and the portrait of Angela with the top of her head cut off. Snapshots of the two of them before and shortly after their marriage, smiling at each other, embracing, laughing, each accompanied by a cryptic handwritten note. And the other photos, sometimes mixed with the snapshots, sometimes sent separately, of funerals and dead women in coffins and bloody aborted fetuses.

Enough, Hollis thought. No more. He closed the file, relocked it in the desk drawer. No more letters, phone calls, drop-bys, drive-bys, confrontations, presents, photos, bullshit, lunacy, fear, uncertainty, desperation. No more!

He switched on his computer, pulled up the Chesterton file. Nice little plum for Mannix & Hollis, and mostly his baby: a 4,500-square-foot house and outbuildings in the Paloma Mountains east of town. Money no object, full creative control. Shelby Chesterton owned a Silicon Valley computer software company, had tired of living in the South Bay rat race, liked the slower pace of the North Bay, and was preparing to relocate both his company and his family to Los Alegres. He'd bought a large chunk of real estate on the mountainside, complete with a private lake, and interviewed a dozen architectural design outfits in the county before handing the job to Mannix & Hollis. Hollis had gotten along well with him from the first—they saw eye-to-eye on other subjects besides modern architecture—and he'd been given carte blanche. The result was an environmentally friendly, innovative, regionally styled home that employed elements of Maybeck's vision with his own unique method of detailing. The Chestertons had been ecstatic. Mannix & Hollis had already gotten one other job as a result of their enthusiastic recommendation to friends. There might well be more if and when the finished house was featured in one of the trade magazines.

Construction had begun three months ago. He hadn't been to the site in nearly a month because of Angela and Rakubian; he checked the most recent progress report from PAD Construction. Some of the foundation slabs had been poured, but the report didn't say which ones; the rest were scheduled for this week and next. He'd have to go up there, see for himself—

Knock on the door. He swiveled his head as it opened and Gabe Mannix poked his bushy head inside. "Busy, Bernard? Or can I come in?"

Bernard this morning. Other mornings it was Paul. Gag born twenty-plus years ago, when they'd worked together in the city, that Mannix refused to let die of worn-out old age. The two early-twentieth-century California architects who had most influenced Hollis's own style, one a white Paris-trained bohemian, the other a black, mostly self-taught traditionalist, were Bernard Maybeck and Paul Williams.

"Come ahead. You're practically in already." He clicked off the Chesterton file, shut down, and swung his chair around as Mannix flopped into the cubicle's one other chair.

"So the asshole showed up here last night."

"Yeah."

"Your place, too, Gloria says."

"McLear Park before that. Angela was there with Kenny. He threatened her outright this time."

"In front of witnesses?"

"Not unless you count Fritz."

"What'd he say exactly?"

"That he'd kill them both if she doesn't go back to him."

"Miserable fuck! So that's why she's ready to run and hide."

"That's why."

"You're not going to let her go?"

"I can't stop her, Gabe."

"If you don't, you might never see her or Kenny again. Even if Rakubian doesn't find her, she'll go to ground so deep she won't dare surface."

"It's her decision."

"Is it? You know what I'd do if I were in your place. Buy a gun and use it."

He kept a poker face. He'd heard this before; Mannix hadn't made any secret of how he felt. Of all the people who knew about the situation, Gabe was the one he'd come closest to confiding in. But he hadn't been able to do it. Not before last night and not now, either.

"Don't you think I've considered it?"

"Seriously considered it?"

"Damn seriously.

"And?"

He shook his head, made a helpless gesture.

"Yeah, I know," Mannix said. "Suppose I do it for you?"

". . . You're kidding."

"You think so? You know how I feel about you and Cassie and Angela. I wouldn't have any qualms about it, moral or otherwise. Same as shooting a rabid dog."

Hollis studied him for a time, trying to decide if he really did mean it. Gabe Mannix was not an easy man to read. They'd known each other twenty-two years, worked side by side at Simmons Glenn Associates for eight before going into partnership on their own, but there was still an ambiguous closed-off part of the man he couldn't quite figure out. Big, shaggy, easygoing, with an endless repository of anecdotes and bawdy stories . . . but he could also be moody, cynical, and unpredictable in his personal life. A brilliant if conventionally minded architect, with a degree from the Pratt Institute in New York, yet he preferred to handle the more mundane jobs that came their way—office buildings, shopping malls, apartment complexes—and to let Hollis have the more challenging individual designs like the Chesterton home. Twice married, twice divorced, now a confirmed bachelor and "connoisseur of one-night stands," yet he seemed to envy Hollis's stable relationship with Cassie. And the way he looked at Angela the past few years—wistfully, tenderly, with a sad little light in his eyes— indicated that he wished he was twenty years younger and she was somebody else's attractive daughter.

"I'd do it," he said. "No lie and no bull."

"It's not your fight, Gabe."

"The hell it's not."

"I wouldn't ask you. Not a thing like that."

"Meaning you don't condone the idea?"

"I didn't say that."

"Guys like Rakubian don't deserve to live," Mannix said. "Do the world a favor, take him right out of the gene pool."

"You sound like a vigilante."

"Maybe I am. Maybe you'd better start thinking like one yourself."

If you only knew, buddy.

"Can we drop this now? It's not doing either of us any good."

"Drop it if that's what you want, but one of us better pick it up again. Before it's too late."

"Gabe, look—"

Mannix shoved onto his feet. "Off to the salt mines. Emerson's bitching again about the changes in that mall design."

"Some work to do myself. I'll be out pretty soon."

"Take your time. You've got more important things to worry about than pencils and slide rules."

When he was alone Hollis pulled up the Chesterton file again and rechecked the progress report and the site plan. All right. If the hillside work hadn't progressed far enough or they'd poured the wine cellar slab ahead of schedule? Cross that bridge if and when.

The rest of the plan now. Nothing specific he could use in the dossier on Rakubian, but there was enough in the nonspecifics. Massive ego. Never admits to being wrong, to any fault or deficiency. Fearless—believes he's smarter than anyone else, indestructible. Pull all of that together and you had a literal-minded man vulnerable to the right kind of approach.

Fitting. The son of a bitch's own massive ego was going to help bury him.

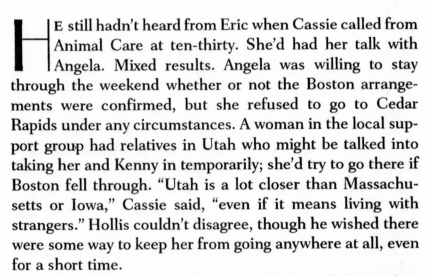

4

E still hadn't heard from Eric when Cassie called from Animal Care at ten-thirty. She'd had her talk with Angela. Mixed results. Angela was willing to stay through the weekend whether or not the Boston arrangements were confirmed, but she refused to go to Cedar Rapids under any circumstances. A woman in the local support group had relatives in Utah who might be talked into taking her and Kenny in temporarily; she'd try to go there if Boston fell through. "Utah is a lot closer than Massachusetts or Iowa," Cassie said, "even if it means living with strangers." Hollis couldn't disagree, though he wished there were some way to keep her from going anywhere at all, even for a short time.

It was almost noon when Eric finally called. By then Hollis was fidgety and not working well. He took the call in his cubicle, and started things off wrong, in spite of himself, by saying too sharply, "What took you so long to get back to me?"

"Hey, don't bite my head off."

"Didn't Larry give you my message right away?"

"He gave it to me. Urgent but not serious. Angie told you about Boston, right?"

Angie. Eric was the only one in the family who called her that. "Yes. You haven't talked to her today?"

"I tried the house just now. No answer."

"She's at a support group meeting. About this Boston business. I know you're trying to help, but—"

"It didn't work out," Eric said.

"No?"

"I thought I had the apartment all set for her, but Jeff went stupid on me and told his folks the reason. They don't want a woman who's being stalked staying in their apartment, they don't want any trouble, the usual crap."

Relieved, Hollis said, "It's just as well."

"Uh-huh. And I suppose you want me to stay out of it from now on?"

"I wish you would."

"I'd set something else up if I could."

"Eric—" He bit that off. "She may have another place to go," he said, and explained about Utah.

"Sounds okay for the time being," Eric admitted. "So you and Mom aren't trying to talk her out of leaving?"

"We're not standing in her way, no."

"But you don't much care for the idea."

"Of course not. Running away isn't going to save her from Rakubian."

"Neither is staying home where he can get to her any time he feels like it."

Hollis was silent. Same old pointless argument.

The line hummed and crackled emptily. Then Eric said in a cold, flat voice, "I hate that crazy son of a bitch. I'd like to smash his fucking head in."

"Knock off that kind of talk," Hollis said sharply. "You know better than that."

"Don't tell me you don't feel the same way."

"Violence isn't the answer." You goddamn hypocrite, he thought.

"Then what is? I can't help thinking . . ."

"What? What're you thinking?"

"Nothing. Never mind."

"Listen to me, son. Don't go getting any wild ideas."

"I don't know what you mean."

"I think you do."

"I won't lose it, don't worry."

"I do worry."

Long pause. "I'm coming home for a couple of days," Eric said then, "and don't tell me not to, okay?"

"Why?"

"The obvious reason. To see Angie before she leaves."

Hollis gave this a few seconds of thought before he said, "All right, no objection. When are you driving up?"

"After my last class tomorrow. Friday traffic'll probably be a bitch, so don't expect me until after dinner."

"Call when you get close to San Francisco. We'll wait dinner if it's not too late."

After he put the phone down, Hollis sat slumped in his chair. He hadn't seen his son in six weeks; it would be good to have him home again for a while. Make Cassie happy, too. But could he trust Eric to stay away from Rakubian? Better impress it on him again, in person, as soon as he could get him alone. If all the pieces of the new plan came together . . . Saturday was the target day. There was a lot to do before then, and any number of potential complications to screw up the timing and logistics. He couldn't afford to let his hotheaded son become another one.

Thursday Afternoon

The Paloma Mountains, like the Los Alegres River, was a misnomer. In fact they were a spine of tallish foothills spotted with oak and madrone, green in the winter but already beginning to brown off now in late spring, that separated this valley from the lush Paloma Valley to the east. Along the lower slopes were scattered ranches, rolling cattle graze, private homes on large parcels. Farther up, where the terrain steepened, boulder-size rocks littered the hillside, the folds between rounded hummocks cut deep to form shadowed hollows choked with trees and brush, and the number of working ranches and private dwellings dropped to a widely spaced handful. Stretches of woods ran near and along the ridgeline, hiding three small lakes and miles of deer trails on the privately owned sections, hiking and horseback trails on several thousand acres that belonged to the city.

The Chesterton parcel was better than two-thirds of the way up, one of the highest and choicest homesite locations. His seventy-two acres had cost him a couple of million; the home, outbuildings, and extensive landscaping he had planned would run about the same. Four million to Shelby Chesterton was like four thousand to Jack Hollis: He was no Bill Gates or Steve Jobs, but the pile he'd made in the technology market was massive and still growing. More power to him. He wasn't your typical high-rolling Type A corporate egomaniac; on the contrary, he was down-to-earth, surprisingly easygoing, a nice guy. Working with him had been a pleasure.

For that reason, because he liked and respected the man, Hollis felt bad about this part of the plan. It amounted to a betrayal, and the fact that Chesterton would never know it was cold comfort. A matter of expediency, yes—the only safe and certain means open to him on short notice. But that did not make the reality taste any less bitter. Another little piece of his integrity torn away and lost because of David Rakubian.

The road ran more or less straight at the lower elevations, turned crooked and then narrow and twisty as he climbed through stands of dusty-looking trees, rocky fields where dairy cattle grazed in the sun. He had the window rolled down and the afternoon breeze was warm, heavy with the smells of madrone, dry grass, manure. Behind him he could see the valley spread out below, the town with its east side suburban sprawl, the river, and Highway 101. From up at the Chesterton site, the view was spectacular. On a clear day you could see Mt. Tam, San Pablo Bay, parts of San Francisco Bay, and the city's skyline forty miles distant.

The pitch of the road grew even sharper; on the south side the terrain began to fall away, gradually in some places, more steeply in others. He made a corkscrew turn through a cutbank, driving at a crawl now because of the blind curves and the fact that the strip of rough asphalt was so narrow here two cars could not pass abreast. This road and most of the others in the Paloma Mountains had been built in the twenties to accommodate the ranchers, and they were little used by anyone except residents and kids looking for a private place to drink beer and get laid. He and Cassie had come here more than once, nearly thirty years ago . . . high school sweethearts, high school heat. It was where she'd given him her virginity, in fact.

Was it also where Angela had given hers to Ryan Pierce? The thought bothered him more than it should have and he wasn't sure why.

At nearly five miles by his odometer, the road split in two: the right fork dead-ending at the gate of one of the cattle ranchers, the left fork following a brushy ravine uphill. That one had brand-new gates standing wide open; the road surface there was gravel and would eventually be paved. Hollis turned in on it, raising clouds of dust that hung and shifted in the clear air like slow coils of smoke.

The house site was another half-mile along, on a wide, deep shelf extending out from a pair of oak-studded folds. Four leveled and graded acres that in another six months, if the weather cooperated, would contain the main house— two-storied, redwood and fieldstone with a cross-gabled roof and an interior of sharp-angled walls and huge rough-sawn boxed beams; five outbuildings in the same general style but with subtle alterations to make each one unique; and an eighty-foot-square stone terrace and swimming pool, tennis courts, and two formal gardens. Right now the acreage was a jumble of earthmoving equipment, dump trucks, pickups, office trailer and toolsheds, portable toilets, stacks of lumber, piles of rock and gravel and dirt, Pete Dulac's twelve-man crew, and all the other components of a medium-size construction site.

Hollis found a place to park near the trailer and attached, steel-reinforced sheds. The noise level was high: grinding gears, pounding engines, backup beepers, men shouting. It must have been a bitch getting some of the trucks and equipment up here, Hollis thought as he went looking for Pete Dulac. The teamsters, especially those who'd hauled the cats and scoops and trailer up East Valley Road, were really earning their pay on this job.

Dulac found him before he was halfway to where the main house was staked out and partly slabbed. PAD Construction's owner was a burly, jowly man in his late fifties, the 49ers cap he habitually wore tilted back on his head, a tool belt slung around his waist. He'd worked for the old man once, long ago, but that wasn't the reason Hollis favored him whenever he could. Dulac was the best and most reliable general contractor in the county. He seldom finished a job late or overbudget; drove his crews hard, but no harder than he drove himself.

"Saw you pull in," he said. "How they hangin', Jack?"

Damn sour joke now, but Hollis went along with it. "A little lower every day."

"Wait till you get to my age. Come up for a reason?"

"Just a look-around to keep Chesterton happy."

"Well, we're still pretty much on schedule."

"Never any doubt of that."

"I'll be in the trailer for a few minutes," Dulac said. "Give a holler if you want me."

Hollis roamed the site, stopping once to talk to a workman, another time to feign an inspection of a foundation slab, a third time to enter one of the portable toilets. What urine he could produce caused a burning and flowed in thin interrupted spurts, as if his bladder were on some kind of timer switch. Frustration made him slam his hand against the inner wall, and when he came out a man working nearby gave him an odd look. He pretended not to notice.

From there he wandered back to the excavation for the big wine cellar. Forty by sixty feet, cut deep into the shale rock of the hillside; all the digging finished, the walls and ceiling shored and framed with plywood. The floor slab hadn't been poured yet, he saw with relief. The hard-packed dirt was overlaid with loose plywood sheets.

Inside, he bent to lift one of the center sheets and then squatted with his back to the opening. He knew that they hadn't hit bedrock anywhere on the site, but he had to be sure the earth wasn't too rocky here for easy digging. He burrowed two fingers into the pack, sifted dirt between his fingers. It would take a pick and shovel easily enough, but there was no way of telling for certain how far down he'd be able to go. Just have to take it on faith that it would be far enough without too much effort.

He replaced the plywood, went back outside. The nearest mound of earth and rock was fifty yards distant; he noted its location and the fact that there was a wheelbarrow near the pile. Then he went to the trailer to talk to Dulac again.

"Everything looks good, Pete. Pouring the rest of the slabs next week, right?"

"Right," Dulac said. "Should have 'em all done by a week from tomorrow."

"One in the wine cellar looks like it might be a little tricky."

"Shouldn't be. We'll have that one down Monday or Tuesday."

"Fine," Hollis said. "Oh, one more thing. Pretty good chance Chesterton and his wife will be driving up on the weekend. If they do, they'll want to check progress for themselves. So I'd better have your spare key to the padlock on the gates."

"Sure, no problem." Dulac got it for him. "You coming up with them?"

"Probably not."

"Well, better remind Chesterton to lock up again when they leave. Remote site like this, we don't want anybody getting in here that don't belong."

"No," Hollis said, "that's the last thing we want. Somebody here who doesn't belong."

5

WHEN he came down out of the hills he drove straight home. Three-thirty already; not much time left in the workday, even if he'd been inclined to return to the office. What he needed right now was to talk to Angela, break the news that Boston was no longer an option and reinforce the argument that she wait awhile before leaving home.

Only she hadn't returned from Santa Rosa yet; there was no sign of her little Chevy Geo. Cassie wasn't home, either. But parked in front was an unfamiliar Dodge pickup, old and a little battered, and as Hollis started his swing into the driveway a rough-dressed man appeared on the porch, stepping out from behind the screen of bougainvillea. Recognition thinned and tightened Hollis's mouth.

Angela's first big mistake.

Now what the hell?

He stood waiting as Ryan Pierce came down the steps and approached him. Tall kid, on the gangly side. And on the scruffy side now: beard stubble, brown hair curling well below his collar, stained cowboy boots and Levi's and a western-style shirt. Not much to recommend him, today or any day, except a pair of soft brown eyes and an ingratiating smile. Little gumption, no real focus or ambition. Hollis had never understood what Angela saw in him. Cassie thought it was gentleness, hidden depths that she'd been able to tap into. Maybe. His own best guess was that Pierce appealed to the strong maternal side of her; that she'd believed she could make something of him, teach him how to be a husband, father, man. Well, she'd been wrong. He had kept right on being immature, directionless through four struggling years of marriage and most if not all of the time since—no damn good to anyone, including himself.

"Hello, Mr. Hollis. Long time."

Not long enough. "What're you doing here?"

"Looking for Angela. You knew I was coming, right?"

"Wrong. If I had I'd've told you to stay in Wyoming."

"Montana. I told her in my last e-mail I was getting ready to drive down. She didn't tell you?"

"No." And he'd ask her why she hadn't, although he was pretty sure he knew the answer.

"I heard she left the guy she married in San Francisco, about all the trouble she's been having with him. Not from her, from my sister Rhona. It sounded messy and I couldn't get her to talk about it and I've been worried about her and Kenny. I quit my ranching job even though we were in the middle of—"

"Worried. Sure you were. How long has it been since you saw your son? Eighteen months? How many phone calls in that time? How many cards or letters?"

"Look, Mr. Hollis, I know I've been a lousy father—"

"Damn right you have."

"—but I'm not the same person I was before Angela and I broke up and I moved away. I've learned some things since I've been out on my own. Done a lot of growing up."

"Is that a fact."

"Yes, sir. I know you don't believe it, and I can't blame you, but I care about her and my son. I never stopped caring. Now . . . I'm ready to start being a father to Kenny. I mean that. Angela must've told you about the money I've been sending the past few months for his support."

"Is that what you think being a father is? Sending a check for a couple of hundred dollars every month?"

"No, sir," Pierce said. "That's why I'm here. I want to he part of his life from now on."

"Just like that. And on your say-so we're supposed to welcome you with open arms."

"I don't expect that. All I'm asking is that everybody give me a chance to prove how much I've changed."

"Your timing is lousy, Pierce. You say your sister told you about David Rakubian. Well, you don't know half of how bad the situation is. Angela's trying to cope with the biggest crisis of her life, and you showing up, trying to wiggle back into her good graces, is only going to make matters worse."

"I wouldn't do anything to cause more problems for her. That's the last thing I want."

"What you want doesn't matter. What's best for her and the boy does."

"Why're you so sure that couldn't be me?"

"Your track record, that's why."

"I told you, I've changed. I really have."

"Start proving it when this Rakubian business is finished. Until then, leave her and Kenny alone."

"Kenny's my son."

"And my grandson. I didn't walk out of his life eighteen months ago; you did. I'm the one who's been here for him."

"I don't want to fight with you, Mr. Hollis."

"Then stay away from my family."

"I can't do that," Pierce said. "I'm sorry, but I can't—not anymore. They're my family too."

"Listen to me—"

"No, sir. Just tell Angela I was here and that I'm staying with Rhona and her family. Will you do that?"

"No."

"I'm going to see them, both of them. Whether you like it or not."

Hollis's anger began to spill over. He moved forward, trying to crowd Pierce without actually touching him. The kid surprised him by standing his ground. "If you bother her, upset her in any way, I'll make you regret it. Now get off my property before I throw you off."

Pierce met his eyes for a ten count before he turned and walked slowly to the pickup.

Damn him! Hollis thought. After eighteen months and at the worst possible time. Maybe Pierce *had* changed, grown up some and learned a sense of responsibility; those brown eyes hadn't been as soft as they once were. But he was still a sorry-ass loser. Incredible how a sweet-natured, levelheaded girl like Angela could have such rotten taste in men.

He left the car where it was, went up onto the porch. And what he found next to the door pushed Ryan Pierce out of his mind. More flowers. A big flashy arrangement, yellow and red roses, half a dozen other varieties, including orchids, all done up in an open vase that must have weighed four or five pounds—a hundred dollars' worth, at least. And that wasn't all. A white rectangular box was propped there, too, with the same local florist's name printed on it.

He plucked an envelope bearing Angela's name off a long plastic fork stuck into the arrangement. Almost didn't open it, thinking that what he would do was take all this sweet-smelling crap into the garage before Angela or Cassie got home, bag it, and hide it in the garbage can where it belonged. He could predict what the message said anyway. But then, on impulse to see if he was right, he yanked the card out of the envelope. *With greater love hath no man.* Not the exact wording he'd had in mind, but close enough.

Crumpling the card, he bent to lift the white box. Might as well open that, too. It was in his hands before he realized that the address label on it did not carry Angela's name. Mr. and Mrs. Jackson Hollis.

He tore the lid off. And stood staring, his rage burning high, at what lay within—at the silk-ribboned funeral wreath and the card that read in small, neat script: *With deepest condolences on the loss of your loved ones.*

He was sitting in the living room, slumped down in his big leather armchair, when Angela and Kenny came home. He had been there for some time, unmoving and so inwardly focused that he was no longer aware of his surroundings. Lost and alone inside his own head, wandering in and out of the shadows. No, not quite alone. Rakubian was there, and Pierce, and the old man with his censorious eyes and critical mouth and the disappointment leaking out of him like a rancid oil. And Ma—the one recurring image of her that he could never drive away, that was as sharply detailed after thirty-six years as if it had happened yesterday.

He'd been ten that summer, inside a hospital for the first time, the medicine smells, sick smells, death smells making his head swim—peering down at Ma in her white bed in the white room and thinking: *She looks so small lying there. She looks like they put her in a pot and boiled her up and shrunk her.* Her voice had been shrunken, too, a weak pygmy voice saying, "Don't you worry now, honey, I'm going to be fine. Good as new in a few weeks, you'll see." And him so scared, seeing her that way, that he blurted out, "Do they *have* to cut you open, Ma?" And the old man looming there big as a house, blinking his censorious eyes and saying with his critical mouth, "It's the only way they can get the cancer out. Quit that sniveling now, boy. Nothing's gonna happen to your mother except she won't be sick anymore when it's over."

She died on the operating table.

They killed her on the operating table.

They wheeled her into a scrubbed white room full of lights and tubes and gleaming instruments and they cut her open and she hemorrhaged, she had some kind of virulent reaction to the anesthetic, and she died and he never saw her again because he wouldn't look at her at the funeral, he closed his eyes when he walked past the coffin—he could not bear to see her dead, it was bad enough remembering her boiled up and shrunken in that other white room with the smells of medicine and sickness and death.

It was not going to happen to him like that. He was not going to die on a goddamn operating table with his body sliced open, or in a hospital at all if he could help it. Surgery was not an option for him. There'd be no prostatectomy; no brachytherapy, the implantation of radioactive seeds; no transurethral resection, that swell-sounding little procedure where they shoved a tool with a tiny wire loop through your pecker and down into your prostate to scrape up the cancerous cells. External beam radiation . . . yes, all right, he could stand that even though it might eventually make his impotence permanent. Hormone therapy was okay, too. But he would not permit Stan Otaki or any other doctor to cut into the center of him. There were no guarantees with surgery anyway. Even if he survived an operation, the cancer could still spread and kill him sooner or later. . . .

He didn't hear the Geo pull into the drive, didn't realize they were home until they came in through the front door. Kenny bounded in first, saw him, shouted "Granpa!" and came running. He launched himself from a couple of feet away, and if Hollis hadn't caught him, hunching and turning his body as he did, he'd have taken a knee where it would have done his prostate the least good. Six weeks ago, after being under Rakubian's thumb for so long, the boy had been quiet, skittish, clingy to his mother; now he was the child he'd been before the marriage, a bundle of energy, a nonstop chatterbox. Amazing how quickly kids his age could recover from a bad experience, if they were gotten out of it before there was any permanent scarring.

"Hey, tiger. What's got you so excited?"

"Me and Jimmy Eilers played video games all day on his iMac," Kenny said. "He's got a brand-new iMac, well, his mom does. Tangerine, yuck, I like blueberry. Blueberry's cool."

"Is that so. Who's Jimmy Eilers?"

"Joyce Eilers's son," Angela said from the doorway. "She's in the group."

"The one with the relatives in Utah?"

"Oh, Mom told you about that. No, that's April Sayers."

"I won him every game," Kenny said. "I mean I beat him every game. Well, most games. Hey, neat. Cool. 'Way, man. Dag! Far out, dude."

"Where'd all that come from?" Hollis asked. "Jimmy?"

"His sister taught him. She's ten and wears glasses and she's got a big butt."

Angela said, "Kenny, that's not a nice thing to say about Tina."

"Well, she does. Humongous, man. Awesome buns."

Hollis set him on his feet. "Go get yourself a Coke. You look like you can use one."

"Nah, I'm not thirsty. I had six Cokes with Jimmy."

"Upstairs and play, then. I want to talk to your mom."

"Grown-up stuff?"

"Grown-up stuff."

"Okay. Mom, why don't we have an iMac?"

"We can't afford one right now. Someday."

"Can I go boot up our crappy old computer?"

"Boot up." Angela rolled her eyes. "Yes, go ahead. And it's not crappy, it's a perfectly good—"

Kenny wasn't listening; he was already running for the hall. He let out a whoop and went racing up the stairs. The way he did it reminded Hollis of Teddy, the addled brother in *Arsenic and Old Lace*, and his "Charge!" up "San Juan Hill."

Angela sat in Cassie's chair, tucked her feet under her. "What is it, Dad?" Warily.

"I talked to Eric this morning. The Boston apartment fell through."

"Oh, damn!"

"Don't look at me like that—I didn't have anything to do with it. His friend's folks changed their minds when they found out why you wanted to stay there."

She sighed, pressed thumbs against the edges of her eyes. "I guess I shouldn't be surprised. It sounded too good to work out."

"Utah might be better. It's a lot closer than Boston."

"Utah may not work out either."

"No?"

"April's relatives have a limited amount of space. They live in a mobile home park."

"So they wouldn't be willing to put you up for a while?"

"They might be. April isn't sure."

"When will you know?"

"As soon as she talks to them. If the answer is no . . ."

"You can still stay right here."

"Daddy . . ."

"Okay, forget I said that. Where in Utah?"

"I'd rather not say. Even if I go there, it's better if you and Mom don't know exactly where we are."

He needed to go to the toilet again; he stayed where he was, crossing his legs. "Your brother's driving up for the weekend," he said. "To see you, mainly."

That put a smile on her mouth. Such a radiant smile she had, like her mother's; when the two of them were happy and laughing, they lit up a room. "When's he coming?"

"He'll be here tomorrow around dinnertime."

"It's been a long time since we've all been together. I just wish . . . well . . ."

"I know," he said. Then he said, "You may as well know that Eric's not the only one who wants to see you. I found your first ex hanging around when I got home this afternoon."

"Ryan? Oh God, he's *here?*"

"Why didn't you tell us he was coming?"

"I didn't expect him this soon. . . . I thought we'd be gone before he showed up. You didn't say that I'm taking Kenny away?"

"No. It's none of his business, as far as I'm concerned."

"I wanted to tell him, but I was afraid to."

"Why? He wouldn't try to stop you?"

"I don't know, he might. He wants to be a father to Kenny again, be part of his life."

"So he kept telling me. That, and how much he's changed. I don't believe it."

"I think he has, Dad. I hope he has. It's not good for Kenny to grow up without a father, his real father."

"You don't have to see him or let him see the boy before you leave."

"But I should, now that he's here. He has a right to."

"Does he? After all this time? Kenny barely remembers him."

Angela gnawed her lower lip. "Where's he staying, did he say? With Rhona?"

". . . Yes."

"Is he going to call or stop by again?"

"One or the other, I suppose."

"You weren't . . . nasty to him, were you? I mean—"

"We had words. What did you expect?"

"I'd better go call April," she said. She got up and left the room so quickly he wondered, frowning, if it were Pierce she was hurrying to call instead.

Thursday Evening

Alone with Cassie, Hollis said, "You see the look on Angela's face after she talked to Pierce? If I didn't know better, I'd think she still has feelings for him."

"You don't know better. She's still in love with Ryan."

"Are you serious? After all this time and the way he behaved?"

"Nobody's rational where love is concerned, you know that. Angela least of all."

"For Christ's sake. How long have you known about this?"

"All along."

"Why didn't you say something?"

"I didn't see any reason to. He left town and then she married Rakubian on the rebound."

"You don't suppose she'd . . ."

"What? Start up with Ryan again?"

"He hurt her once. He'd do it again."

"He's not a kid anymore, and neither is she."

"That's not an answer."

"If Rakubian stops being a threat," Cassie said, "she might turn to Ryan, yes. Depending on whether he really has changed as much as he claims, and if she were sure enough of him and his feelings for her and Kenny. She'd say it was for the boy's sake, but it'd be just as much for her own."

As though he didn't have enough to worry about as it was. . . .

6

Friday Morning

RAKUBIAN'S law offices were on Harrison Street in South Beach, a warehouse district off the Embarcadero when San Francisco was still a viable port city, now a gentrified mix of upscale restaurants and clubs, small businesses, professional offices, expensive condos and lofts. The old three-story structure had been born as a ship chandlery, spent decades of service as a storage warehouse, and in the early eighties been converted and face-lifted into an office building. The architects hadn't done much of a job on the design; conventional was the kindest word for its facade. The same was true of many of the other buildings in the area, in Hollis's professional opinion.

His watch read eight minutes past nine when he turned onto Harrison. Commute traffic had been heavier than usual this morning, in the city as well as on the way down; the hopes he'd had of getting here before Rakubian, approaching him on the street instead of having to do his talking inside, were long gone. The bugger was obsessively punctual; he would already be at his desk, unless he had an early court appearance scheduled.

At this hour there was still street parking in the vicinity. Hollis jockeyed the Lexus into a space, sat there for a time after he shut off the engine. He'd gone over what he would say to Rakubian a dozen times last night and this morning; he went over it yet again. Ticklish part of the plan. If he didn't handle this just right, the rest of it was worthless.

He wished there was a safer way to brace Rakubian. On the street would have been best; he cursed himself for not leaving home earlier than he had. Walking into those offices again, after his half-out-of-control tirade weeks ago, was a calculated risk. It might work in his favor if he made the right impression on the secretary and paralegal this time, but it would still call attention to himself.

No other way now. Phoning him here or at home was a fool's gambit; for all he knew Rakubian recorded every one of his incoming calls—it would be right in character—and he couldn't afford to chance having anything he said pre-served on tape. If he went to St. Francis Wood tonight, he had no guarantee Rakubian would be home; and he did not want to risk being seen in the neighborhood again if he could avoid it.

Quit stalling, he told himself. There's risk in everything you do from now on.

Out of the car, dodge through traffic, enter the building. Elevator to the top floor. A couple of deep breaths at the door marked David Rakubian, Attorney-at-Law, then walk in with his shoulders a little rounded, his face carefully ar-ranged to project both reluctance and restraint.

The suite was small—anteroom, two offices, supply and copy room—and designed to reflect businesslike compe-tence. Muted colors, minimum of furnishings and decora-tion, no frills of any kind. The anteroom was empty except for the attractive young secretary, Janet Yee, seated at her desk. The door to Rakubian's office was closed; the other office door stood partway open, giving Hollis a glimpse of hawk-faced Valerie Burke at her desk as he came forward.

The Chinese woman's professional smile froze when she recognized him, then melted into an uneasy frown. "Oh," she said. "Mr., um, Hollis."

"Don't worry, I'm not here to make another scene. I need to see Mr. Rakubian if he's in."

"Do you have an appointment?"

"No, I don't."

"Well, his calendar is full this morning—"

"If he's in, please tell him I'm here and that it's important I talk to him. Very important."

"More accusations and threats, Mr. Hollis?"

He turned his head. The paralegal was standing now in the doorway to her office—a thin, homely brunette in a mannish suit, her arms folded across her chest, her eyes behind gold-rimmed glasses radiating disapproval.

"On the contrary," he said. "What I have to say this time is something he'll want to hear."

"And that is?"

"Between him and me." He looked at the secretary again. "Ms. Yee?"

She glanced at Valerie Burke, as if for confirmation, and picked up her phone and punched a button. "Mr. Jack Hollis to see you, sir. He says it's very important." Pause. "No, sir, Mrs. Rakubian isn't with him."

Mrs. Rakubian. Just the sound of it grated on Hollis.

"No, sir, he's not." Pause. "Yes, sir." Ms. Yee put down the phone and said stiffly to Hollis, "Mr. Rakubian will see you. Go right in, please."

The two women watched him cross the room; he could feel their eyes on his back. He didn't blame them for their mistrust, after the fit he'd pitched on his last visit. If Rakubian had told them anything about the situation, it had been distorted to make himself out to be the injured party, Hollis the obstacle in the path of a reconciliation.

He opened the door marked Private without knocking, went in, and closed it behind him.

Rakubian's office was almost as large as the anteroom, just as functional but with his dark stamp on it. One wall covered with law books, bank of windows providing an oblique view of the Ferry Building and the bay in the distance, a replica of one of Goya's "black" paintings on another wall. And on a pedestal, squatting atop the helmeted head of the Greek goddess Pallas Athena, a foot-high black raven. It was a wonder he hadn't hung a sign around the raven's neck reading "Nevermore!"

Rakubian stood behind his dark mahogany desk, stiff and straight, no discernible expression on his olive-toned face. He wasn't particularly tall, but he gave the impression of height, of looking down on everyone and everything out of eyes as black as charred wood. His hair and brows were also black, as thick and wiry as animal fur. Square chin, aquiline nose, white smile when he felt like turning it on. Women found him handsome, but if you worked at penetrating the surface you could see what lay beneath, squirming and crawling like maggots. One long look at him standing there and Hollis felt the hate rise; he could taste it in the back of his throat, hot and metallic.

"Why are you here, Hollis?" No preamble, no pretense. The deep voice was neutral except for the undercurrent of contempt that was always there, that had been there from the first moment they'd met. Homo superior talking down to homo inferior. "We have nothing more to say to each other."

"I wish that was true, but it's not. I came here to tell you you're going to get what you want."

"Yes?"

"Angela's given in. You wore her down to the point where she feels she has no other choice."

Nothing changed in Rakubian's expression or demeanor. He was not surprised or pleased or relieved because he'd expected nothing less, sooner or later. He said, "Then why didn't she come with you? Or alone or with Kenneth?"

"She's not ready yet."

"Meaning you're not ready to permit it?"

"She makes her own decisions," Hollis said. "I think it's a big mistake. I tried to talk her out of it, but she won't listen to me anymore. But there are conditions before she'll reconcile with you. Her conditions, not mine."

"And they are?"

"A meeting with you first—not alone, with me present. To settle some things to her satisfaction. The main one is that you agree never to lay a hand on her again for any reason. Put it in writing, signed and witnessed."

"A document like that is not legally binding."

"She knows that and so do I. Are you willing to sign one anyway?"

"I've never mistreated Angela," Rakubian said. "Discipline is not mistreatment."

Hollis held his hands flat against his thighs to keep them from fisting. "Either you agree to no more physical *discipline*, in writing, or she won't give you another chance. I won't let her give you another chance. If your answer is no, say so right now and I'll walk out of here."

"You've made your point, Hollis."

"You'll sign the agreement? Live up to it?"

Rakubian shrugged. As if he found the notion ridiculous and of no particular import one way or the other. "I love Angela. I would do anything for her."

"As long as she does exactly what you want."

"I don't understand your meaning."

"The park the other night. Remember what you said to her?"

"Not offhand, no."

"You threatened her. And my grandson. You said you'd kill them both rather than give her up."

"A man says things in the heat of passion he doesn't always mean."

"What about doing things in the heat of passion?"

"I would never harm my wife or her son."

"Under any circumstances?"

"Angela is my life, I love Kenneth as if he were my own. What do you think I am, Hollis?"

A fucking monster.

"She wants your promise, also in writing, never to threaten her or Kenny or anyone else in our family again."

A sigh this time. "Is that all?"

"Yes, except that if you violate the agreement in any way, she'll leave you immediately and you'll never see her again. Guaranteed."

Rakubian came out from behind his desk, went to stand at one of the windows looking out. He had a feline way of moving, sinuous and gliding, like a predator on the stalk for prey. Watching him, Hollis tasted his hate again.

Close to a minute passed before Rakubian swung around to face him. As if there had been no gap in the conversation he said, "In return I demand a signed document from you that you will leave Angela and me alone from now on. No interference of any sort in our relationship."

Hollis pretended to think this over. "All right, if that's what it takes to get you to treat my daughter like a human being instead of a possession."

"A gross exaggeration, whether you believe it or not. I

have never thought of Angela as a possession. I respect her feelings and her intelligence."

Bullshit. The only intelligence you respect is your own; the only feelings you care about are the ones you have for yourself.

"Settled, then? You'll meet with us?"

"Yes, but I want to speak to Angela first. Privately."

"Why?"

"To hear her tell me herself she has come to her senses. She can call me here or at home tonight—"

"No," Hollis said.

"No?"

"She won't talk to you on the phone. In person only."

"Her terms or yours?"

"Hers. She'll confirm it when we meet."

No response. Those black eyes were as cold as death.

"Well?"

"Where and what time?"

"Our cottage on Tomales Bay. Two P.M. tomorrow."

"Why not here? Or my home, or yours?"

"The cottage is a neutral site. It also happens to be where she's been since yesterday morning."

"Is that so? Alone?"

"Not alone. And not with Kenny. So don't go getting any ideas about driving out there before two o'clock tomorrow."

Rakubian turned back to the window. Thinking it over. *Come on, damn you, it sounds good, it sounds like you're getting exactly what you think you deserve, say yes—*

"I'd prefer to meet here," Rakubian said.

Shit! "Why?"

"The agreements can be more easily drawn up here."

"They're not legally binding, isn't that what you said? What difference does it make where they're written or what they're written on? Bring along some of your stationery if you like. For Christ's sake, Rakubian, we're not preparing a brief or taking depositions. We're trying to put your marriage back together."

"I'm well aware of that."

"The cottage, then. Two o'clock. It's what she wants, can't you bend a little for once to get what *you* want?"

Faint smile. Smug, condescending. Hollis could almost read his mind: *I always get what I want.*

"Very well," the son of a bitch said. "Two o'clock at Tomales Bay. How do I get to this cottage of yours?"

In the car, on his way across the city to the Golden Gate Bridge, Hollis used his cell phone to call North Bay Transit in Santa Rosa. The woman who answered said yes, there was regular bus service on Sundays, San Francisco to Los Alegres. Leaving from the Transbay Terminal, Mission and First Streets, every half hour from noon until 7 P.M.

Okay. One more arrangement to make, and he'd have the problem of what to do about Rakubian's car solved.

He took care of that arrangement as soon as he reached Mannix & Hollis. Gabe was out at a meeting, which made it easy to brace Gloria. Easy to weave another little web of lies around someone he cared about.

"I hate to ask this," he said, "but are you free for a couple of hours Sunday morning?"

"What's up on Sunday?"

"I need a ride to Tomales Bay. Our cottage out there. The foundation's shaky, needs shoring up, and I'm scheduled to meet a local contractor at noon. And now my car's acting up."

"If it rains, it pours," Gloria said sympathetically.

"He's got something going on in the morning, the contractor, I mean, so he can't come in and pick me up. Cassie and Angela are both tied up, too. I suppose I could cancel out. . . ."

"Hey, no problem. I'll be glad to do it. We're always home from church by ten-thirty and no plans after that. How long do you think it'll take?"

"No need for you to wait. Just drop me off. Contractor'll drive me home when we're done."

"You sure? I don't mind waiting. . . ."

"Running me out there is enough of an imposition."

"Imposition, my fat ass. Pick you up at your house at eleven?"

Better if it was someplace other than the house, but he couldn't think of a place or an excuse. "Eleven's fine. Thanks, Gloria."

"De nada. What are friends for?"

Late Friday Afternoon

When he got home Cassie was already there, sitting in the living room with Fritz alert at her feet, one of their big spiral-bound photo albums open on her lap. Angela and Kenny were upstairs. The reason she was home early, Cassie told him, was that she'd agreed to work until two at the clinic tomorrow so one of the other vets could visit an ailing relative. He took the opportunity to mention that he'd be working tomorrow afternoon himself, some last-minute design changes at their Larkfield site. Her only comment was that it was too bad they wouldn't be able to spend the entire day with the kids.

He gestured at the photo album. "How come?"

"No particular reason. Feeling nostalgic, I guess."

"Which one is it?"

"Come sit and look. Yosemite," he said, sitting beside her.

"And Mono Lake and Virginia City. One of our best trips."

"I remember. Must've been . . . what, nearly twenty years ago?"

"Eighteen. Angela was seven, Eric four."

"Time," he said, and shook his head.

They flipped pages, pointing out individual snapshots that triggered memories: El Capitan, the Ahwanee Hotel, Tuolumne Meadows, the tufa towers at Mono, the Bucket of Blood saloon in the old mining town. By the time she closed the album Hollis felt almost calm. A rush of tenderness filled him; he tilted her chin toward him and kissed her, deeply.

"Hey," she said, smiling, "what was that for?"

"Twenty-six years of putting up with me."

"And counting."

"Yes, and counting. I love you, Cass."

"I love you, too."

"Why? I mean, what did you ever see in me?"

"You can't imagine the number of times I've asked myself that question."

"Seriously."

"Well, for one thing you're terrific in the sack."

"Seriously, Cass."

"All right. You're gentle, sensitive, caring. A good man in all the ways that count. You're also pigheaded, moody, and inclined to jump to conclusions, but hey, nobody's perfect."

"You come pretty close."

"Uh-huh. My list of faults is longer than yours and you know it."

"I can't imagine my life without you. Without the kids."

"Devoted family man. That's another of your good points."

"I mean it," he said.

"I know you do. Don't you think I feel the same way?"

"Yes. I just wanted to say it."

"We're a team, buddy," she said. "And we're going to keep on being a team for a lot more years."

"A lot more," he agreed, and wondered if she believed it any more than he did.

Friday Night

Eric called from Colma, south of San Francisco, a little before six-thirty. He'd made better time through the San Jose commuter bottleneck than expected and he thought he'd be home before eight. They agreed to wait dinner. Cassie and Angela were both in upbeat moods—because Eric was coming and Rakubian had left them alone for the day, and on Angela's part because her friend's Utah relatives had agreed to act as short-term landlords and because she'd met with Pierce today and the meeting had gone well. At least Pierce was being understanding and supportive, a positive force in her life for a change.

Eric arrived at ten of eight. On close inspection Hollis liked what he saw. His son was lean and fit and sun-browned: tennis, jogging, hiking. He seemed more self-confident, too, with a ripening sense of humor—both signs of maturity. He hadn't completely lost the sudden broody lapses into silence, or the vaguely defensive, combative attitude when he was alone with Hollis, but these traits were less pronounced every time he came home. If the father-son closeness still wasn't what it should be, the distance between them had narrowed so that they were within touching distance. Being out on his own had been good for Eric. At eighteen he'd been a difficult boy; at twenty-one he was developing into a man to be proud of.

Dinner. All of them trying a little too hard to be cheerful, Eric teasing Kenny and making him the giggling, chattering center of attention. But the strain was there, a faint but tangible presence at the table even though they avoided mentioning Rakubian or Angela's moving away. Still, it was good to see his kids laughing again, even if some of the laughter was forced. A foretaste of the way things would be once the David Rakubian threat had been neutralized.

Hang on to that thought, Hollis. Hold it close tomorrow and there won't be any buck fever this time, you won't have any trouble doing what needs to be done.

But he slept little that night. And when he did drop off, his dreams were horrorscapes sprinkled with blood.

7

Saturday Afternoon

THE Tomales Bay cottage had been part of his inheritance after Pop's death. It was also where the old man died, of a sudden heart attack at the end of a day of fishing near Hog Island—keeled over on the dock float after tying up his dinghy, fifty-eight years old and nobody around to see it happen but the sea gulls. The cottage had been his getaway spot, his pride and joy, built with his own hands in the fifties on the wooded stretch of land south of Nick's Cove. Hollis's memories of the place when the old man was alive were mixed. He'd never much cared for fishing or boating, hadn't enjoyed being dragged along for long weekends alone out here with Pop. On the other hand, there had been some good times; he remembered huge plates of both raw and barbecued oysters, long walks on the headlands and along the shore, curling up with a book in front of a blazing fire, the three-room box smoky and warm, on nights when fog blanketed the water and pressed in close against the windows.

He and Cassie had had some good times here, too, after

they were first married and while the kids were still young. But few enough the past ten years or so. Neither Eric nor Angela cared for the place as they grew older—too remote, the weather too often cold and misty—and Cassie had taken on more of a workload at the clinic, developed other interests. The cottage was mostly his now, and still little used. Yet he'd never been able to bring himself to sell it. He wasn't sure why. The good memories, partly, he supposed. And because it had been Pop's place. And because every now and then, when he felt peopled out, it became *his* male retreat.

Now it would serve another purpose.

Now, today, another man would die here.

No close neighbors, trees screening most of the property from Highway 1, a separate garage without windows. Oh, it was the perfect place, all right, to commit murder . . . no, to commit an act of self-defense. He wondered if he would feel the same about it after today, if he would ever be able to come here again. Probably not. The smart thing to do would be to put it on the market and be done with it. Another piece of himself lost. Another sacrifice.

What would Pop say if he knew? Hell, Hollis thought, he'd be all for it. Would've done the same thing himself, in this kind of situation—just bulled right ahead instead of planning it out, the way I almost did Wednesday night. Man of action, take the bull by the horns, kick ass and never look back . . . that was Bud Hollis, a monument built of clichés. He'd be proud of me, by God. More proud of me for killing a man, eliminating a threat to the family, than he ever was for anything I accomplished while he was alive or since.

Hollis slowed, made the turn off the highway onto the rutted access lane. The trees, mostly pine and cypress, were old and bent from the constant buffeting of the coastal winds; passing through them, he had a sense of retreating backward in time. The cottage added to it: redwood boards, sagging roofline, creaky pilings sunk deep into the bayshore mud and supporting both the rear deck and the crookedly attached dock, everything weathered gray and unchanged —except for the new roof—since his boyhood. As he approached, he would not have been surprised to see the old man appear in the doorway, straight-spined and unsmiling, a fishing rod in one gnarled hand and a can of Bud in the other.

He pulled up in front of the ramshackle garage, sat looking through the gap between it and the shack at the whitecapped bay. The wind was strong today; he could hear it rattling and soughing in the trees, smell the briny odor of the bay even with the windows rolled up. After a time he opened the glove compartment, removed the chamois-wrapped Colt Woodsman. Sat a few seconds longer, taking stock of himself.

The sense of fragmentation was there again, and an edginess, and a hollow feeling beneath his breastbone. Emotional push-pull: resolve and repugnance, necessity and uncertainty. He'd taken a good long look into the center of himself the past few days and he had little doubt that he was a man capable, in extremis, of taking a human life. But that didn't mean he could or would when the time came. He might freeze up again; he might shoot Rakubian dead without a moment's hesitation. There was just no way to be sure. He would not know the full sum of Jack Hollis for another sixty minutes or so. Two o'clock, the hour of reckoning.

He went first to unlock the garage. Not much in there except the two items he'd remembered—a short-pronged pick and a rusty shovel. He'd hide Rakubian's BMW in the garage so Gloria wouldn't see it when she brought him out tomorrow. Then he'd drive it to San Francisco and leave it in one of the parking garages downtown—Union Square or

Sutter-Stockton—and take a North Bay Transit bus back to Los Alegres. Simple. No one would notice or remember him; parking garages and buses were places that harbored anonymity.

He hefted the pick, swung it once to make sure the wood hadn't rotted where the head was attached. He would have no trouble using it or the shovel; the summers Pop had made him do scut labor on his construction sites, to "toughen him up," would finally serve a useful purpose. He carried the tools to the car, put them in the trunk with the other items he'd stowed in there at home this morning. Now he had everything he needed—perhaps more than he needed. The more prepared he was, the more likely he would be able to follow through.

A strong mingling of dust, must, salt damp, and dry rot assaulted his sinuses when he let himself into the cottage. It had been months since his last visit. He set the .22 on the table in the kitchen alcove, opened the folding blinds and then the sliding glass door to the balcony to let in light and fresh air. Nostalgia stirred in him as he surveyed the cramped living room and kitchen areas. Everything the same as it had been before the old man died, some of the original furnishings unchanged and unmoved. Forties Sears & Roebuck, fifties kitsch. Yellow-and-brown linoleum on the floor, worn through in places. Yellow Formica-topped dining table and matching chairs, ancient coil-topped refrigerator, two-burner propane stove. The horsehair sofa and Pop's overstuffed Morris chair, the fabrics on both torn and showing their insides here and there. Claw-foot smoking stand, ugly lamps, faded and poorly done seascapes, the stuffed and mounted trophy fish over the blackened stone fireplace. That fireplace . . . it smoked no matter how clean the chimney was. On windy days it let drafts down the warped old flue that made freakish whistling, howling noises and blew ash all over the floor. "He could hear the noises now; they made him feel cold. I can't do it in here, he thought. Outside. The sound of the shot won't carry, not with this wind.

He stepped onto the spongy boards of the deck, rested his hands on the railing without leaning on it. A handful of sailboats whitened the bay, one close by Hog Island, the others near the anchorage at Inverness and up near the state park on the opposite shore. The tide was out; the mud stakes marking the oyster beds far to the south were visible a hundred yards offshore. Quiet here except for the wind, the chatter of gulls, the distant hiss and rumble of cars on the highway. Peaceful.

He glanced at his watch—twenty minutes to the hour—and then went back inside, leaving the sliding door open. He unwrapped the Woodsman and checked the loads, the way the old man had taught him. Set the gun on the mantelpiece, where he wouldn't have to look at it when he was sitting down. Drink? Better not. But he went to the alcove anyway, found the half-full bottle of Bushmills in the cupboard, poured a double shot and took it to the Morris chair, and set the glass on the smoking stand without drinking from it. Later, maybe. If he needed a little last-minute Dutch courage.

The musty, closed-up smell evaporated as he sat there. Funny, though . . . he could have sworn that every now and then he had a faint whiff of the old man's latakia pipe tobacco. After seventeen years? Ghost scent. Or maybe not; Pop had smoked that stubby briar of his incessantly, no doubt a major contributing factor in his fatal coronary, and old fabric like the chair's absorbed and retained odors. Now that he thought about it, he remembered other times when he'd sat here and caught the same ephemeral tobacco scent.

Pop. Tough love—what passed for love in him anyway—

but always tempered with those censorious eyes, that critical mouth, the ooze of disappointment. Tried so hard to please him, never seemed to measure up to his expectations. Like with the hunting, the fishing. *You haven't got the guts for a man's sport.* Like with his career choice. Pop had wanted him to be a builder, join him in his construction business. Hollis & Son, General Contractors. Pop's view: building things was man's work; designing them, "fiddling with blueprints and slide rules," had a faintly effeminate taint. He'd wanted half a dozen strapping, brawling, sports-minded, beer-swilling chips off the same rough-hewn block; instead all Mom had given him was one medium-sized, independent, unathletic, bookish son with tendencies that in his eyes smacked of latent homosexuality. *What are you, boy? A goddamn fag?* In his heart of hearts he'd never forgiven his only son for being what he was instead of what he was supposed to be.

"Hey, Pop," Hollis said aloud, "how's this for a *real* blood sport? If I go through with it, will I finally measure up? Be a chip off the old block after all?"

He sat humped forward in the chair, listening for the sound of Rakubian's car.

Two o'clock.

And Rakubian didn't show.

2:05.

2:10.

He took the Woodsman off the mantel, went outside with it hanging down along his leg, and stood peering up through the trees toward the highway. Cars passed, little blips of color and movement, but none slowed or turned in.

2:15.

2:20.

Something had gone wrong. Rakubian wouldn't be this late if he was coming. Anal-retentive control freak, always punctual . . . he should've been here *before* two, smug and gloating because he thought he was getting his prize possession back.

All of Hollis's screwed-up courage was gone now; his nerves were raw and jumping. Frustration, anger, bewilderment—and underneath those emotions, another that he couldn't deny. Relief. The kind a condemned man must feel when he's given a temporary last-minute reprieve.

Some kind of traffic problem, maybe that was it. No, Rakubian would have left the city early, to ensure getting here on or ahead of schedule. Accident? Blowout or engine failure of some kind? Or . . . he wasn't fooled yesterday after all, guessed it was a trap? What would he do in that case?

Figure Angela was still home and go after her there?

Fear crowded away the other feelings. He sat heavily on the front step, laid the .22 down beside him, and dragged the cell phone out of the case attached to his belt. He'd decided it was best to leave it on this time. No calls from home—that was a good sign, wasn't it?

It rang in his hand.

He said, "Shit!" and had to jab twice before he connected with the answer button. "Hollis."

"Jack, it's me." Cassie, sounding upset. "I'm not sure I should be bothering you, but—"

"What is it, what's wrong?"

"Maybe nothing, I could be overreacting—"

"Cass, for God's sake. Angela and the boy, are they all right?"

"Yes, yes, that's not it."

"Rakubian?"

"No, it's Eric. He found that damn evidence box in the

garage, read some of Rakubian's letters, and listened to a few of the tapes. Angela said he was pretty upset."

"What did he say to her?"

"That's just it, he didn't say anything. It was the look on his face . . . you know the look he gets when he's brooding. It was so intense it scared her."

"Let me talk to him."

"He's not here. He left when she did—she took Kenny to see his father again. Eric wouldn't tell her where he was going."

"When was this? What time?"

"More than two hours ago. She got home five minutes ago, just after I did."

"Eleven-thirty, twelve, twelve-thirty?"

"Before noon," Cassie said. "She doesn't think Eric will do anything crazy—that's why she didn't call one of us. But I'm not so sure. He hates Rakubian and I keep thinking about that temper of his. . . ."

A temper that could be explosive; Eric was as capable of violence as his father and grandfather. And no sign of Rakubian here or in Los Alegres. Before noon . . . and it was less than an hour's drive from Los Alegres to St. Francis Wood. Eric *could* have gotten there by twelve-thirty, even a little earlier. Before Rakubian was ready to leave . . .

Hollis switched the phone to his left hand; his right was slick with perspiration. The blood-pound in his ears made Cassie's voice sound far away.

"Jack," she said, "am I overreacting or not?"

"Probably. I hope you are."

"What should we do?"

Try not to panic, he thought. He said, "You call Eric's friends, his old haunts, anyplace you can think of he might be. I'll see if I can get hold of Rakubian."

"What'll you say to him?"

"Let me worry about that."

He could not remember Rakubian's home number, finally got it from San Francisco information. The line hummed and buzzed and clicked—a dozen rings, no answer, and his answering machine wasn't on. That really scared him, the machine being off. Rakubian always kept it on when he was away from home; compulsive about it, according to Angela. Hollis called information again, this time for Rakubian's office number, and tried that. The answering machine there was on; he hung up immediately.

Two-forty now. Rakubian wasn't coming, no longer any doubt of it. Eric . . . no, he wouldn't let himself think the worst. Whatever the reason for the no-show, it was pointless to wait here, pointless to speculate. Go down to the city, find Rakubian, camp on his doorstep if he had to. Relieve his mind about Eric, and then figure out another way to do what had to be done.

He drove too fast over the back roads from Marshall to Nicasio, from Nicasio across the hills and down to Highway 101. Telling himself to slow down, there was no real urgency; half-skidding the Lexus through the curves anyway, as if his body were acting independently of his mind.

Cassie called again just before he reached San Rafael. "I can't find him anywhere," she said. "Nobody's seen him all day. Did you talk to Rakubian?"

"No answer at his house or office."

"Oh, God, I don't like this."

"It doesn't have to mean anything. He could be anywhere . . . as long as he's not in Los Alegres harassing you and Angela."

"There hasn't been any sign of him here. No calls or anything, either."

"That's a relief."

"It sounds like you're in the car. Are you coming home?"

He hesitated. Tell her the truth? It would only increase her anxiety, and he did not want her to know he was anywhere near Rakubian or Rakubian's house today. "No. On my way to Paloma for a meeting with one of the Larkfield people. Nick Jackson."

"Can't you get out of it?"

"I can if there's any real need. I don't think there is, Cass. Eric's impulsive, but he knows better than to start any kind of trouble with Rakubian."

"I'm not so sure. . . ."

"I am," he lied. "Stop worrying, everything's going to be all right."

Fog crawled over the city, turning the sky west of Twin Peaks the color of dirty silver. He turned up Sloat, then up St. Francis to Monterey, slowing to a near crawl as he approached Rakubian's property. Cars were parked at the curbs along there, but none was Eric's bright red Miata. He'd have been even more alarmed if he had spotted it; it was after four now.

He crept past the Spanish stucco. Nothing to see in the jungly front yard or on the visible part of the porch; driveway empty, garage door shut. He drove another block, made a U-turn, and parked on the downhill curve just out of sight of the house. He was on his way out of the car before he remembered the Woodsman. Not thinking clearly; the sense of fragmentation was acute, as if he were starting to come apart inside. His carefully engineered plan had already come apart but he could still put it back together and himself back together with it. If Rakubian was home . . .

He unwrapped the .22, slipped it into his jacket pocket.

Out then and downhill through the blowing fog. No cars moving, nobody in the neighboring yards or in the nearby park. He crossed the street, forcing himself to take a casual pace, and went up Rakubian's walk and rang the doorbell. Chimes, and another sound audible to him: heavy, atonal music playing somewhere inside. He strained to hear footsteps, his right hand on the gun in his pocket.

All he heard was the faint percussive music.

He rang the bell again, waited, rang it a third time. The chimes, the music, the wind. Now what? First thing: check the garage, see if Rakubian's car was there. He left the porch, followed the path around to the driveway. No windows on either side of the garage; he went to the door on the near side, tried it. Unlocked. He put his head inside.

The silver BMW was a gleaming hulk in the shadows.

Oh, God, he thought.

He tried the side door to the house, found it locked. Went back to the front, half running. At the door he did what he hadn't done before—depressed the old-fashioned latch. And it clicked and the door creaked inward.

His heart hammering, he stepped into the darkened foyer and shut the door behind him.

The music was loud enough here to be identifiable: classical, atonal, oppressive. Mussorgsky. *Boris Godunov*. Rakubian's favorite, played it over and over, wouldn't shut the damn piece off any of the times Hollis and Cassie had visited Angela. Coming from the combination library and office that opened off the central hall.

"Rakubian?" Shouting it above the pound of the music.

No response.

He moved ahead, his footsteps making little clicks on the terra-cotta floor. A light burned in the library; he saw the pale glow as he neared the archway. "Rakubian?" Through the arch, one pace into the library. And his stomach heaved, his legs jellied; blindly he clutched and hung on to the jamb to steady himself.

Rakubian was there. On the dark-patterned Sarouk carpet in front of his desk, sprawled on his back with arms outflung and one leg bent under him, and his head—

Blood, brain matter. Streaked and spattered over his white shirt and blue tie, his face, his shattered skull, the carpet, a black raven statuette on the floor close by. A real-life horrorscape sprinkled with blood.

I hate that crazy son of a bitch. I'd like to smash his fucking head in.

Eric, Eric, what have you done!

8

Early Saturday Evening

FOR a minute, two minutes, Hollis was incapable of movement. His mind worked now, but in a stuttery, off-center way: piecemeal thoughts, disoriented perceptions. Everything in the room—Rakubian lying there dead, all the gore, the pale light and shadows, the oppressive symphony, the dark furnishings and dark-spined books and ugly statuary and bleak wall hangings—seemed to lose reality in his eyes and ears, to blur and distort. It was as if he had suddenly become trapped in one of Rakubian's paintings—a Goya "black" of screaming souls in torment, a surrealist interpretation of a scene from Dante's *Inferno*.

Paralysis and disorientation ended at the same time, in an abrupt convulsive tremor that tore him loose from the archway and carried him two steps into the library. He saw clearly again: the room, the body, all of it just as it was. His thoughts were clear but fast-running, like a ticker tape unwinding at accelerated speed across a screen. The music beat at him in thudding waves; he detoured around the dead man to the old-fashioned record player, found the reject switch and the off button. The sudden silence seemed to carry dissonant echoes in a long diminuendo.

Up close, then, to where Rakubian lay, careful to avoid the blood spatters. He'd thought that when he stood looking down into that dead face he would feel relief, vindication, even a kind of terrible elation. He felt nothing except revulsion. No, another emotion, too. Fear. The enemy was dead, Angela and Kenny were safe . . . but now Eric was in jeopardy. Crazy, bitter irony: his son had switched places with him and with his daughter, become both avenger and victim. Even dead, David Rakubian was a threat to them all.

He squatted, forced himself to touch and then lift one wrist, using his thumb and forefinger. Cool flesh. Stiffening. Dead at least three hours, lying here all that time with *Boris Godunov* playing over and over like a funeral dirge. With rigor mortis setting in, it would be difficult to move him before long. Hollis felt his gorge rising; he tightened the muscles in his jaw and throat, released the dead wrist, stood again, and hurried back through the archway into the hall.

The guest bathroom, he remembered, was at the end of the hall on the left. He made it there just in time to drop to one knee in front of the toilet. Dry heaves, mostly; all that came up was a thin stream of the whiskey he'd drunk at the cottage. When the spasms ended he flushed the toilet, pulled himself upright over the sink. He splashed his face with cold water, made a cup of laced fingers and rinsed the sick taste from his mouth. An inadvertent glance at the mirror showed him an old man's face: hollowed cheeks, grayish skin, eyes with too much white glistening like curdled milk.

He found his way to the utility porch at the rear. Rakubian had been as much of a control freak in his home as anywhere else: a place for everything and everything in its proper place. That made it easy to locate the items he would need. Heavy-duty trash bags, the big 33-gallon kind. A spool of strong twine. A roll of paper towels. All of these he carried back into the library.

Except for one leg, Rakubian's body was full on the Sarouk rug. Six feet by four feet, that rug, the nap thick and tightly woven; much of the residue from the shattered skull had soaked into a portion of the design that was the color of burgundy wine, so that there did not seem to be much of it until you looked closely. Seeped through to the tiles? He prodded the one leg onto the carpet, bent to pick up the lower end, and then dragged rug and body a few feet toward the arch. None of the blood had leaked through; the tiles where Rakubian's head had lain looked dry and were dry to the touch.

Hollis shook two of the garbage bags open. He could not stand to look any longer at that broken, red-streaked face. As much as he'd hated the man in life, there was something almost pathetic about him in violent death. Shrunken, a crude and empty shell, with all the obsessive craziness reduced to coagulating red and gray fluids. How could you hate a broken shell, a clotted stain on a fine old carpet? Even if he'd done this himself, he would not have been able to go on hating what the husk had contained.

Lifting the heavy shoulders, getting the trash bag over the head and upper body was stomach-churning work. Sticky blood on his hands when he finished, sweat matting his clothing to his skin. Stuffing legs and lower torso into the second bag wasn't as bad, but his hands shook so much by then that he had trouble looping twine around the corpse, tying the bags together in the middle and at both ends. Done, finally. He groped his way to the black leather sofa, sat there with his stained hands clasped between his knees until the shaking stopped.

The sweat continued to seep out of him. Too warm in there . . . Rakubian kept the heat turned up, no matter what the weather. Thrived on it like a frigging spider. Hollis remembered Angela telling him how sometimes at night she would wake up unable to breathe and beg Rakubian to turn the heat down or at least to let her open a window. Of course, he'd refused and berated her for being childish. Everything for himself, always.

Not anymore.

Hollis stood, went past the body without looking at it. In the bathroom he washed his hands, washed them a second time, then scrubbed out the sink and soap dish to make certain there were no traces of blood left. He dried off on one of the guest towels, used the towel to wipe the toilet bowl, vanity counter, sink and the faucet handles, then folded and replaced it on the rack. For the first time he grew aware of an insistent pressure in his bladder; he nudged the seat up with a knuckle and urinated . . . tried to urinate. Interrupted flow, burning. He flushed the evidence away.

On the utility porch again, he unlocked the outside door and tested the knob to satisfy himself that it was open. Back to the library. The .22 had become a heavy dragging weight in his pocket; he shrugged out of the jacket, laid it on the couch. Then he opened the third garbage bag, used a piece of paper towel to prod the raven statuette inside. *Nevermore!*

He knelt with the towel roll, scrubbed at the drops and spatters on the tiles. The stains were mostly dry; they wouldn't clean up fully without water. To the bathroom once more to wet a few of the paper towels. More scrubbing, and dry sheets to dry the floor afterward. Used towels into the garbage bag. Crawl around on hands and knees, looking for any stains he might have missed. Blip of himself doing it: grisly image with the bagged corpse there beside him, like a scene from a horror movie.

When he was satisfied he stood and scanned the room. No signs of violence remained. The only false note was that the floor in front of the desk seemed unnaturally bare with the carpet moved away. Do something about that later. He bent to grasp the fringed edge of the Sarouk, began to drag it and its burden into the hallway.

His cell phone went off.

In the too warm silence, the eruption of sound was startling enough to jerk his fingers loose from the rug. His heart skipped, banged, skipped; it took a few seconds to pull his breathing under control. Ring. Ring. All right, get a grip, it's probably Cassie. And for God's sake don't let her hear anything in your voice. He blew out a breath, yanked the phone from his belt and clicked on.

"Hollis."

"Jack, Eric's home. He came in five minutes ago."

Careful, now. Careful. "Where was he?"

"He went for a long drive, he said—the Russian River, out to the coast. To cool off."

"You believe him?"

"I want to."

"But you're not sure?"

"Yes, but still . . . you know how he gets. Closemouthed, withdrawn. He still seems to be on edge, wrought up."

On edge, wrought up. He crushed a man's skull this afternoon.

"I'll talk to him later," Hollis said. "Main thing is, he's home safe and nothing happened."

"This time," she said.

"Everything else okay? You know what I mean."

"So far. When will you be home?"

"I . . . don't know yet. I may be late."

"Why, for heaven's sake?"

"Nick Jackson wants me to have dinner with him."

"Beg off, can't you?"

"It's more business than social, so I'd better not. There's no good reason for me to, is there?"

"I suppose not, but—"

"I'll be home as soon as I can," he said, and disconnected. Before he replaced the unit he switched it all the way off. No more calls until he was finished with Rakubian. No more little shocks, no more big lies.

He caught hold of the carpet again, dragged it down the hall and through the kitchen onto the porch. Left it near the outside door, then retraced his route to make sure there were no telltale marks on the floor. Some ridges and speckles of dust was all; these he erased with more dampened paper towels.

At the front there was a formal living room, seldom used, as darkly furnished as the library. Two Oriental rugs in there, the largest of them, three by five feet, spread out before the fireplace. He moved a couple of tables, rolled the rug, rearranged the tables and two chairs so that the empty floor space didn't seem conspicuous. Shouldn't matter anyhow. Rakubian had permitted only a handful of visitors in the first few months of his marriage, and none at all in the last four or five. A loner—no close friends, few acquaintances. His home was his castle, the kind with a moat around it. Who'd notice anything out of place in here? Or in the library, but Hollis knew he'd never feel secure unless another carpet covered the space where Rakubian had died.

He wiped the tiles in front of the fireplace, took all the soiled paper towels to the porch, and stuffed them into the open trash bag. Carried the rolled carpet into the library and laid it down. Better, much better. It didn't seem too small for the space, and its pattern resembled the blood-soaked one's.

Finished. This part of it.

The rest . . . Don't think about the rest yet.

He put his jacket on, zippered it to the throat. In the foyer he cracked the front door and peered out at the street. Nobody in sight. He stepped through quickly, shutting the door behind him. When he came out to the sidewalk he saw someone in the park, an overcoated man walking a dog on a leash, but the man wasn't looking his way. Still he felt exposed, vulnerable as he turned up the street.

Eyes front, same measured pace as before: a man who belonged in this neighborhood as much as the dog-walker. The cold wind beat at him, moaning in his ears, freezing his sweat. By the time he reached the Lexus he was chilled.

Inside, he locked the .22 in the glove compartment. Panicked moment then: he couldn't find his keys. They weren't in either jacket pocket, what if they'd fallen out in the library? Right pants pocket, no, left pants pocket . . . why had he put them there, he never put his keys there. He fumbled the ignition key into the slot.

A car came down Monterey behind him; he heard it, then saw it in the rearview mirror. Passenger car, nondescript, two people inside. He turned his head as it passed, as if he were hunting for something on the seat. It continued on without slowing. He waited until it was two blocks away before he started the engine.

Downhill past Rakubian's driveway, stop, reverse— telling himself to do this casually, not too fast or too slow, he had every right to be here. He cut the wheel too sharp on the first try, almost ran into the bushes bordering the drive. Come on, come on! Second pass was better, in more or less straight; adjust, back up slow and straight. The street in front of him remained empty. Stop a few feet from the garage . . . there.

He stood for a few seconds after he stepped out, checking his surroundings. Tall shrubs and trees hid the near neighbor's property; only the roofline of the house there was visible. More trees at the rear, beyond an expanse of lawn, created a thick screen. It was as if he were standing in a pocket, with the street the only open end. Okay. But he still felt conspicuous as he went around to unlock the trunk and raise the lid.

One thing about a Lexus, it had a wide, deep trunk. He moved the tools and other items, pushing them all against the inner wall. Then he shook out and spread his Cal Poly blanket over the cleared space.

To the porch door, inside to what was left of Rakubian trussed up in the black body bags—not a man anymore, just so much trash to be taken away and disposed of. He bent to work his hands under the bundle, dipped his knees, lifted. Not as heavy as he'd expected: Rakubian hadn't been a big man except in his own eyes. The slick feel of the bags, the deadweight, brought his gorge up again; he swallowed it down. Check the street. Clear. When he stepped outside he did it too quickly and stumbled, nearly dropped his burden. *Careful!* But then, in his haste and revulsion, he lowered the body too soon when he reached the open trunk; it struck the edge with a loose thumping sound and flopped in crooked, one end caught on the locking mechanism. The head . . . the head was still hanging out. He shoved and tugged and finally got all of the bundle inside, curled and bent like an inverted S.

Jesus!

He backed off, sweating in the cold, and turned again to the porch door. And froze. Car on the street, gliding by in the thickening fog. The driver didn't glance his way—or did he? He couldn't be sure.

Only a few more things to do. Get the bag containing the waste towels and statuette, pitch it into the trunk. Roll up the bloodstained rug, tie it with a piece of twine, wedge it in on top of the corpse. Close the lid, test the lock. Into the house for one last walk-through to reassure himself that he hadn't overlooked anything and to test the dead-bolt lock on the front door. Back to the porch, use his handkerchief to wipe the inside doorknob and push-button lock. Set the lock, wipe the outer knob, pull the door shut, test it.

Into the car, start the engine.

Drive.

Don't think, just drive.

9

Saturday Evening

THE ride across the city to the Golden Gate Bridge: splintered, freakish, as if he were making it dead drunk. Little flashes of awareness—somebody honking at him because he was going too slow on Nineteenth Avenue, another car cutting him off inside the park, the murkiness of the tunnel under the Presidio, the lighted line of tollbooths and the wall of fog obscuring the bridge towers. Followed by blank periods, lost time during which he functioned in an unconscious state. It was not until he was halfway across the bridge, poking along in the slow lane, that he came jolting back to himself to stay. The gaps in his recent memory frightened him. What if he'd hit a pedestrian, had some other kind of accident? Concentrate, Hollis. Get off the road if you can't drive without blanking out.

He was all right after that. Too aware, if anything: the white lane markings, the noisy traffic, the big shopping malls and strip malls and housing tracts flanking the freeway, the fogbanks giving way to cloudy blue once he reached the foot of Waldo Grade—all of it too sharply detailed, too bright, too loud, as though his sense perceptions had been cranked up to the maximum.

Despite the urgency in him, he could not make himself drive past fifty. Every time the speedometer edged above that mark, his foot eased up on the accelerator. Slow, slow . . . lines of cars whizzing by. None of the other drivers paid any attention to him, but he still felt nakedly exposed. As if the car bore external signs of the trunk's contents.

The trip seemed interminable. Corte Madera, San Rafael, Terra Linda, the Napa-Vallejo cutoff, Novato . . . each creeping by. Maximum fifty all the way. The sun slid down behind the hills west of Novato, light began to fade out of the sky. It would be near dusk by the time he reached Los Alegres; full dark when he finished the long climb through the hills to the Chesterton site. Burial by flashlight. Bad enough in the daytime, but in the dark . . . ghoul's work.

I must be crazy, he thought. Cassie was right—I must've been crazy all along.

Paloma County line. And finally, finally, Los Alegres. He took the first exit, Main Street, get off the damn freeway. Long loop along the river and beneath the highway overpass into town. Right on D Street, across the drawbridge, out Lakeville past the industrial parks and housing tracts and onto Crater Road. Headlights on now, boring into the gathering darkness. Oncoming beams reflecting off the windshield, jabbing his eyes with bright splinters. Stop and go, stop and go, and the Paloma Mountains did not seem to be getting any closer, seemed instead to be moving farther away. Optical illusion: stress, the light, the dark.

What am I going to say to Eric? Letting himself think about it now, for the first time. *Come right out and tell him I know? Hint around, prod him into confessing what happened? Or pretend that nothing happened? A thing like*

this . . . there's no right way to handle it. Father and son, con-
spirators no matter what either of us says or does. No, wait,
suppose his conscience gets the best of him and he decides to
turn himself in? Taught him the difference between right and
wrong, my own damn moral code turned upside-down. Can't
let that happen—

Sudden flickering light in the car.

Red and white pulsing light.

His gaze jerked upward to the mirror. Frosty prickles on
his neck and back, body going rigid, hands in a death grip on
the wheel. Behind him, close . . . rooftop pulsars throwing
out red and white, red and white.

Police!

A wildness surged through him. He came close, very
close, to jamming his foot down on the acclerator, turning
himself into a fugitive in the single twitch of a muscle. *Don't*
panic! Like a shriek in his mind.

He jerked his foot off the gas pedal, onto the brake. Easy,
tap it, that's right. Tap it again, ease over to the side of the
road. The police car did the same. He shoved the shift lever
into Park, his breath rasping in his throat. Slide the window
down—inhale, exhale, slow and deep. Don't say or do anything to give himself away. The old man: Cops are like dogs,
let 'em see fear and they'll jump all over you.

Footfalls, flashlight beam slanting past; shape outside
the window moving closer, swinging the light, bending
down. In the reflected glare the cop's face was young, not
much more than twenty-five, his expression neither friendly
nor hostile. Neutral voice to match: "Evening."

"Good—" The word caught in Hollis's throat; he
coughed and got the answer out on the second try. "Good
evening, Officer." His voice sounded all right, the strain an
undercurrent too faint to be discernible. "Did I do something wrong?"

"That stop sign back there. You ran it."

Stupid! "I didn't see it. I guess . . . I guess I wasn't paying enough attention."

"License and registration, please."

He removed the license from his wallet, handed it over. No choice then but to open the glove box. He leaned over, trying desperately to remember if he'd wrapped the Woodsman in the chamois cloth earlier. The flash ray followed his movements. Even if he had wrapped it, and the light picked up the shape and made the cop wonder—

Open. The bulb light inside showed him that the gun was wrapped and that he'd shoved it back deep; the flash beam didn't reach it, because the cop didn't say anything. He let out the breath he'd been holding, fumbled up the registration, quickly shut and locked the compartment again.

The cop studied his license, then the registration. "Mr. Hollis. Jackson Hollis."

"Yes." His voice shook, but the cop didn't seem to notice. "Yes, that's correct."

"Keokuk Street address current?"

"Yes."

"West side. Not on your way home, then?"

"Out for a drive. Truth is, Officer, I had a fight with my wife. A real screamer. If you're married, you know how it can be sometimes."

"I'm married." Empathy in his tone? Maybe a little. "Alcohol involved? Before, during, or since?"

"No. Nothing all day."

"Mind stepping out of your car?"

"Not at all. If you'd like me to take a Breathalyzer test . . ."

"Just step out, sir."

He obeyed, unbending in slow segments, standing ruler-backed with his arms at his sides. The cop held the light on him for a few seconds, then told him to wait there and returned to his cruiser. Hollis squinted against the glare of the headlights. He couldn't see what the cop was doing inside, but he thought he knew: checking to see if there were any outstanding warrants against him.

Another car crept by, the driver's face framed briefly in the side window, gawking. *Felon by the roadside, caught.* He shook the thought away, tried to will himself into a kind of sleep mode the way a computer is programmed to do. No good; his mind kept churning. Was there anything to make the cop suspicious? No, not even an unpaid parking ticket on his driving record. He had nothing to worry about if he just cooperated, kept his head, masked his emotions.

It seemed a long time before the cop emerged again. He didn't approach Hollis; instead he stood just off the Lexus's rear bumper, in the headlight wash, and began writing in a slender book. Ticket . . . writing out a ticket. He took his time doing it, glancing up a couple of times. One of the glances seemed to hold on the trunk. No, not the trunk, the license plate. Hollis could feel sweat trickling on him, in spite of the cold night air. Less than five feet between the cop and what lay inside the trunk . . . what if a sixth sense told him something was wrong? What if he came up and said, "Mind opening your trunk, Mr. Hollis?" All over then. Nowhere to run, nothing more to cover up except Eric's involvement. He'd say that he killed Rakubian, he'd say he went to the city to talk to him and they argued and Rakubian attacked him and he'd acted in self-defense. . . .

The cop finished writing and moved toward him. Hollis stood rigid.

And the cop said, "Okay," and extended the ticket. He took it automatically; a little gust of wind tried to tear it from his fingers and he tightened his grip. "Sorry to have to write you up, but running a stop sign the way you did can cause a serious accident."

"Yes.

"Better be more careful from now on."

"Yes."

"Might want to go on home instead of doing any more driving around. Patch things up with your wife."

"Yes." As if his brain had slipped into a one-word loop.

"Good luck," the cop said, and made a little gesture with his forefinger that was half warning and half salute, and turned away.

Hollis shut himself inside the Lexus. Good luck. Jesus, good luck! It took him two tries to turn the ignition, a few seconds more to steady himself before he eased out onto the road.

The cop followed him. He'd expected that; he drove well within the legal limit, straight down Crater Road to the intersection with East Valley Road. Full stop at the sign there, flick the turn signal for a left onto East Valley. He made the turn, and again the cop followed, hanging back by a hundred yards or so and matching his speed as he accelerated.

Hollis's eyes kept skipping between the road and the rearview mirror. *What if he follows me all the way home? I can't go home with Rakubian in the car, I can't do that. Have to stop somewhere, 7-Eleven, service station . . . shake him somehow and pray I don't run into him again. If he spots me driving back this way he'll wonder what I'm up to, maybe pull me over again, demand to look inside the trunk. . . .*

The trailing lights abruptly cut away: the cop had turned off onto the road paralleling Crater, heading back toward town.

He was alone again, safe again, with Rakubian's corpse.

The corkscrew climb into the hills seemed to go on and on endlessly. He felt exposed up here, too, like a bug crawling across a piece of glass; headlights on these mountain roads could be seen for miles, all across the valley and the town. But not tonight—he kept reminding himself of that, for all the good it did. Tonight there was haze in the valley and along the spine of the hills, a thin river of fog flowing down from the north that blurred the distant lights. Another thing in his favor, another reminder: nobody paid any attention to headlights in the Paloma Mountains, took them for granted. If he came upon another car, even a county sheriff's patrol, the occupants would assume he lived here or was visiting someone who did. The only thing he had to worry about now was driving slow and careful on the sharper turns.

He was still afraid.

The encounter with the cop had solidified his fear, jammed it down tight inside him. It would not break loose until he was finished with Rakubian, maybe not even then. He wondered if it would stay with him long after tonight, for as long as he lived, a different kind of cancer inexorably eating away at him.

He needed to pee again. His bladder felt huge, an overin-flated sac with needles attached to the outside . . . bloated and stabbing pains both. Partway up the winding road, in a little copse of trees, he stopped the car and got out and un-zipped. The burning, this time, was acute enough to make him grit his teeth. But he was done quickly for a change, and the pains were gone by the time he started driving again.

He reached the gate to the Chesterton property without seeing another set of headlights. Unlock the gate, drive through, relock it behind him. Tires crunching gravel as he crawled along the newly built road. The construction site loomed ahead, dead-still and full of broken shadow shapes. Thin curls of mist drifting through the headlamp beams made it seem an even eerier place—like a cemetery in the dead of night. Some of the shapes appeared and disappeared as he swung in among them, and his mind turned them into graveyard images: foundation slabs and staked sections became burial plots, portable toilets became headstones, Dulac's trailer and the heavy equipment became chimerical crypts.

His mouth was dry, his face hot, as if he might be running a fever. His consciousness began to shrivel again. Defense mechanism, and he didn't fight it this time. The only way he would be able to get through what lay ahead was to do it mechanically—an android drone functioning on programmed circuitry.

He braked long enough to orient himself, crawled ahead at an angle toward the wine cellar excavation. The beams picked it out; it might have been a mine shaft cut into the hillside, or an unfinished mausoleum. Tiered rock and dirt gleamed a short distance to the right. He drove as close as he could to the hillside, turning the wheel to bring the rear end around and his lights full on the earth dump. When he shut them off, the darkness pressed down so thickly it was as though he'd gone blind. The illusion brought a brief twist of panic; he opened the door to put the dome light on, kept it open for several seconds after he swung out. Then he stood blinking, scanning left and right, until his eyes adjusted.

Cold up here, but not as cold as it had been in San Francisco. Not as much wind, either, the fog moving in slow, sinuous patterns. Cricket sound rose and fell; the wind carried the faint rattle of disturbed branches, the odors of pine, madrone, damp earth. The lights of Los Alegres were smeary pinpricks in the ragged veil of fog.

Top of the world, Ma.

He shivered, swung around to open the trunk. He didn't touch the body, not yet. Pick, shovel, disassembled push broom from the garage at home. Utility lantern. Pair of bib overalls, pair of heavy work gloves, pair of old galoshes to protect his shoes, a worn khaki shirt. When he had all of these on the ground, he shed his jacket and pullover and tossed them onto the front seat; donned the shirt, overalls, galoshes, and gloves. Then he lighted the lantern, followed its beam to the earth dump.

The wheelbarrow wasn't where he'd seen it on Thursday. Took him a couple of minutes to track it down, over on the far side. He ran it back to the car, the lantern riding inside so that its long ray jumped and wobbled and threw crazy shadows against the fog. He loaded the tools, humped the barrow over bare ground, over a pair of poured slabs and inside the excavation.

In there he positioned the lantern so the beam held steady on the center section of the floor. Lifted one of the plywood sheets, propped it against the wall out of the way; did the same with a second sheet. The cleared space . . . long enough and wide enough? Yes. He flexed the muscles in his arms and back. Not thinking now, all but shut down inside.

He hefted the pick and began to dig.

10

Saturday Night

PICK. Shovel. Loose dirt piled on the plywood to one side. Clods and chunks of rock into the wheelbarrow. Pick. Shovel. Loose dirt. Clods, chunks. Full barrow out to the dump and back again empty. Pick. Shovel . . .

He lost all sense of time. His perceptions narrowed to light and dark, cold and sweat-heat, aching strain in arms and shoulders and lower back, chink of metal on stone, thud of metal biting into earth. One barrow full, two barrows full, three barrows full. And the hole growing wider, deeper— standing in it, climbing out, dropping back in until one loose, sloping side touched him at mid-thigh. Deep enough. His strength was flagging by then; the pick had grown as heavy as a ten-pound sledge.

He tossed it out, sent the shovel after it and himself after the shovel. His body begged for rest. Instead he lifted the barrow's handles, grunting, and slogged it out and across to the earth pile; emptied it, then wheeled it around to the rear of the Lexus. His eyes stung with sweat and grit. He wiped them clear on his shirtsleeve as he opened the trunk.

Getting the body out of there and into the wheelbarrow was a grim struggle. It had stiffened in full rigor and he couldn't unbend it from the S curve. Wielding the pick and shovel had weakened his arms and back, so that he was unable to lift the deadweight as easily as he had at Rakubian's house. He jerked, pulled, finally got it over the lip, but when he tried to lower it, it slipped down and upended the barrow with an echoing clang. Blank period after that. He had no memory of righting the carrier, hoisting Rakubian into it; he was halfway to the excavation, wheeling his heavy load, before he came back to himself.

The hole was too narrow. He realized that as soon as he pushed the wheelbarrow alongside. A sound like a hurt animal's whimper came out of him. More digging, another foot or so of width before the bent and bag-wrapped remains would fit into the hole.

Upturn the barrow, body thumping on plywood. Pick. Shovel. Loose dirt onto the side pile. Clods, chunks of rock into the carrier. Pick. Shovel. Dirt, clods, chunks. Wide enough now? Almost. Pick, shovel, dirt, clods, chunks. Pick shovel dirt clods chunks. Climb out and take up the handles and wheel the barrow out of the way.

Roll the dead thing into its grave.

Prod and pull until it was wedged on its side.

It fit in there, just barely. Tight squeeze. The Sarouk carpet still had to go in, but that shouldn't be a problem because the hole was deep enough and overlong by a couple of feet. Plenty of room to spread it and tuck it around the corpse.

He went and got the rug, stumbling a little on enervated legs. Untied and unrolled it and covered the body, working to find room along the sides, wadding its fringed ends into the two-foot open space. He was panting when he finished;

he couldn't seem to take in enough air. He looked at the shovel, said "No" aloud, and crawled over to the side wall and sat motionless with his legs extended, trying to breathe.

Sat there.

And sat there.

Outside somewhere, a night bird made a low screeching sound. It roused him from an exhausted near-doze. His chest ached but he had his wind back. He heaved upright and picked up the shovel, a lead weight in his hands. He plunged the blade into the pile of loose earth, began to fill in the grave.

He had no idea, afterward, how long it took. The pile shrank, Rakubian and the Sarouk and the sides of the hole gradually disappeared. And the cellar floor was once more pounded flat and even. He leaned on the shovel, staring down. Gone. Dead and buried and soon to be gone forever. Not to be forgotten, though, not until Jack Hollis was ready for his own fine and private place.

He felt like puking again.

Still work to be done. Screw the push broom handle into the base, sweep the section of earth so it looked as though it had never been disturbed. Replace the two plywood sections. Sweep out the remaining loose dirt. Carry the tools outside, then shine the lantern around to be sure there was nothing to make Pete Dulac or anyone in his crew suspicious. It seemed all right, but how could he really be certain? So tired, used up—he had no judgment left. Have to take it on faith. They had no reason to suspect anything wrong, did they?

Take the barrow out to the dump, empty it, leave it where he'd found it. Disassemble the broom, load it and the pick and shovel into the trunk. Gloves off, galoshes off, overalls off and into the trunk. Take out the blanket, get his pullover and jacket from the front seat, find his away across to the trailer. Water hookup there, fed by the well that had been dug on the property. He stripped to the waist and splashed icy water on his face and upper body, gasping and shivering, to rid his flesh of the stink and residue of his grave digging.

He dried off quickly with the blanket, yanked on the pull-over and jacket. Back at the car, he started the engine, put the heater on high. Sat hugging himself as warm air began to flood the interior. Kept on sitting there because he did not trust himself to drive yet.

What time was it? He held his watch up to peer at the dial. After ten. Three hours up here. That was how long it took to bury the dead—three hours.

He sat. The chill in him was bone deep; the heater did no more than warm his skin, make him drowsy. His arms and legs, his torso, tingled with fatigue. He shut off the engine—low on gas and he couldn't chance running out on the way home. But his eyelids stayed heavy, his mind dull with torpor. Don't go to sleep, for God's sake.

He slept.

Jerked awake, slept a little more, woke up and stayed awake. Reaction, regeneration: still exhausted but with the edge off, no longer sleepy or muddle-headed. Good because now he was ready for the drive home; bad because his thoughts were focused again.

I did it. I did this. How could I have done a thing like this?

The fear still lived in him. Revulsion, too. And now something close to self-hatred.

He shrank from the thought of facing Eric, Cassie, Angela. If he had to do it tonight . . . His watch told him he'd slept for ninety minutes; it was 11:45. Four and a half hours up here. It would be 12:30 by the time he got home. The kids would likely be in bed, but Cassie? Worried that he was out so late, that he hadn't called, she might wait up for him. Could he hide the truth from her? Not a question of could—

he *had* to. Bad enough what he'd done tonight, but what Eric had done . . . keep that from her at all cost.

He'd be all right in the morning, clearheaded and able to deal with the situation. Just get through the rest of tonight the best way he could. The worst was already over . . . almost over.

Wasn't it?

Except for the porch light, the house was completely dark. So Cassie had gone to bed, too. Even if she was still awake, it would be easy enough to plead exhaustion and go right to sleep.

Dark house, uneventful drive home . . . he should be feeling better now, safer. Instead he felt . . . strange. So drained he'd had to open the window, turn the heater off and the radio on to keep himself alert, but inside he was still wired tight. The tingling that had been in his limbs earlier seemed to have passed by some weird osmosis through skin and flesh, become an internal sensation like a steady, low-voltage electrical pulse. He could feel it in his throat, his chest, down low in his belly.

He let himself into the house. No light in the hall; that meant Cassie was angry as well as anxious. The ticking of the grandfather clock seemed overloud to him; the odors of cooked meat, furniture polish, air freshener, Cassie's perfume were strong in his nostrils. As if his senses had become heightened somehow. He took the stairs in an old man's climb, one riser at a time. Paused in front of Angela's door, resisted the urge to look in on her and Kenny, and moved ahead to the open door to his bedroom.

Cassie was a motionless blob of shadow on her side of the bed. He could hear her breathing and knew from the cadence that she was awake. Not ready to talk to him yet, though; she lay silent as he crossed to the bathroom.

He shut the door, turned on the light. The strange feeling had grown even more pronounced; the inner tingling was urgent, as if any second now his hands, his body would start to twitch and jerk. He imagined himself in a kind of uncontrollable fit, beginning to foam at the mouth; the image, gone in two or three seconds, left him cold all over. He stripped naked, threw his clothes into the hamper, turned on the hot water in the shower. The thought came to him then, standing there next to the toilet, that he hadn't had to urinate since he'd stopped on the road into the Paloma Mountains after the incident with the cop. Nearly five hours up there, the drive home, even now standing here . . . no pressure at all.

In the shower, under a stream as hot as he could stand it, he scrubbed himself with a thick lather. Hands, face, arms, underarms, upper body. The soapy washcloth took away the last of the sweat-stink, but he didn't feel clean. And now his skin seemed too tight, sensitive to the touch, prickly on the surface again—sensations that had nothing to do with the steamy water.

He kept scrubbing with the cloth, working downward across his abdomen. The instant it touched his privates, the inner tingling became something else—a carnal heat that flared the way a torch ignites. His erection seemed to leap up all at once, sprong! Like Dan Quayle's anatomically correct doll in *Doonesbury*. He stood staring down at himself in disbelief. Weeks of virtual impotence, and tonight, after all that had happened, all the nightmarish things he'd done this day . . . a massive hard-on, sudden and unbidden. As though the acts had temporarily, perversely repaired him: bladder, prostate, sexual apparatus.

It disgusted him and at the same time he was more excited than he'd been since his first sexual experience in high school. A great, screaming urgency that was need and fear and self-loathing and a clutch of other emotions all mixed up together, his phallus so high-jutting and engorged it was like something that had attached itself to his body, a parasitic entity, rather than an extension of himself.

No! he thought. He shut off the water, stepped out, and dried off savagely, punishing his body with the towel. The erection would not diminish, the urgency remained like a consuming fire. It shut down his thoughts, engulfed his will to resist, left him with nothing but the clamant heat.

He shut off the light, padded out into the dark bedroom. Cassie stirred as he approached, started to sit up, and he heard himself say, "No, don't put on the light." His tone more than the words caused her to lie still. He drew the bedclothes back and slid in beside her, whispered her name, moved to fit his body against hers. Heard her suck in her breath when she felt him like iron against her thigh.

"Jack, what . . . ?"

"I need you," he said in somebody else's voice, "please, baby, I can't . . . I need . . . it's been so long . . ."

She lay stiffly while his fingers fumbled with buttons, groped inside her pajama top to encircle her breast. "What is it, what's happened?"

"Nothing's happened."

"Why're you so late? Why are you like this?"

"I just need you . . . please Cass please . . ."

She yielded to him, not gradually but all at once, turning her body against his, her nipple hardening under his palm, her hand stroking down between their bodies to grip and guide him. She gasped as he filled her, clutched him tight with her hands, arms, legs, began to move with him in all the practiced rhythm of twenty-six years of lovemaking. But it was nothing at all like it had ever been before—not slow and tender, no murmured endearments. It was fierce, fast, insistent, an almost desperate coupling punctuated by pants and groans, Cassie's as well as his, fast fast until he came with a crying moan that she managed to half stifle with her mouth, a climax as intense as a backdraft in a burning building, as if he were ejaculating jets of fire. When it ended it left him burned out inside, an empty hulk that collapsed against her. She neither moved nor let go of him, clinging just as fervently until his pulse rate began to slow down. The embrace was all hers; he no longer had the strength to return it.

He knew she was waiting for him to speak first and he groped for words. The only ones he found were "I love you. I love you so much," in a frog's croak.

"I know you do."

"I'm sorry, I couldn't help it, I—"

"Don't be sorry for that. I needed you too."

Gently she disengaged herself and sat up. He sensed she was going to switch on her bedside lamp and he lay with his eyes shut. He could almost feel the sudden radiance against his lids, her gaze probing his face. But there was nothing there for her to see, nothing left inside him to show through.

"Talk to me," she said. "If something did happen—"

"Nothing happened."

"Then why are you so late? Jack . . . did you really go to Paloma to see Nick Jackson?"

"I told you I did."

"Not the city . . . Rakubian . . ."

"No. Of course not."

"I was so worried. I thought—"

"You thought what?" Hollis opened his eyes and sat up weakly, blinking, to face her. "I didn't confront or harm that psycho, if that's what's bothering you. Do you want me to swear it? All right, I swear it on Angela's life, Kenny's life."

She believed him because she wanted to believe. She said, "Do you blame me for worrying, thinking the worst?

First Eric disappeared, all upset, and then you do the same thing. . . ."

"No," he said, "I don't blame you."

"Where have you been? Why didn't you call?"

"Dinner lasted longer than I expected. Afterward . . . I just felt depressed. Angela leaving, that business with Eric today, Rakubian. I needed to be alone. I went to a movie, drove around for a while afterward . . . avoided coming home, as lousy as that sounds."

The lies rolled out glibly; oh, he was becoming a fine god-damn liar. Cassie believed them, too. She said, "I understand, but you still should have called."

"I know it. I'm sorry."

"Didn't you think about Rakubian? That he might show up here again, do God knows what?"

"He didn't, did he? Show up or call or anything?"

"No. But he could have."

"I'm not myself these days, Cass, not thinking straight. One minute I function more or less normally, the next I'm half crazy, the next I'm like a teenager in heat. Schizoid. That's not an excuse, just an explanation, such as it is."

Cassie sighed and said, "I feel the same way." Then she touched his face, tenderly. "You look so tired."

"Exhausted."

"Sleep now, both of us." She flicked off the lamp.

In the darkness, on the edge of sleep, holding her and hating himself, he thought: Keeping them safe, that's all that really counts. No matter what it costs me, no matter what it takes . . .

11

Sunday Morning

ON the patio after breakfast, last night's mist already burned off and balmy spring smells in the crisp air, Cassie and Angela inside out of earshot.

"Is there anything you want to tell me, Eric?"

"Like what?"

"About yesterday."

Pause. "You mean Rakubian?"

"Yes. Rakubian."

"There's nothing to tell," Eric said. Looking him straight in the eye. "All that stuff stored in the garage . . . I admit it really freaked me. I felt like driving straight to the city and beating the shit out of him."

"But you didn't."

"I didn't. Kept my cool and went for a long ride in the opposite direction. I suppose you were afraid I might've done something stupid?"

"I'd stand behind you if you did, you know that."

"Well, you don't have to worry. I'm not a kid anymore."

"No, you're not." You're an adult liar and pretender, just like your old man.

Eric was silent for a time, that brown-study silence that always made Hollis a little uncomfortable. "Poor Angie," he said at length. "Every time I look at her, see how afraid she is. . . ." He shook his head, as if shaking off a painful mental image. "What's the use talking about it? We've talked it to death."

Hollis sat back, watching his son brood. Outwardly, Eric seemed all right. His eyes were clear, as though he'd slept well enough; hands steady, body language more or less normal. But inside? Frightened, worried . . . yes. Heartsick? Probably. Remorseful? Maybe. The same emotions Hollis himself was feeling—and concealing. The two of them sitting here as if this were any Sunday morning at home, one not a murderer, the other not an accomplice after the fact, yesterday any Saturday rather than a turning point in both their lives. Hiding the truth from each other because neither could bear to face the other with it.

His son, his flesh and blood—a killer. How do you reconcile a thing like that? Answer: In an evil time, evil things happen—good people are driven by both external and internal forces to do things they would never do in ordinary circumstances. Maybe that was a rationalization, not really an answer at all, but there was no other way to look at it that would allow him to hold himself together. He was a sadder, more bitter, somewhat diminished man today, and he suspected Eric saw himself in the same way.

Rakubian's death made no real difference in how he felt about his son. Still loved him as much as ever, would do anything to protect him. Twinges of disappointment and shame, no denying that, but none greater than his own. He could live with what Eric had done. But could Eric?

Conscience and anger management, those were the

keys. The anger was something they could talk about, but at another time—not this close to all that had happened yesterday. For now, they'd each keep their secrets and go on telling the lies they'd have to tell. . . .

"Dad? You okay?"

"Yes. Why?"

"Funny look on your face. Like you're in pain."

"Just thinking about Angela and Kenny.

"Yeah. Me, too."

Hollis asked, "You planning to drive back to San Luis today?"

"No, I thought I'd leave in the morning when they do. Make sure they get on the road okay. I only have two Monday classes and I can blow them off." Pause. "Your prostate giving you trouble?"

He frowned at the abrupt change of subject. "What makes you ask that?"

"The way you walk, sit, the look you get sometimes—like just now."

One secret he didn't have to keep any longer, at least from Eric; one lie he didn't have to go on telling. "Yes, it's giving me trouble."

"Same symptoms?"

"Mostly."

"What does Dr. Otaki say?"

"I haven't been to see him recently."

"Christ, why not?"

"Too many other things on my mind. But I'm going to make an appointment this week. You haven't said anything to your mother about this?"

"Uh-uh. I guess you haven't, either."

"I didn't want to worry her. I'll tell her after I see Otaki, have a new batch of tests run." But it occurred to him that if the signs had been obvious enough for Eric to pick up on

them in just a couple of days, they surely must have been obvious to Cassie all along. Then why hadn't she said anything?

"Will you let me know the test results?"

"Of course. Why wouldn't I?"

"No reason. Making sure, that's all."

They had nothing more to say to each other after that.
Just sat there sipping coffee and not making eye contact—
conspirators alone with their secrets in the spring sunshine.

When he was sure Gloria had had enough time to get home
from church, he shut himself inside the garage and called
her on his cell phone. Trip to Tomales Bay canceled: he
wanted to spend the day with Angela and Kenny, he said,
since she'd decided to leave tomorrow. Gloria was sympathetic. She said to give them her love, she'd pray for them every day. Pray for Eric and me, too, Hollis thought. We're the
ones who need it now.

He made quick work of emptying the Lexus's trunk. Pick
and shovel into a corner of the garage behind some other
tools; Colt Woodsman into the locked storage cabinet; overalls and galoshes and gloves and soiled khaki shirt and Cal
Poly blanket into a trash bag. He stuffed the bag into the
bottom of one of the trash barrels.

Nothing left to do now but wait.

Sunday Afternoon

Two visitors, to say good-bye to Angela and Kenny.

One was expected. During breakfast she had said tentatively, "Ryan is going to drop by this afternoon. He asked and
I said I thought it'd be all right. Please don't be angry with
me, Daddy."

"I'm not angry."

"He won't stay long. Just to see Kenny again before we go."

Hollis promised he'd be civil to Pierce and he meant it. Little enough in the way of a favor, if it would help ease her through the next twenty-four hours. She seemed raw-nerved today—not because of the long drive to Utah or the prospect of living with strangers, he thought, but because she was apprehensive that Rakubian might show up at the last minute, do something crazy before she could escape. He longed to take her in his arms, tell her she never had to be afraid of David Rakubian again, tell her escape was no longer necessary. Keeping up the pretense was almost as painful as what Rakubian alive had put them through.

The other visitor, the first to arrive, came unannounced. Gabe Mannix. Hollis was in his study with Kenny playing Pokémon on the computer. The boy was much less animated than usual; resigned to the move—Angela had had a long talk with him—but not really understanding or liking the idea.

"I don't want to leave you, Granpa," he'd said, his thin arms tight around Hollis's neck. "I wish I could stay here with you and Granma."

"I wish you could, too. But it's only for a little while."

"Will you come and visit us?"

"Maybe we won't have to. Maybe you and your mom will be back home before it's time for a visit."

"Really?"

"Cross my heart."

"How soon? Two weeks?"

"Not that soon."

"Before the Fourth of July fireworks?"

"We'll see. If you promise to be good and take care of your mom."

"I will. I promise, Granpa."

More longing, more painful pretense.

When Hollis heard the doorbell he thought it was Pierce and stayed where he was. Then Cassie appeared and told him it was Gabe. He left Kenny to his video game and went out to the living room.

Mannix was seated on the couch beside Angela, holding her hand and talking earnestly. Whatever he was saying had spawned a wan smile. She'd always been fond of him; said more than once that he was like an uncle to her. The expression on Mannix's craggy face was anything but avuncular. If any other middle-aged man had looked at his daughter with that kind of wistful yearning, Hollis would have resented it. Not so with Gabe. They'd been friends too long—and his feelings for her were not only unspoken but close to worshipful besides. He was a lusty bugger with every woman except Angela. And Cassie, too, of course.

He gave Hollis a crooked grin, still holding her hand. "I was in the neighborhood," he said.

"Sure you were.

"Well, I couldn't let them leave without saying good-bye, could I?"

"No, and I'm glad you didn't. If I'd been thinking straight, I'd've invited you. Cup of coffee?"

"You don't mind, I'd rather have a little hair of the dog."

"Big night?"

"Big night with small people. Scotch, single malt."

Hollis poured three fingers of Glenlivet for Gabe, resisting the urge to do the same for himself. In his fragile and volatile state, alcohol was a dangerous additive. The four of them sat talking desultorily, each avoiding the subjects of Rakubian and the temporary relocation. After a time Eric came downstairs to join them.

Then Pierce showed up.

At least he wasn't as scruffy-looking as last week. Hair trimmed, clean-shaven, an old corduroy sport jacket and slacks in place of the western outfit. Ill at ease, though, and seeing both Gabe and Eric didn't help him any. Eric had nothing to say to him; ignored his tentative greeting and went back upstairs. Mannix's reaction was a surprised double-take and then a fixed scowl. Pierce seemed to sense that offering to shake hands was inviting rebuff. He didn't try it with Hollis, either.

He perched on a chair nearest Angela, who moved away from Gabe and closer to him. Cassie, the social arbiter, went to fetch Kenny, but the boy's presence did little to ease the strain in the room. He seemed no more pleased to see Pierce than the rest of them.

Pierce ruffled his hair, something he didn't like adults to do, and asked, "How's it going, sport?"

"Okay," Kenny said. Then he said, "Are you really my dad?"

Pierce's smile sagged; his answer sounded defensive. "Sure I am. You know that."

"Then why don't you live with us? Why'd you stay away so long? Why aren't you going away with us?"

Cassie fielded that, saying, "Kenny, how about showing your father how good you are at Pokémon. Your mom'll go along, too."

Angela took the hint and the three of them went out, Pierce rubbing shoulders with her and holding the boy's hand—as if for him the past eighteen months had been wiped off the slate and they were a family again. Watching them, Hollis wished he'd poured Scotch for himself after all. Mannix didn't like it, either. He drained his glass and got to his feet.

Cassie said, "You're not leaving already, Gabe?"

"Things to do. No rest for the wicked."

"Go in and say good-bye to Angela before you go."

"I already said my good-byes."

He pecked Cassie on the cheek, glanced at Hollis as he turned. The look said he wanted to talk. Hollis followed him to the door, out onto the porch.

As soon as they were alone: "What's that little prick doing here, Jack? When did he come crawling back?"

"A few days ago."

"You should've warned me."

"I know. Just not tracking like I should."

"Well, what the hell is he sucking around for?"

Hollis gave a terse explanation.

"Changed?" Gabe said. "Him? Bullshit."

"Angela seems to be buying it."

"Yeah, I noticed. Looks to me like he's trying to worm his way back with her. You don't think she's naive enough to let it happen?"

"She isn't naive. She's scared."

"Meaning she might?"

"Meaning I don't know. Cassie thinks she's still in love with him."

"Christ! After all this time?"

"I don't want to believe it, either."

"You can't let her get involved with him again."

"What do you want me to do, spank it out of her? It's her life, Gabe. Her choices."

"Damn poor choices when it comes to men," Mannix said. "First Pierce, then Rakubian, now Pierce again. Did she tell him where she's going?"

"She's not telling anyone the exact location, including Cassie and me."

"Suppose he follows her?"

"That's not going to happen."

"He showed up here, didn't he."

"She'll take precautions. She won't allow anything to jeopardize the relocation."

"I hope you're right. Little pissant. The way he treated her and the boy . . ."

"Get off Pierce, will you?" Hollis said. "He's not the main problem here."

Mannix ran a hand over his face, worked his mouth as if he were tasting something sour. "Yeah, Rakubian. What're you going to do about him?"

Hollis said carefully, "If I had the answer to that I'd've done it long ago."

"You've got the answer. You just won't face up to it."

"Get off that, too, all right?"

Mannix looked at him for several seconds, his expression unreadable. Then he shrugged and said, "All right. I'll be around if you want to talk some more. Right now I need another hair of the dog. Hell, the way I feel I may try to swallow the whole frigging pelt."

Monday

He kissed his daughter and grandson good-bye a little before seven-thirty. She was anxious to get on the road early, drive as far as Winnemucca today so she could get to Salt Lake City tomorrow night. Dark smudges under her eyes, twitchy movements, her gaze darting to the street the entire time he and Eric were helping load her car as though she half expected Rakubian to come roaring up in his BMW. Eric wasn't in much better shape today. Withdrawn, mostly silent. Conscience working on him, too, Hollis thought.

The good-byes were brief and awkward. Quick kisses that were little more than pecks, even Kenny's. Eric's hand dry in his, and the contact broken in an instant. Thin smiles, hurried promises, halfhearted reassurances. Angela and Eric left together, a two-car procession with her in the lead; he would follow her all the way to Highway 80, to make certain she had no pursuit. It twisted Hollis again to know that there was no need for any of this and yet he was powerless to stop it.

He stood with Cassie in the driveway, her arm tight around his waist, watching both cars pass from sight, and for some time after they were gone. When he felt her looking at him he made eye contact.

She said, "I feel a little lost right now. You know what I mean?"

He knew, all right. He felt that way himself.

All that morning, working at his drafting board, he was on tenterhooks. Had he overlooked anything at the Chesterton site to make Pete Dulac's crew suspicious? He was unable to conjure up a clear image of the way the excavation looked when he'd finished cleaning up. Saturday had begun to recede in his memory, the details to blur, as if he'd been an observer rather than a participant—like with a movie he'd seen, or one of those queer omniscient dreams in which you stand apart and watch yourself doing things that make little or no sense.

Every time the phone rang he paused to listen to Gloria's end of the conversation, imaginary dialogue running on a loop inside his head: "Oh, yes, Pete, he's right here" and "Jack, Jesus, we found a body up here, somebody got in over the weekend and buried a dead guy in Chesterton's wine cellar." It didn't happen. None of the calls were from Dulac or anyone else connected with PAD Construction.

His tension was obvious to Gloria, but she took it to be a

reaction to the kids' departure; she left him alone and took care of most of the callers herself. Mannix wandered in at ten-thirty, looking even more hungover than yesterday. He had little to say, worked less than an hour, and wandered out again before noon.

Hollis insisted on staying in between twelve and one. To give Gloria a chance for a restaurant meal instead of her usual brown-bag lunch, he said, but the real reason was that he could not have choked down a bite of food without gagging. The phone didn't ring at all during that hour. He should have begun to relax by then; perversely, the waiting and the uncertainty increased the strain. By the time Gloria returned, he'd had as much as he could stand. He went into his cubicle and called Pete Dulac's cell phone number.

"Jack Hollis, Pete. How's it going?"

"Same as last Thursday," Dulac said shortly. "On schedule."

"Well, I just wanted to tell you Chesterton was pleased. Nothing but good things to say about you and your crew."

"I'd be damn surprised if he'd had any complaints."

"He particularly liked the way the wine cellar looked."

"Yeah, well, rich people and their priorities. Listen, Jack, I'm glad about Chesterton, but I'm busy as hell here. They're pouring the slab right now."

"You mean in the wine cellar?"

"That's what I mean. Anything else you wanted?"

"No," Hollis said. "No, nothing else."

He sat slumped in his chair. The release of tension made him feel light-headed, as if he were melting inside. Pouring the slab right now: sealing Rakubian in his grave. The murder weapon, the bloody carpet, the body with its shattered skull . . . all hidden where no one could ever find them, under two feet of solid concrete. Eric was safe. Angela, Kenny, Eric—all safe.

Not himself, though, not yet. Still wriggling on the hook. He wondered how long it would be before Rakubian was reported missing and the San Francisco police got around to him.

12

Tuesday Evening

APRIL Sayers, the woman from the Santa Rosa support group, called before dinner with a brief message: Safe arrival. No incidents, no difficulties. They'd be receiving an e-mail shortly.

Now, at least for the time being, he could quit worrying about Angela and Kenny.

Wednesday Afternoon

Stan Otaki was a well-regarded urologist and usually too busy to make short-notice, nonemergency appointments. But Hollis had known him for thirty years—they'd been classmates at Los Alegres High—and when he apologized for canceling his last two appointments and indicated he was ready to begin treatment, Otaki squeezed him in at one o'clock.

He disliked doctors' offices almost as much as hospitals—the medicinal odors, the gleaming equipment, the admixture of sterility and implied suffering. He sat uncomfortably in Otaki's private office, offering another round of weak excuses and answering probing questions about urination, erectile dysfunction, levels of pain and discomfort. Then he submitted to a teeth-gritting rectal exam, a check of his blood pressure and vital signs. Otaki was not much for his words in the examining room; he waited until they were back in his office.

"Of course, I can't tell you how far the cancer has progressed until we do a blood workup," he said, "but my guess is that it hasn't reached an advanced stage. If that's the case, and your health is otherwise good, we should be able to control it with aggressive treatment."

Advanced stage. Number III on the chart: cancer cells have spread outside the prostate capsule to tissues around the prostate, possibly into the glands that produce semen. It was probably too soon to worry about Stage IV—cancer cells have metastasized to the lymph nodes or to organs and tissues far away from the prostate such as bone, liver, or lungs—but then, you never knew with cancer; it could spread like wildfire. Number III was bad enough. Number IV was the next thing to a death sentence.

"I won't make a definite recommendation until I see the test results," Otaki said. "If they show no radical change, however, your best option is still going to be a prostatectomy. And the sooner the better."

"No."

"Look, Jack, you've made it plain how you feel about surgery, but—"

"No," he said. "I'm not going to let you or anybody else cut me open, no matter how far the cancer has progressed. There's radiation therapy, isn't there?"

"Yes. Five days a week, six to seven consecutive weeks. Are you willing to undergo that kind of rigid schedule, endure the probable side effects?"

"If necessary."

"Well, the decision is yours," Otaki said. He ran a knuckle over his neat salt-and-pepper mustache, a gesture Hollis took to be disapproving. "Your body, your health."

"Are you telling me radiation probably won't work?"

"Of course not. It may well do the job."

"And if it doesn't?"

"Ruling out surgery under any circumstances radically increases the risk factor. That's a fact—that's what I'm trying to make you understand. If you doubt me, get a second or third opinion—"

"I don't need any other opinions. I don't doubt you."

"Will you at least give it some more thought? Talk to Cassie about it?"

"Yes, all right."

But he knew he wouldn't.

Thursday Morning

There, at last, on page 3 of the *Chronicle*:

PROMINENT S.F. ATTORNEY
REPORTED MISSING

It was the second item in the Bay Area Report section devoted to minor news stories. Less than three column inches —another good sign. He read the paragraphs avidly.

David J. Rakubian, 35, personal injury attorney known for his tenacious courtroom tactics . . . last seen late Friday afternoon at his South Beach offices . . . reported missing by his paralegal, Valerie Burke, on Monday afternoon . . . mandatory waiting period before police could take official action . . . Rakubian's car found in the garage of his St. Francis Wood home . . . no evidence of foul play . . . recently divorced from his wife of nine months . . . arrested in Los Alegres three weeks ago for public battery on his ex-wife . . .

No evidence of foul play. That was the key phrase. The police hadn't found anything suspicious in the house; it would take a thorough forensic examination to bring out blood traces, and it wasn't likely there'd be one without something concrete to support it.

The paralegal would be the source of information about the marriage breakup, coloring it to favor Rakubian; the part about public battery probably had been dug up by the reporter. The police had Hollis's name from Valerie Burke, too, and a full account of his angry outburst in Rakubian's office, plus the fact of his second visit last week. It would not be long before he was contacted—today, tomorrow at the latest. Unless he took the initiative first.

He glanced across the breakfast table. Cassie was sipping coffee, reading the Datebook section. He drew a breath, then rattled the newsprint and said explosively, "My God!"

Her head jerked up. "What?"

"Look at this," he said. He passed her his section, tapping the article with his forefinger.

She looked. And then she looked at him, looked past him—a bleak, distant stare. After a few seconds she said, "What does this mean?"

"I wish I knew."

"Coincidence, Jack?"

"Coincidences happen. One could've happened to him."

"Such as what? A convenient accident?"

"That, or something else. A shyster like him must have plenty of enemies. He paused. "There's another possibility, too."

"Yes?"

"It was voluntary," he said. "What if he found out somehow about Angela going away?"

It was like a slap; she winced, stiffened. "You mean he might've gone looking for her, hunting her?"

"I hope to God that's not it." The lies were like fecal matter in his mouth, hurting him as much as they were hurting her. He went on with it, hating himself again. "But I wouldn't put anything past him."

"How could he have found out?"

"How does anybody find out anything?"

"But he couldn't know where she went."

"No. There's no way he could've followed her, with Eric right there. We'll e-mail her, tell her what's happened, warn her to be extra careful. Alert April Sayers, too."

Cassie nodded. But then she said, "I don't know. I don't know, Jack."

"Don't know what?"

"His car . . . the paper says it's in his garage. If he's gone looking for Angela, why didn't he take his car?"

"Decided it was too conspicuous, maybe. Or he went somewhere by air."

"That doesn't sound like Rakubian. To just drop out of sight that way—no calls to his office staff, leaving everything behind."

She was thinking too much. Too smart for her own good. "He's psychotic, Cass. You can't predict what a psycho will do."

"He's been consistent all along, hasn't he? Disappearing when he can't possibly have any idea where Angela went . . . it just doesn't sound right."

He couldn't push it any more; it would only arouse her suspicions. He said, "If something did happen to him, accident or otherwise, it's good news—the best news we could ask for. A kind of miracle."

"Is it?"

"If he turns up dead, or doesn't turn up at all, it means

Angela and Kenny can come home. It means we can all stop being afraid."

"I don't know," she said again. "I don't like this."

"What don't you like? You can't want Rakubian to still be alive somewhere."

"I've wished him dead a hundred times."

"Well?"

"If he's dead . . . why? What happened to him?"

"The details aren't important—"

"They are if he was murdered."

"By a stranger? What does it matter who?"

"Suppose it was Eric?" she said.

His first call was to April Sayers. She'd already seen the piece in the *Chronicle*, had just gotten off the phone with her Utah relatives. Angela and Kenny were fine. Extra precautions were being taken, just in case. And all for nothing, Hollis thought as he rang off. He could imagine how upset his daughter must be over this. Consoling himself that it was only temporary, that the end result justified the additional anxiety, was cold and bitter comfort.

Second call: Eric. It was early enough so that he was still in his room and his line was free. Hollis would have preferred to talk to him alone, but Cassie insisted on picking up the extension. Her fear that Eric was responsible had rocked him. He should have seen it coming, but he hadn't. He'd managed to allay the fear somewhat, enough to keep her from saying anything to Eric; she let him do most of the talking. Eric's reaction may have reassured her, but it bothered Hollis. No hint of surprise that Rakubian had been reported missing, not found murdered in his home. Concern about his sister and nephew, cautious optimism—the same outward pose as Hollis's. But was he handling it *too* well?

Not feeling as much guilt and remorse as he should, perhaps thinking that what he'd done was wholly justified?

The third and last call was to the Hall of Justice in San Francisco, Missing Persons division. The inspector in charge of the Rakubian case, he was told, was Napoleon Macatee, but he wasn't at his desk. Hollis left a message, supplying both home and office numbers. Now he was on record as having made first contact.

Inspector Macatee called him at Mannix & Hollis shortly before noon. Polite, soft-spoken, voice inflections that indicated he was African American. No, Hollis said, he had no information about David Rakubian's disappearance. He'd seen the news story, he was concerned because of the potential danger to his daughter.

"You know he assaulted her in public a few weeks ago," he said, "and we had to get a restraining order against him. He's been getting more and more irrational, calling at all hours, showing up here, making threats."

"His office staff paint a different picture of the man," Macatee said.

"Sure they do. They only saw his public face. We have tapes of all his calls, his letters, everything. If you'd like to go through the . . ."

"Pretty sure I'll want to do that. Mr. Hollis, I understand you went to the man's offices last Thursday morning. Mind telling me why?"

"The obvious reason. One last futile attempt to get him to stop harassing my family. It was a waste of time, like talking to a piece of stone. As far as he's concerned, he isn't guilty of anything except trying to get his wife back. He's obsessed with her. He's not only a control freak and an abuser, he's a dangerous psychotic."

"Psychotic's a pretty strong word."

"Not for Rakubian. The last time he showed up in Los Alegres, he caught my daughter alone and threatened to kill her and my grandson both if she didn't go back to him."

Macatee digested that before he asked, "Anyone else there at the time?"

"Just Kenny, my grandson. But my daughter wouldn't make up a story like that. She doesn't lie and she doesn't exaggerate. She said he meant it, and I believe her."

"Did you know about this threat when you went to talk to him on Thursday?"

"I knew and I called him on it. He denied it, of course."

"You make any threats against him in return?"

"No. I lost my head the first time I went there—I guess you know about that—and I was determined not to let it happen again. But I came close to losing it, I'll admit that."

"Angry, frustrated . . . that how you felt when you left?"

"Wouldn't you be if it was your family, Inspector? I should have known better than to try to reason with a man like him. But no matter how I felt and still feel, I didn't have anything to do with his disappearance."

"See him again anytime since Thursday?"

"No."

"Talk to him?"

"No."

"Your daughter have any contact with him?"

"No. She was home with us all weekend."

"She at home now?"

"Not since Monday morning," Hollis said, and went on to explain about Angela's decision to relocate, the arrangements she'd made. "I can't tell you exactly where she is. My wife and I don't know ourselves."

"But you can get in touch with her."

"Yes. She already knows that Rakubian is missing. What

worries my wife and me is that he found out she was relo-
cating and dropped out of sight to hunt for her."

"How would he've found out?"

"I can't answer that. I sure as hell didn't say anything to
tip him off. But he's a shrewd bugger and he has plenty of
contacts. For all we know he hired somebody to watch her. I
doubt anyone could've followed her when she left on
Monday, but how can we be absolutely sure?"

"I'll want to talk to your daughter," Macatee said. "Ap-
preciate it if you'd get word to her, have her contact me as
soon as possible."

"You won't try to force her to tell you her whereabouts?
Or to come back here?"

"Not without good cause."

"All right. I'll e-mail your name and number to her."

Macatee asked a few more questions, none of them, as
far as Hollis could tell, motivated by anything other than
routine. He said he and Angela would both be in touch and
rang off.

End of round one. A draw, he thought—the best he
could have hoped for.

Friday Afternoon

Stan Otaki called with the results of his PSA blood test. "The
good news," he said, "is that the cancer hasn't spread outside
your prostate."

He clung to that for a few seconds. Then he asked,
"What's the bad news?"

"The growth rate is definitely accelerating. My advice,
like it or not, is a 'first cut' to remove and test the lymph
nodes surrounding the gland."

"Surgery. I won't do it, Stan."

Otaki made a breathy, rumbling noise. "So be it. Then I

suggest we begin radiation therapy right away."

"No argument there."

"I'll make the arrangements."

"And meanwhile," Hollis said, "what should I do? Start putting my affairs in order, just in case?"

"Don't make light of this, Jack."

"I'm not. Just trying to keep a smiley face."

"A positive attitude is important. We've discussed that."

"I haven't forgotten. My attitude's positive," he said, and he meant it. "I'm going to beat this thing, one way or another."

"That's the spirit."

After all, he thought, this malignancy can't be any worse than the one I buried on Saturday night.

Friday Evening

Cassie sat quiet when he finished telling her, no show of emotion of any kind. He thought her eyes were moist, but he couldn't be sure in the lamplit living room.

After a time he said, "You knew, didn't you."

"That it's been getting worse? Yes."

"Why didn't you say anything?"

"You've had enough on your mind without me nagging you about the cancer. I knew you'd see Stan eventually—talk to me when you were ready. You're stubborn and foolish sometimes, but you've always been a fighter. You'd never give in to a life-threatening disease."

"No way."

"So it's radiation, then."

He nodded. "You won't try to talk me into having surgery?"

"Would it do any good?"

"You know how I feel. I couldn't stand to go through an

operation. I break out in a cold sweat just thinking about it."

"Then I won't say a word. But I want you to do one thing for me in return."

"If I can."

"Don't lie to me anymore. Don't evade the truth, or stretch it, or hide behind it. We're a team, remember? Don't fight *me* anymore."

"I won't," he said. And he wouldn't, where the cancer was concerned. Eric and Rakubian were another matter. Hiding that truth was a necessity—an act of mercy, an act of love.

Monday Afternoon

Napoleon Macatee drove up from the city to examine the evidence of Rakubian's stalking. Hollis and Cassie met him at the house at two o'clock. He was a black man in his fifties, stocky and solid as a barrel, with eyes like brown wounds. Those eyes had seen a great deal and would never be surprised or shocked by anything again. At once the eyes of a cynic and a martyr.

He seemed forthcoming enough when Hollis asked if there were any new developments. The short answer, he said, was no. He'd spoken to Angela twice (as they had; she'd called after her first talk with Macatee, again a few days later). He'd spoken to Eric, a fact he mentioned briefly and without a hint of suspicion. He'd spoken to dozens of Rakubian's neighbors, business associates, and individuals who might have cause to do him harm. No leads so far. Nothing to indicate accident, voluntary disappearance, or foul play.

Cassie said, "It doesn't seem possible he could have vanished without any trace."

"Happens more often than you might think," Macatee said. "Fifty thousand disappearances in this country every year. Men, women, children. Across the board when it comes to social and financial status, race, religion, age. Known reasons, too. David Rakubian's case isn't so unusual."

"How likely is it he'll be found?"

"Depends. If it was voluntary and he covered his tracks well enough, odds are he'll stay lost unless he decides to resurface on his own. If he was a victim of violence, evidence of it may turn up sooner or later. It's not as easy to dispose of a dead body as people think."

Not unless you're very, very lucky.

They showed Macatee the evidence box, the dossier Hollis had brought home from the office. He sifted through the letters, cards, poems, time logs; listened to two tapes at random. Hollis watched him closely the entire time. Macatee's expression remained neutral, but there seemed to be compassion in the brown-wound eyes when he looked at Cassie. He asked if he could take the dossier and several other items along with him, wrote out a receipt, thanked them for their cooperation, and left them alone. The interview had lasted little more than an hour.

Hollis was convinced that if Macatee had any suspicions, they were without any real basis. Fishing in the dark. Perhaps even doing no more than going through the motions. The dossier, the tapes and letters, confirmed what a sick bastard Rakubian had been. Could a cop who'd seen all sorts of human misery honestly care what happened to a wife abuser and stalker, as long as he stayed missing? Hollis didn't see how. The inspector had struck him as a good man; if anything, he had to be on their side.

Monday Night

He had the dream for the first time that night. There had been others in the past nine days, disturbing but vague and

134 ◆ BILL PRONZINI

jumbled, and he recalled little of them afterward. This one was vivid, murky in background but sharp in every detail, as if it were a terror-laced memory or precognition.

He was walking in a formless place of shapes and shadows. Wary but not frightened. Ahead he saw a wall, and as he neared it an opening appeared. He walked through the opening and found himself in a cave with wooden walls and a concrete floor. He stood looking down at the floor's smooth black surface. And as he looked, cracks began to form there, to lengthen and widen, and the fear came in a rush as the concrete crumbled. A hand reached up through one of the cracks, fingers clawing toward him, then the entire arm, a shoulder, a head—Rakubian's shattered head, Rakubian's face grinning in a savage rictus. Then, like a bloody monolith, dripping dirt and fragments of rotting skin, all of the dead man rose up out of the broken floor and started toward him, whispering his name. He tried to run, stood rooted, and the clawed fingers closed bonily around his throat—

He jerked awake damp and shaking, his breathing clogged. Only a dream, a nightmare, but it remained hot and clear in his mind. He could still see Rakubian's face, the death's-head grin, the bulging eyes; still feel the pressure of those skeletal fingers. His throat ached as if the strangulation had been real.

There was no sleep for him after that; he lay staring blindly into the darkness. And the feeling that crept over him was as strong and irrefutable as any he'd ever experienced. A product of the dream, of guilt filtered through his subconscious . . . but he could not make himself believe it. The feeling was too visceral, too intense to be easily dismissed.

He and Eric weren't safe. None of them were.

Somehow, someway, Rakubian was still a threat to them all.

Part II

Early to Mid July: Phantom

13

Thursday

NGELA and Kenny came home two days after the
Fourth of July holiday.

They had exchanged daily e-mails with her, and as
time passed she'd grown less afraid of Rakubian's sudden re-
appearance and more willing to end her voluntary exile.
Finally she'd agreed to set the Fourth as her own indepen-
dence day. And stood by that decision when the time came,
packing Kenny into her Geo early on the morning of the
fifth. The little car rattled into their driveway just before
dusk on the sixth.

The six long, difficult weeks of radiation therapy had
made Hollis listless and depressed. Now that they'd ended,
and he was no longer quite so fatigued or prone to sudden at-
tacks of diarrhea, he had begun to regain both stamina and
optimism; he'd gone back to work for the first time just before the holiday. Angela's and Kenny's safe return was just
what he needed to boost his spirits, energize him.

She looked good. Smiling often again, the haggard look

erased, the fear reduced to a shriveled presence deep in her eyes. Not her old self yet by any stretch; it would take time for a complete healing. But she was alive again, and seeing that made it a little easier to live with what he and Eric had done that Saturday in May.

Cassie had been right about his conscience: no matter how many rationalizations he used to erect a protective wall, his guilt and his knowledge of Eric's continued to breach it. Doubts, nightmares, sleeplessness . . . they all plagued him. He was a changed man, forever changed. His sins, actual and intended, would torment him to one degree or another until the day he died.

That was the way it was for him, but evidently not for Eric. There had been no indication over the past several weeks that *his* conscience was tearing him up. On the phone today, bemoaning the fact that he couldn't be there to welcome Angela and Kenny in person, he'd sounded happy and secure. The summer job he'd taken with a respected engineering firm in Santa Barbara was working out well; he bragged about an active love life, too. The seemingly too easy adjustment troubled Hollis. He wished they weren't being kept apart by the summer work and his cancer treatments. If he could see his son in person he'd be better able to judge his mental state, and to broach the anger management subject.

He'd talked to Inspector Macatee four times since his May visit, playing the role of worried parent checking for any new information. There'd been none to be concerned about. Rakubian's law offices had been closed at the end of June, the secretary gone two weeks before that, the paralegal hanging on until there was nothing left for her to do. Angela, in her divorce suit, had waived all rights to community property in perpetuity, so Rakubian's house would remain closed up, his possessions untouched, until the bank that held the mortgage eventually foreclosed for nonpayment. Otherwise, the status was unchanged. Macatee had lost interest—it was in his quiet cop's voice. He had other missing persons cases to deal with, dozens of them; Rakubian's had been back-burnered, soon enough would be relegated to an inactive file and forgotten.

So why did Hollis keep having that dream about Rakubian heaving up through the concrete floor, coming after him with hooked fingers and revenge-hungry eyes?

Why was he still afraid?

Friday

Pierce showed up before they were finished with breakfast. He'd made a couple of tentative overtures to Hollis and Cassie while Angela was away, but for the most part he'd had the good sense to keep his distance. He was still living with his sister, but he'd taken part-time work on the Gugliotta cattle ranch in Chileno Valley—back in Los Alegres permanently, it seemed. Angela must have kept in touch with him by e-mail. The only way he could have known she was coming home was if she'd told him.

He hugged her and she let him get away with hanging on to her longer than was necessary, then kissing her. The look she gave him had heat and shine in it. Hollis stood from the table and went outside so he wouldn't have to watch them. After a couple of minutes, Cassie came out to join him.

"Another pretty morning," she said.

"It was."

"Still cool, though. You should put on a sweater."

"Don't fuss over me." Then, "You were right, Cass."

"About what?"

"About Angela still being in love with him. Did you see the look on her face when he started pawing her?"

"I wouldn't call it pawing."

"As good as."

"He cares about her. That's obvious."

"Does he? Maybe he just wants to sleep with her again."

"I don't think so. He's trying, he really is."

"Trying to what? Get her to marry him again . . . another damn Rakubian? Or just live with him this time?"

"Make up for his mistakes, be a father and a man. Give him a chance to prove himself. Everybody deserves a second chance."

"If he really has changed. Maybe he's just better at hiding what he's been all along."

"Don't be a curmudgeon. She's home, Kenny's home, Rakubian's gone God knows where, and you're done with the radiation and making progress. That's a lot to be thankful for."

"I just don't want her to make another mistake."

"Neither do I. But if she does . . . well, it's her business."

He had a sudden flash of the wine cellar, Rakubian's bagged corpse wedged into the shallow grave. "Until it becomes our business," he said.

Late morning. Gabe Mannix arrived with a bouquet of welcome-home flowers for Angela, a video game for Kenny, and some designs he'd done for a new proposal request the firm had received. If they landed the job, it would be their biggest and most lucrative in years—a planned retirement community on the edge of the Dry Creek Valley, several hundred units on a thousand acres of prime real estate. The work perfectly suited their talents, Gabe's because of its size and Hollis's because the initial site survey indicated the need for harmonious blending into the rolling hillside tract. There would be strong competition, so their conceptual designs and the rest of their submission had to be just right.

Mannix was excited about the proposal; his preliminary

designs showed more innovation than usual, more flair. Some of his enthusiasm rubbed off on Hollis. He spent two hours poring over the schematic site plan and fee schedule, adding his own vision to the designs. The work cheered him. And didn't tire him much at all.

Monday

Angela drove to Santa Rosa to see Joyce Eilers, another of the women in the support group, and came home full of news. Joyce worked in the bookstore at Paloma State University, had arranged an interview for her for a job opening there. If she got it, she'd be able to start immediately on a part-time basis and to work full-time once the new school year began in the fall.

"It's the best thing that could happen," she said to Hollis. "I can rent a place of my own, and go back to school nights—work on my teaching degree."

"You mean move out right away? There's no need for that. You know you're welcome to stay here as long as you like."

"I know, but I don't feel right about it. You and Mom have done so much for us already."

He waved that away. "Think of the money you can save. Apartments are expensive and you'd have to put Kenny in day care until he's ready for school. . . ."

"I need to be on my own, Daddy. I need to start living like a normal person again. You understand, don't you?"

He understood. And he offered no more argument, because he knew she was right.

Tuesday

Another session with Stan Otaki, to discuss his most recent blood test.

"So far so good," Otaki said. "But we're not out of the woods yet."

What do you mean *we*, Kemosabe? "You just said so far so good. Arrested growth and no indication of spread outside the prostate."

"It's under control for now, but the cancer hasn't gone into remission. It can still grow, still spread, at any time."

"What, then? More radiation?"

"No. The body can stand only so much zapping."

"We're back to slice and dice, is that it?"

"Surgery is still my recommendation."

"And my answer's still no."

"Then the next step is hormone therapy."

Hormone therapy. Use of drugs such as LHRH-agonists to decrease the amount of testosterone in the body, or antiandrogens to block the activity of the testosterone. Upside: These drugs cause cancer cells to shrink. Downside: possible cardiovascular problems, hot flashes, impotence and loss of sexual desire.

"Any objections to that?" Otaki asked.

"No," Hollis said bleakly, "no objections. When do we start?"

Wednesday

Angela landed the job in the Paloma State bookstore. She would begin work and Kenny would begin day care the first of next week.

Friday

Pierce took Angela out to dinner to celebrate her new job. Not Kenny, just her—him in a suit and tie and her all dressed up and glowing like a high-school girl on her first big date. They stayed out fairly late; Hollis and Cassie were still up when he brought her home. She didn't have much to say to them before she went upstairs, wouldn't quite meet their eyes. And the glow was more pronounced, almost a flush.

"I knew it," Hollis said. "She went to bed with him."

"Oh, now."

"You saw that humid look on her face. She let him screw her again."

"Well, what if she did? She's a grown woman, with normal appetites."

"Pierce," he said. "For God's sake."

"She was married to him for four years, Jack."

"And that makes it all right?"

"Whatever Ryan is or isn't, he's several steps up the ladder from David Rakubian. He can't possibly be as bad for her, can he?"

In bed a while later, he realized that it wasn't really his daughter's sex life that was upsetting him, it was his own. He hadn't had an erection since the night of Rakubian's burial, not even a weak twitch from the old soldier. His sex drive was already gone, cancered and radiated away. But it wasn't himself he was sorry for, it was Cassie. She had always been as highly sexed as he was; enjoyed him as often and as enthusiastically as he enjoyed her. She had to be twice as frustrated. Yet she hadn't complained, and when he'd offered to give her release in one of the other ways she'd said no, it wouldn't be any good for her if he couldn't share the pleasure. Still, he felt bad for her, and guilty even though he had no control over the situation. It wasn't fair. She deserved much better than this.

In that uncanny way she had sometimes, she seemed to intuit what he was thinking. She moved closer to him, put her head on his shoulder and her hand on his chest, not touching him with her body. "Don't worry about me," she said. "Just having you here next to me is all I need."

Trying to make him feel better. It wasn't enough, dammit. Not for a whole woman with half a man.

Saturday

Cassie took Angela apartment hunting, and when they returned they were all smiles. They'd looked at places in Santa Rosa, Rohnert Park, and finally found one right here in Los Alegres—on Sunnyslope, not much more than a mile away. One-bedroom, ground-floor apartment with a tiny fenced rear yard. Five hundred a month, which was pretty reasonable for a furnished apartment these days. Cassie had paid the first and last months' rent and the security deposit—a loan Angela promised to pay back at twenty or twenty-five dollars a month. She would, too. Scrupulously.

The find pleased Hollis as well. She and Kenny would still be close by; he would not have to start missing them all over again.

Sunday

He felt pretty good, so he insisted on helping with the move. Angela had little in the way of essentials; everything fit into her Geo. Some kitchenware, sheets and towels, a few other items came from Cassie's stock. Twenty-five years old, two marriages, a son, and all she had to show for it were a few articles of clothing for her and the boy, a box of personal items, an outdated PC, and an eight-year-old car. If she took up with Pierce again, she'd never have much more. Thinking about that prospect didn't make him angry, it just made him sad.

And of course Pierce showed up at the apartment as they

were moving her in. Kenny seemed to have accepted him completely now; called him Dad and spent as much time hanging around him as he did his granpa. I'm going to lose the boy, too, Hollis thought, and then told himself he was being selfish. He wanted them to be happy, didn't he? Even if that meant being with Pierce?

Yes, as long as he treated her right this time. If he didn't—

If he didn't, what, Hollis? You and Eric will kill *him* and bury his body under another concrete slab?

The thought was depressing. And made him be nicer to Pierce than he'd been since the kid's return.

Tuesday Morning

He came home from his weekly visit with Stan Otaki at eleven-thirty. During his six weeks of daily radiation doses, he'd needed someone—Cassie, Gabe, Gloria, taxis on a few occasions—to transport him to and from the hospital. Now that that ordeal was over he was able to drive himself places again, as long as he didn't overdo it with any lengthy trips. He hated being dependent on others; the one thing he needed almost as much as his family was the ability to fend for himself. Which was another reason why the thought of surgery started him trembling inside: He'd be helpless, completely at the mercy of one casual acquaintance and a team of strangers.

The mail had already been delivered; he fished it out of the box, sifted through it as he let himself into the house. Bills, junk, a charity solicitation, two mail-order catalogs. And a white, business-size envelope, with his name and address typed or computer printed, he couldn't tell which; first-class postage, no return address. More junk, probably. He set the other mail on the hall table, tore open the envelope, and shook out the single sheet of white paper it contained.

In the upper middle of the sheet was a single line of type, in capital letters:

WHAT DID YOU DO WITH HIS BODY?

14

T was like a blow to the head: sudden numbing shock, a few seconds of disorientation. He stared at the words until they began to shimmer and blur, as if they were breaking up on the paper.

Somebody knows.

His mind struggled against the thought. How could anyone know, even suspect? *Now*, almost two months after the fact? Why would anyone send a one-line note like this, more taunting than accusing?

Unless—

The police? Macatee?

Almost immediately, he rejected that. Two months . . . Rakubian's disappearance shunted into an inactive file by the volume of new missing persons cases. Strong new evidence would have to practically fall into Macatee's lap to stir up fresh interest. And there was no way that could have happened. Dammit, no way. Two months dead, two months buried. Construction on the Chesterton site

148 + BILL PRONZINI

moving ahead on schedule, no clues left to find there, and nothing at Rakubian's house to connect Eric or him to the disappearance. And the bottom line: Cops don't send anonymous messages, for any reason. They don't operate that way; can't afford to, the laws and judicial system being what they are. If Macatee's suspicions had been aroused somehow, he'd have shown up with questions, if not outright accusations.

Then who?

Why?

Hollis squinted at the postmark on the envelope. North Bay, which meant it had been mailed in Paloma County or Marin County. Somebody who lived up here? Or somebody who'd driven from elsewhere to mail the note?

He was beginning to feel light-headed. He went into the living room, sank into his chair, and stared again at the single line of type. *What did you do with his body?* He couldn't imagine anyone caring enough about Rakubian to resort to a thing like this, or any reason for waiting until two months after the fact. What was the motive? Revenge? Rakubian had no friends, no relatives—he'd been an egotistical loner disliked, hated by those who knew him. Money . . . some kind of extortion scheme? Not without proof of guilt, and there was no proof. A sick, twisted game?

That recurring dream . . . like a prophecy fulfilled. His formless fear had shape now, if not yet a name. The new threat wasn't Rakubian but Rakubian's legacy. As if it was his evil that had risen from the grave, entered a human host, and set out to wreak vengeance on the ones who'd put him there. Fantastic notion, but it made the back of Hollis's neck crawl just the same.

Two months. That was what made the least sense of all, the time lapse. Two months, and no conceivable way anyone could have found out the truth. Only two people knew what happened that Saturday, himself and—

Eric.

Eric?

"Nonsense," he said aloud, but the word had a hollow ring. Convulsively he was on his feet, moving, needing to move. He paced the room in plodding steps, telling himself his son couldn't possibly be responsible. And yet . . .

Suppose Eric's apparently easy adjustment was a facade? Suppose all along his conscience, like Hollis's, had been ripping him apart to the point where he'd begun to crack up? He must suspect who had disposed of the corpse; might be afraid Hollis hadn't done a proper job and it would eventually be found. He was a deep kid, his mind worked in convoluted patterns that were sometimes bewildering. If he was unable to admit his guilt and his fear, it *was* possible he'd resort to a roundabout method to force the issue. Irrational act, done in extremis. An anonymous cry for help.

Wait . . . the postmark. Eric wouldn't have flown up from Santa Barbara just to mail a letter, would he?

No, but a friend could have forwarded it as a favor.

But why go to that much trouble? If he was sick, desperate, the postmark wouldn't matter to him. Just mail the goddamn thing in Santa Barbara.

Another explanation occurred to Hollis, brought him up short. What if Eric wasn't the perpetrator but another victim? What if he'd received a note like this as well?

What if somebody knew or suspected that he'd murdered Rakubian?

Tuesday Afternoon

Eric sounded fine on the phone, just as he had the last time they'd talked. No hesitancy in his voice, no unease. "You caught me in the shower," he said. "Man, what a day."

"Everything all right?"

"I'm frazzled. They had me running back and forth between here and Ojai all day."

"I meant with you, personally."

"Well, I've got a date this weekend with a girl I met at one of the clubs. My hunch is she's married, and I'm not sure I ought to—"

"I'm not interested in your love life, son."

". . . No, of course you're not."

"I didn't mean that the way it sounded." Handling this badly, dammit. He never seemed able to find the right words, the right approach when he was trying to have a serious talk with Eric. "I'm just wondering if there are any problems, anything important happening in your life."

"Well, the answer to that is no. Why?"

"Would you come to me if there were?"

"I might, if I thought you could help."

"How would you do it? Call or what?"

"Phone, e-mail, whatever."

"You wouldn't write a letter?"

"Snail mail? Come on, Dad."

"So you're sure there's nothing you want to talk over."

"Not a thing."

"Nothing out of the ordinary that might've happened recently?"

"Other than the prospect of getting laid by a married woman, no. What's going on? Why all these questions?"

Hollis thought: This is crazy, both of us tiptoeing around, pretending, playing the secrets game. It's got to stop. For a moment he considered dragging the truth out himself, forcing Eric to admit his part; but he couldn't do it. Not on the phone, not on the basis of what might be nothing more than a crank note. The important thing was that Eric was neither responsible for the note nor had received a similar one himself.

If he was telling the truth.

If all that calm wasn't a front, like a layer of Sheetrock to hide a crumbling wall.

He said, "I worry about you, that's all. Just want you to know I'm here if you need me."

Longish pause. "That goes both ways, Dad."

"Yes. Both ways."

Tuesday Evening

He called Angela at her new apartment, to find out if everything was all right with her. Yes, fine. High spirits. She chattered on about the university, her job, how much Kenny liked day care, how well Pierce and the boy were getting along, how glad she was to be home.

It neither reassured nor cheered him.

Wednesday

He couldn't work, couldn't concentrate. Couldn't sit still. He drove down to Mannix & Hollis for no good reason, came back and took Fritz for a walk, went by himself to McLear Park and spent an hour watching a middle-aged foursome play a bad set of tennis doubles.

What did you do with his body?

Like an endless echo in his mind.

Thursday

Gabe took him to lunch at a new Thai restaurant that had opened downtown. Mild pumpkin curry, steamed rice, a bottle of Singha beer. The food was tasteless—he had no appetite these days—and the beer did nothing for him. What he really wanted was a double Irish, but Stan Otaki had warned him against drinking hard liquor, even in moderation, during his cancer treatments.

They talked business for a while, the Dry Creek Valley project and a potential drainage problem the geologist's report had pointed up with the rocky, nonabsorbent soil. As hard as he tried, he couldn't seem to focus on the details. He kept losing the thread of the discussion, blanking out completely for a few seconds. Mannix was not the most observant or sensitive of men, but even he couldn't help but notice.

"You seem preoccupied, Bernard. Something bothering you?"

"No. Just a little spacey today."

"The cancer? Everything okay there?"

"Status quo."

"Angela? Kenny?"

"They're fine. I'm thinking of getting Kenny an iMac for his birthday."

"He'll love it. How's her new job?"

"Just what she wants for now. She's already signed up for evening classes in the fall—start working for her MA so she can teach."

Mannix said reminiscently, as if he were picturing Angela in his mind, "She looks so much better now that that fucking psycho is out of her life. Her old self again."

"Not quite, but she's getting there."

"You did the right thing."

". . . Right thing?"

"You know what I mean."

"I don't, Gabe."

Mannix shrugged. "Status quo there, too," he said, and signaled the waiter. "I don't know about you, but I can use another beer."

It wasn't until later, after he'd been dropped off at home, that he realized what Mannix had meant by "the right thing."

Gabe thought his advice had been taken after all; he thought Hollis was the cause of Rakubian's disappearance.

Thursday Afternoon

He was resting on a chaise longue on the patio, the Thai food heavy in his stomach and an afternoon breeze cool on his skin, when he heard the truck pull into the driveway. Loud exhaust, rumbling engine—Ryan Pierce's old Dodge.

Now what?

Reluctantly he stood and went along the side path. Pierce was just getting out of the pickup, wearing stained Levi's, a khaki shirt, a battered straw cowboy hat. The Dodge's bed was stacked with bags of feed and blocks of salt.

Pierce saw him and took off the hat. The way he stood there, hat in hand, made Hollis think of a none too bright farm boy. He shook the thought away. He was trying to be fair and equable with the kid these days, wasn't he?

"How're you, Mr. Hollis?" Still formal and polite. You had to give him that much.

"Holding up. What brings you here?"

"Well, I had to get some supplies and I thought I'd swing by, see if you were home. I've been wanting to talk to you."

"Yes? What about?"

"Angela. Kenny, too."

"What about them?"

"I guess you know I've been seeing a lot of them since they came back. Does it bother you and Mrs. Hollis?"

"Would it matter to you if it did?"

"I'd like to know."

"You can hardly expect us to be jumping for joy, given your track record."

"I suppose not. But my reasons aren't selfish. It's because I care about them and I want to do what's right for them."

"And just what do you think that is?"

"Start over again, the three of us. Be the family we never were before. I owe it to Angela, to my son."

Hollis stared at him. "What're you saying?"

"I'm going to ask her to marry me again."

"Christ, Pierce! Are you crazy?"

"Never more sane. I love Angela, I love Kenny, I was a sorry damn fool for ever letting them out of my life. The three of us belong together. Whether you think so or not, Mr. Hollis."

Anger kindled in him. He smothered it. Pierce was serious, earnest, and he was capable of the willful stubbornness of a mule. A show of anger would accomplish nothing, probably lead to a public shouting match.

He said slowly, keeping his voice even, "Does Angela know about this?"

"Not yet. I haven't said anything, at least not directly. Seemed like a good idea to tell you first."

"Ask me for her hand?" Hollis couldn't keep the sarcasm out of his tone. "You never bothered the first time, you just went ahead and knocked her up."

A muscle ticced on Pierce's cheek; otherwise his face was stoic. "I made a lot of mistakes back then. I'm trying not to make any more, anyway not the same ones."

"Trying to convince Angela to marry you again is a damn big mistake. You know what she went through with her second husband. The last thing she needs is another commitment, another go-round with you."

"I understand how badly Rakubian hurt her," Pierce said. "Makes me sick every time I think about it."

"You hurt her, too, once. Remember?"

"I'm not likely to forget. It won't happen again, I swear that to you. I want to make up for what I did and what Rakubian did."

"And I'm telling you, this is the wrong time to pressure her into a committed relationship."

"I won't pressure her. I wouldn't do that. I'll let her set the date when she's ready. Until then, I'll be there for her—however she wants me, anytime she wants me."

Hollis waited until he was sure he could speak normally before he said, "Don't say anything about marriage to her now. Give her time. She needs time, Pierce."

"I want her to know how I feel, same as I wanted you to know."

"Listen to me. I'm warning you, if you upset her, make her life difficult again—"

"I won't. I told you that, and I meant it. Take care of yourself, Mr. Hollis, okay? You can't take care of Angela anymore, but I can. And I will."

After he was gone, Hollis trudged back to the patio. Weary, shuffling steps. *You can't take care of Angela anymore.* Damn Pierce! Damn him because he was right.

15

Friday Afternoon

THE second note came in Friday's mail.

He didn't see it until almost four o'clock. It had been one of his better days; no queasiness or discomfort when he woke up, mental faculties in sharper focus, some of his old energy. As long as he didn't think about it too much, he could pretend that he was just another reasonably healthy, forty-six-year-old man. He left the house when Cassie did, surprised Gloria by showing up at the office at his usual time, surprised himself by putting in better than six hours of work on the site plan and conceptual designs for the Dry Creek Valley project. It was three o'clock before fatigue and a dull headache caught up with him. He considered pushing it another hour, decided that would be foolish, and left for home at three-thirty.

The envelope was the top one in the box. Same type, no return address. He was neither surprised nor upset when he saw it; he'd expected that there would be more. There was a sense of fatalism in him, of things going and already gone irreparably wrong. Buried under sublimating layers of hope and evasion most of the time, now up and crawling close to the surface again.

One thing to be grateful for, he told himself as he took the mail into the house: he'd gotten home before Cassie. She would not have opened a piece of mail addressed only to him—respect of privacy was part of their mutual respect for each other—but she'd have wondered and probably asked him about it, and then he'd have had to lie to her again.

In the kitchen he opened a bottle of Sierra Nevada, emptied half of it in two swallows. Then he tore the envelope open.

YOU WON'T GET AWAY WITH IT. YOU'LL SUFFER FOR WHAT YOU DID.

He sat at the dinette table. Drank more ale, made a face and set the bottle down; it tasted foul now, as if by some alchemy it had been changed into dog piss. He peered at the postmark on the envelope. Smeared, as sometimes happened when the post office machines were freshly inked. It might have been North Bay again, but he couldn't be sure.

He forced himself to think clearly, logically. Would Eric have sent a message like this one? It didn't read like a plea for help; it seemed to be both accusation and threat. No sane reason for Eric to threaten him . . . no *sane* reason. Or maybe it wasn't meant to be a threat. There was another way to interpret it. If Eric was too guilt-ridden to admit the truth outright, he might conceivably switch pronouns, substitute "you" for "we." *We won't get away with it. We'll suffer for what we did.* Accusing himself as well as his father; threatening himself, if anyone, because at some visceral level he sought punishment and expiation.

And maybe, Hollis thought, that's what I want, too. Punishment and expiation for *my* sin.

But not like this. Not by Eric, and not by party or parties unknown.

Bad enough if Eric was responsible, but in that case at least he understood the reasons behind it—he could find some way to help him. Worse if it were someone else, because it was like fighting blind. Even Rakubian had been a known quantity; it had been clear what needed to be done in order to protect his family and himself. How do you stop, what safeguards do you take, against a phantom?

Friday Evening

The doorbell rang a few minutes past five.

Hollis was in the living room, hiding himself and his bleak thoughts behind the *Examiner*; Cassie, home just fifteen minutes, had gone upstairs to shower and change clothes. He put the paper aside as the bell sounded again. It rang twice more as he crossed to the hall, an urgent summons that quickened his steps. He pulled the door open without checking through the peephole.

Angela stood there.

He blinked at her; she had a key, she didn't need to ring the bell. Then he saw her, really saw her. White-faced, eyes slick-bright, one hand on the doorjamb as if for support, the other clutching her purse against her chest. He felt an inner twisting, a spurt of fear.

"Daddy," she said, almost moaning it.

She was alone, he realized. "Kenny? Is he—"

"He's all right, I haven't picked him up yet. I drove straight here. I couldn't . . . I had to . . ."

He looped an arm around her shoulders, felt the quivering tension in her, and drew her inside. There was a creaking and thumping on the stairs as he shut the door: Cassie had heard them and was coming down. He maneuvered Angela into the living room, sat her down on the couch. Sat beside her with his arm still around her shoulders. Before he could say anything, Cassie came hurrying in.

"What's going on? Honey, what—"

"He's back," she said.

"Back? Who's back?"

"David. He's alive and he's back."

Hollis heard Cassie's breath suck in. He didn't, couldn't look at her. He knew then what had happened, what was coming, and with the knowledge the feeling of fatalism returned, stronger, darker, like a black hole opening in his mind.

"My God," Cassie said, "you mean you saw him?" She sat heavily on Angela's other side. "He showed up at school or your apartment—"

"No, but he knows where I'm living."

"How could he know?"

"He *knows*, Mom. He's after me again."

"Did he call you, is that it?"

Angela shook her head, fumbled at the catches on her purse and rummaged inside. The taste of ashes was in Hollis's mouth as he watched the crumpled sheet of paper materialize in her hand.

"This was in my mailbox when I got home."

He snatched it from her, uncrumpled it. Same paper, same typeface. Two lines, identical to the ones on the note he'd received today. *You won't get away with it. You'll suffer for what you did.*

Cassie reached for the paper. He couldn't prevent her from reading it; he let her take it without protest. She scanned the lines, kept staring at them as though trying to digest their meaning.

"I almost believed he was gone for good," Angela said dully. The hunted look had returned to her eyes; her face was bloodless. She'd come so far, almost all the way back, and now this. "It seemed he must be after so much time. But he's not, he's somewhere close by, and he wants me to suffer. . . ."

"No," Hollis said.

"Hurt me, hurt Kenny . . ."

"No! Rakubian didn't send that note."

The words were out before he realized what he'd said. Angela and Cassie were both looking at him, their gazes like a pressure against his face; he still could not meet either one.

"Who else could it be?" From Cassie.

"I don't know. Somebody's sick idea of a joke . . ."

"It's not a joke," Angela said, "it's David, you know it is."

"It doesn't sound like him," he said lamely. "Two lines, no mention of your name, no signature . . . it's too impersonal. Why would he send an anonymous note instead of calling, making the same demands as before?"

"He doesn't want me anymore. All he wants is for me to suffer."

"Why two months of silence? It doesn't make sense."

"Yes it does. It's his way of torturing me. He won't do anything right away. There'll be more notes, phone calls, God knows what else." Her voice had begun to rise. "Oh God, I can't go through all that again, I can't!"

Cassie gathered her close, murmured to her and stroked her hair. All the while she looked at Hollis over the top of her head, a steady, unreadable look.

He sat with his hands between his knees. Limp, useless lumps of flesh—like what was left of his manhood hanging higher up. Voices muttered in his head. One said, "It's not Eric, he loves Angela, he'd never do anything to hurt her." Another said, "You don't know him or what he's capable of, you've never really known him." A third, the loudest, said,

"You're not the only target now . . . Angela, maybe Cassie . . . it's just like it was when Rakubian was alive."

Cassie, with little help from him, calmed Angela down; tried to convince her to spend the night there, let Hollis go pick up Kenny. She wouldn't agree to it. She kept saying, "I feel like such a little girl, always running home—I have to stop being a little girl." Cassie finally talked her into a partial compromise: the two of them would fetch Kenny together. Hollis understood that she wanted some time alone with Angela, and that was all right with him. He needed to be by himself for a while.

When they were gone he sat in his study, staring blankly at the architectural prints on the walls while he tried to order his thoughts, shape them as he would one of his designs into a logical, substantive pattern. He hated the feeling of impotence; it was the way Pop had made him feel as a kid, weak, ineffectual, and until now he'd refused to let himself be crippled that way as an adult. He had dealt with all the other crises in his life, he'd dealt with Rakubian, or tried to, the best way he knew how. All right, he'd deal with this new crisis, too.

One thing for sure: He could no longer afford to wait for something else to happen. He had to act, and quickly. And he had to stop shouldering the entire burden himself, no matter who was responsible for those notes or why.

In the kitchen later, picking at a cold dinner neither he nor Cassie wanted:

"I wish you'd been able to talk her into staying with us tonight," he said. "I don't like the idea of her and Kenny alone in that apartment."

"I don't think they'll be alone."

"What do you— Oh. Pierce."

"She said she was going to call him."

"I suppose he spends a lot of nights over there now."

"Some, probably."

"Terrific."

"He wants to marry her again," Cassie said.

Hollis frowned. He hadn't told her about Pierce's visit yesterday. "She tell you that?"

"Yes."

"So he's already asked her."

"Not in so many words. But he's made it plain enough that he intends to."

"She's not going to say yes?"

"She says she isn't ready for another commitment."

"She has some sense left, then. If she means it."

"Anyhow," Cassie said, "it's a good thing she's letting him stay there, isn't it? Now?"

"You think so? My guess is he'd run at the first sign of trouble."

"You're wrong. Ryan's not like that anymore."

"Right, the big change. Now he's got you believing it."

"I have eyes. You'd see it, too, if you opened yours."

He let that pass. "It's not just her safety that's worrying me. It's her mental state."

"She'll be okay. She was when I left her. I wanted to stay until Ryan came, but she'd had enough mothering."

"For tonight. What about tomorrow and the days after that? Suppose there's another note? She's liable to take it into her head to run away again."

"I asked her about that. She said no, it'd take a lot more than a note or two to send her back into hiding. But she's been through so much . . . I doubt she can stand much more."

I doubt any of us can.

"If she does decide to take Kenny someplace safe, I can't honestly blame her. I don't think you can, either."

"Not if Rakubian really is back," he said.

"Why do you keep saying 'if'? I don't see who or why anyone else would send a note like that."

"Neither do I. I want it to be somebody else, that's all. A crank, somebody harmless."

"We have to be realistic," Cassie said.

"Two months, don't forget that. I just can't see Rakubian staying away and keeping silent that long."

"He's crazy and unpredictable. After all the things he's done already, I wouldn't put anything past him."

Except resurrection from the dead, he thought.

Bitterly he said, "Rakubian or whoever, if there's any real danger, running away isn't going to keep her and Kenny safe. Neither is Pierce, if she stays. And neither am I with this goddamn cancer."

"Don't start feeling sorry for yourself. You're not Super-dad, and nobody expects you to be but you. The job isn't yours or mine or Ryan's anyway, it's the police's."

"What the hell can they do? They couldn't find a trace of Rakubian in two months. The note isn't conclusive proof she's in danger from him or anybody else—it *could* be the work of a crank. If we go to the cops they'll make sympathetic noises and tell us not to worry. No. That's not the answer."

"Neither is doing nothing. Maybe we should hire a private investigator."

"To do what, act as a bodyguard? Camp on Angela's doorstep, follow her around wherever she goes?"

"I didn't mean as a bodyguard. I meant to try to track down Rakubian."

"If the police couldn't find him, how is a private detective going to manage it after two months? They're not miracle workers, that's a lot of fictional crap."

Strained silence.

At length Cassie said, "This isn't doing either of us any good."

"No, it isn't."

"I'd give anything if he'd stayed missing, if he really was dead. In my mind I had him dead and buried somewhere for good. Didn't you?"

"Yes," Hollis said. "Dead and buried for good."

Saturday Morning

Eric said, "Oh, it's you, Dad. Jeez, you woke me up." He sounded sleep-fogged and grumpy; he'd never been much of a morning person. "You know what time it is?"

"Seven-fifteen," Hollis said. "I wanted to be sure to catch you home. I tried to call twice last night."

"Date I told you about. I left straight from work, got home late. I didn't get much sleep." A woman's voice rose querulously in the background, close by. "That's why. And she's *not* what I thought she might be. Ms., not missus—"

"I need to see you."

"See me? When?"

"Right away. We have to talk."

"About what?'

"When I see you, not on the phone."

"Something wrong?" Eric sounded more awake.

"Yes. I want you to fly up to SFO this afternoon."

The line hummed.

"I called United," Hollis said. "There's a flight out of Santa Barbara at one-twenty, gets in at two-thirty. I'll pick you up at Arrivals. Reservation's already made in your name and paid for. Round-trip—you can fly back tonight at five-fifty."

Again the line hummed emptily for a few seconds. Hollis tried to imagine the expression on his son's face, what might be going through his mind. And couldn't.

"Okay, if it's that urgent." Calm acceptance, in a voice that betrayed nothing of his feelings. "You sure you want to drive all the way to the airport? I can rent a car, come up there. . . ."

"I'll manage. One thing: This is just between you and me."

"Whatever you say."

"I'll see you at two-thirty. Don't miss the flight."

"I won't," Eric said. "Whatever this is about, you can count on me."

We'll see about that. We'll find out a lot of things this after-noon.

16

Saturday Afternoon

SAN Francisco International, like so many things to him these days, seemed different, strange. It had been nearly two years since the last time he'd been there, and the ongoing airport construction had altered both its shape and its access; the entrance and exit ramps had been moved, the entrance lanes now ran through an underpass beneath one of the new terminal buildings. New signs pointed him to Arrivals, but the Saturday congestion made it difficult to get around to the United terminal. And when he did get there, ten minutes after the scheduled arrival time of the Santa Barbara flight, Eric was nowhere to be seen among the crush of waiting passengers. He tried to squeeze the Lexus into a parking space between a taxi and a limo; an airport security cop waved him off. He had no choice then but to loop all the way back through the maze of lanes and construction for another pass, fighting aggressive and reckless drivers like a participant in a stock car race.

He had to make four passes, better than half an hour's

wasted time, before he finally saw Eric—Cal Poly sweatshirt that clashed with his old maroon-and-white windbreaker— waving at him from the curb. He jammed on the brakes, cut in front of a stretch limo, and stayed put through a series of angry horn blasts until Eric piled into the car.

"Jeez, I'm sorry, Dad," he said. "Plane was thirty minutes late taking off."

"Not your fault."

Neither of them spoke again until they had cleared Arrivals and were in one of the airport exit lanes. Then Eric asked tentatively, "Where're we going?"

"Someplace quiet where we can talk."

They rode in heavy silence after that. Hollis took the north ramp that led to Airport Boulevard, where there were a number of large travelers' hotels. He swung into the parking lot of the first one he saw, slotted the car near the entrance. His shoulder muscles were tight and he had a vague headache; otherwise he felt well enough, too keyed up to be particularly tired yet. Later, after he was done with Eric and the long drive home, he knew he'd be exhausted.

In the hotel lobby he asked, "You hungry?" and Eric shook his head. They bypassed the restaurant, entered the bar lounge. Dark, quiet except for a TV tuned low to a baseball game, only half a dozen patrons lining the bar. Hollis led the way to a back-corner booth. He ordered coffee for both of them, waited until it was served before he opened the discussion.

"We'll start with this," he said. "Have you received any unsigned mail in the past few days? At your office or your apartment, either one."

Eric frowned. "Snail mail?"

"Any kind of mail."

"No, nothing."

"Have you sent me or your sister anonymous notes?"

"Have I— Why would I do a thing like that?"

"Answer the question."

"Of course not. What kind of anonymous notes?"

"This kind."

He took the three sheets from his pocket, the one to Angela and the two he'd received, and laid them side by side in front of his son. Eric's face seemed to harden as he read them, as if his flesh were solidifying from within. When he raised his head his eyes were angry.

"Rakubian," he said.

"You know it's not Rakubian."

"How would I know that? Who else—?"

Hollis said nothing, watching him.

"They sound like his kind of crap," Eric said. "But this one . . . 'What did you do with his body?' What does that mean?"

"What do you suppose it means?"

"Somebody thinks you had something to do with him disappearing, is that it?"

"Well?"

"You didn't, did you?"

"Dammit, you know I didn't kill him."

"Dad . . . I never thought you did."

"Okay, that's enough," Hollis said wearily. "No more lies or evasions."

Eric blinked at him. "Hey, wait a minute. What made you think I might've sent those notes? I wouldn't care if you'd chopped Rakubian up into little pieces and fed 'em to Fritz—"

"That's not one bit funny."

"I wasn't trying to be funny. You know I'd never do anything to hurt you or Angie—"

"Not if you were thinking clearly."

Strained silence for a clutch of seconds. Then, slowly,

"You're afraid *I* had something to do with whatever happened to Rakubian. That's why you had me fly up here."

"It's time, son. Past time."

"For what?"

"To get it out into the open. All of it, on both sides."

"I don't have any idea what you're talking about."

"Eric, I *know*. I've known all along. I was there not long after you. I found him where you left him."

"Where I—"

"Who did you think cleaned up his house, got rid of the body? You must've guessed it was me."

Eric sat without moving, his eyes round but showing nothing of what he was feeling or thinking.

"You can tell me how it happened or not," Hollis said. "That's up to you. The one thing I have to know is whether you went there with the intention of killing him. Did you?"

No answer. Not even an eyeblink.

"Did you, Eric?"

"When?" The word seemed to come from deep within; his lips barely moved.

"When what?"

"When was he killed? When did you find him?"

"I just told you—"

"Dad, you answer *me* now. When did all this happen? What day?"

The sudden sharpness in Eric's voice, more than his words, brought the first stirrings of doubt. Hollis said, "The Saturday before Angela left for Utah."

"The day I found the box in the garage."

"You had every right to be furious—"

"Sure I was furious. But not enough to kill him. I couldn't kill anybody, not even to save Angie. You never did understand who or what I am, did you?" Eric's body seemed to loosen all at once; he leaned forward so abruptly that his elbows banged the table, rattled the coffee cups. "Listen to me, Dad. That day I did exactly what I told you and Mom I did—drove out to the coast, then up along the Russian River. I didn't go to San Francisco. I didn't see Rakubian."

"You . . . didn't . . ."

"I didn't kill him. *It wasn't me.*"

The truth.

Hollis knew it, accepted it all at once. Certain knowledge replacing the false belief, the rush to misjudgment.

Somebody else had gone to Rakubian's home that afternoon, somebody else with a powerful reason to hate him and to want him dead. Somebody else had picked up the raven statuette and crushed his skull. Somebody else . . .

And the corpse, the blood, the carpet, the garbage bags, the cleanup, the nightmare drive, the cop, the gravedigging, the burial, all of it, all of it . . . for nothing.

He'd covered up somebody else's murder.

He sat stunned, the truth like a hammer beating at his senses. There was relief in him . . . *Eric was innocent* . . . but in these first moments it had been dwarfed by the weight of his own mordant guilt.

"Eric," he said thickly, "get me a brandy. Double shot."

"You're not supposed to drink. . . ."

"Just get it. Please."

Eric hesitated, then lifted to his feet. He seemed to be gone a long time. Then the snifter was in Hollis's hand, the brandy inside him in two convulsive swallows. Its spreading heat let him think again.

"Dad? You believe me?"

"Yes. I believe you."

"Why'd you wait so long to talk to me? All those questions at home the day after, on the phone the other day . . . why didn't you say something either of those times?"

"I thought it'd be easier if we just pretended . . . if we kept our own secrets. . . ." He pressed the heels of his hands against his temples. "You were right—I never did know you very well, did I."

"Maybe you didn't try hard enough. Maybe I didn't, either."

He nodded. I'm a goddamn fool, he thought.

After a little time Eric asked, "What happened that Saturday? Did you go to Rakubian's place because you thought I had?"

"Yes." He explained about Cassie's phone call, his discovery of the body. The words came in a rush, hot and acidulous in his mouth. "His skull was crushed . . . and I remembered you saying that was what you wanted to do to him, crush his skull. It never occurred to me that somebody else might've done it. I'm sorry . . . I'm so sorry."

"If I'd been in your place," Eric said slowly, "I'd've thought the same thing. So then you cleaned up everything, to protect me."

"No other reason." Hollis told him the rest of it, everything except the exact location of the grave. Purging himself. When he was done, Eric seemed to be looking at him in a new way. But he couldn't tell whether he'd gained or lost stature in his son's estimation, just that he'd been reevaluated.

"It must've been pretty bad," Eric said. "If that cop had looked in the trunk . . ."

"Might've been better if he had."

"Don't say that."

"I screwed up. Not just that day—before and since, all the way down the line."

"What do you mean, before that day?"

He felt the urge to confess his original plan. I was going to kill him myself, he wanted to say, shoot him down like a dog. And I might have if somebody else hadn't done the job for me. That's the really ironic thing here, you see? Somebody else killed him, not me, not you, a third party took care of the problem, and all I had to do when I found him was walk away or call the police and it would've been over then and there. We might have been suspected, you and I, but there would have been no proof because we're innocent and eventually they'd have found out who did it . . . some little piece of evidence I took away or destroyed. Now it's too late. Now we can't call the cops, we can't dig up Rakubian, and the person responsible not only got away with it but may be stalking us now, like Rakubian stalked us but for no comprehensible reason. All I've done is exchange a known threat for an unknown one.

He put none of this into words. His insane plan to take Rakubian's life—and it *was* insane, he knew that now—was his own private cross. No good purpose would be served in sharing it with his son, with anyone ever.

"Before, after, it doesn't matter," he said. "I screwed up, that's all. Maybe put us all right back in jeopardy again."

"You think whoever wrote those notes is the person who killed Rakubian?"

"Has to be. No one else knows he's dead."

" 'What did you do with his body?' Yeah. Killed him and left the body there in the house, and the next thing he knows the body's gone and everything's cleaned up. Must've been some shock when he found that out."

"A shock, yes."

"But how'd he know it was you? He wouldn't've still been hanging around when you got there."

"May have come back for some reason, saw my car. Or guessed it was me somehow."

"What I don't get is why he waited two months, why he started sending those notes. I mean, he was home free. What's the point of hassling you and Angie?"

Hollis shook his head.

"He sent this one to her at her new apartment," Eric said. "She's been living there less than a week. How'd he know where to find her?"

The answer to that was plain enough. Hollis said nothing, let Eric come to it on his own. It didn't take him long.

"Somebody we know," he said.

"I don't see any other explanation."

"Who? Jeez, Dad, I can't imagine anybody we know hating us that much."

I can. One person.

"Who'd want Rakubian dead besides us? Or care what you did with his body? Or want you and Angie to suffer any more than you already have?"

One person, one motive that makes any sense.

He shook his head again. A headshake was neither a lie nor an evasion.

Eric said, "What're we going to do?"

"*We're* not going to do anything. You're going back to Santa Barbara on the five-fifty flight."

"Listen, I—"

"No argument, please. There's nothing you can do at home."

"I can help find out who's doing this."

"How? What can you do that I can't?"

". . . If you identify him, what then?"

"Cross that bridge when the time comes."

"You can't turn him in without implicating yourself. He knows you got rid of the body, covered up, he'd tell the police—"

"His word against mine," Hollis said. "He can't be absolutely certain it was me and he can't have any idea where Rakubian is buried. He'd never be able to prove he didn't do it himself."

"The cops might still believe him."

"I won't turn him in if I can avoid it. The threat of it alone might be enough to get him off our backs."

"Suppose it isn't? What if he tries something . . . if he has a gun or a knife?"

"I can take care of myself."

"Dad . . . you're not thinking of going after *him* with a weapon?"

Another headshake that was neither lie nor evasion. "There are other ways to protect myself. I may have cancer, but I'm not a cripple yet."

It was the wrong thing to say. Eric's mouth tightened; Hollis could almost see the shutter come down behind his eyes.

"I'm sorry," Hollis said, picking his words carefully now. "I know you're concerned, I know you want to help. But this thing could drag on for a while, turn out to be a hell of a lot less dangerous than it seems. You can't quit your job, put your life on hold indefinitely."

No response.

"Let me handle it. If there's anything you can do, I'll call you right away. I mean that—right away."

Another dozen beats. Then, "What about Mom? Does she know?"

"About the notes, yes."

"But not about Rakubian being dead or what you did."

"No. It would've meant telling her I believed you were guilty, and I couldn't do that to her."

"You going to tell her now?"

"I'm not sure it's a good idea."

"I am," Eric said. "She has a right to know the whole story. So does Angie. Tell them both, Dad. We're all in this together."

Eric's gaze was intense, and Hollis understood that the need for family unity was just as important to him. He'd been able to teach him that much, at least. He understood, too, that if the closeness, the new bond that had formed between them here was to be maintained, he must neither argue nor fail to follow through. He nodded, gripped his son's arm.

"You're right," he said. "We're all in this together, we all need to know what we're dealing with."

Somebody we know.

Ryan Pierce.

Driving home, looking at it from different angles as objectively as he could, he came up with Pierce every time. Motive for killing Rakubian: the same as Hollis's, as Eric's—to eliminate the threat to Angela and Kenny. The old Pierce might not have been capable of violence, but the new Pierce was a different story. He'd changed, all right, only not in the way Angela and Cassie believed; hardened into a man with definite convictions and a twisted set of values. And the one thing he wanted more than anything else seemed to be a new life with his ex-wife and his son. Motive for sending the notes: to make Angela dependent on him, leverage to convince her to remarry him. Secondary motive: to punish Hollis for standing against him.

It had to be Pierce. He *wanted* it to be Pierce, because then there was no immediate danger to anyone in the family and the solution to the problem was relatively clear-cut. The only real danger was in his sticking around, manipulating Angela. Confront him, then, and threaten him—with the law, but also with telling her he was a murderer. Point out that even if he tried to shift the guilt to Hollis, it wouldn't work because she was still Daddy's girl—she would never take his word over her father's. Convince him that his only choice was to pack up and move away and never come near any of them again.

But be careful, don't just bull ahead. Think through how he was going to handle Pierce, exactly what he would say to him. The more prepared he was, the greater the leverage to pry him out of their lives once and for all.

He felt better by the time he reached the Los Alegres exit—empowered again. He had decided something else, too, by then. He was not going to tell Cassie or Angela what he'd told Eric, not just yet. He was still committed to no more lies or evasions; he would simply withhold the truth a while longer. Until he talked to Pierce. Until he had him good and tight by the short hairs.

17

Sunday Morning

CASSIE went to church at ten o'clock.

Hollis went to the garage to clean, oil, and load the Colt Woodsman.

When he was done he rewrapped the .22 and put it in the Lexus's glove compartment. Then he left a note for Cassie, saying he'd gone on an errand, and drove to Angela's apartment.

She and Kenny were there; Pierce wasn't. But Hollis would have known he'd spent the night even if Kenny hadn't blurted it out three minutes after his arrival. Angela was calm today, smiling, the picture of Sunday-morning domesticity. She poured him a cup of coffee, another for herself, while Kenny climbed onto his lap and chattered about some new video game Pierce had given him. That was when the boy made his slip.

"Dad's gonna live with us all the time," he said.

"Oh, he is. Did he tell you that?"

"Uh-huh."

"When?"

"Last night when he tucked me in."

Angela was staring into her cup, two spots of color high on her cheekbones. He watched her until she raised her head, but she wouldn't quite meet his gaze. She said to Kenny, "Honey, you can watch the Cartoon Channel if you want to."

"Hey, cool!"

And then to Hollis, "We can sit in the garden."

The "garden" was a twenty-foot square enclosed by a board fence draped in scraggly wisteria. Brown lawn, a couple of pyracantha shrubs, two strips of flower bed that were mostly hard-packed dirt. She deserves better than this, Hollis thought. Kenny deserves better than this.

They sat in a pair of molded plastic chairs on a tiny rectangle of cracked concrete. Angela asked tentatively, "Are you mad at me, Daddy? About Ryan?"

"No."

"I needed somebody. Not just for protection . . . I mean . . ."

"I know what you mean."

"You understand, don't you?"

"When is he moving in permanently? Be pretty cramped in such a small space, won't it?"

"It's not like that," she said." At least not yet."

"He seems to think it is, from what he told Kenny."

"He wants it that way, the three of us together again. Very much. Last night . . . he asked me to marry him again."

Even though he insisted he wouldn't yet. "And?"

"I didn't give him a definite answer. I'm not sure it's what I want. I still care for him . . . a lot. And Kenny does, too. But marriage so soon after David . . . and the situation the way it is . . . I don't think it's the right time to be making that kind of decision."

"No, it isn't."

"Ryan says he understands. But . . ."

"But what? Is he pressuring you?"

"Not exactly."

"What then, exactly?"

"He's so sure it's the right thing. He swears he loves us, and I know he means it. I can't be as absolutely certain of my own feelings, that's all."

"Did you tell him about the note?"

She nodded. "I felt he should know."

"What was his reaction?"

"He said he'd make sure nothing happens to us."

"Uh-huh. Where is he now?"

"He left about nine. He had some things to do."

"What things?"

"He didn't say."

"Be back when?"

"He didn't say."

"Just went off and left you and Kenny alone."

"He can't watch over us every minute. . . ."

"I want to talk to him," Hollis said.

"About his proposal? Please, Daddy, don't interfere. It won't do any of us any good."

"That isn't what I want to talk about. You have any idea where he went?"

"Well, Rhona's, maybe. Most of his things are still there. . . ."

Right, he thought. No need to move them over here just yet. A razor, a toothbrush, some clean underwear, a couple of packages of condoms—what else would he need?

He stood. "I'd better be going."

"Can't you stay a while longer?"

This was the last place for his showdown with Pierce; it had been a mistake to think he could manage it anywhere near Angela and Kenny. Neutral ground, someplace where he could stay focused and maintain a tight grip on his emotions.

"Things to do myself," he said. "We'll get together again later."

She seemed subdued as they went back inside; she probably thought he *was* mad at her, even though he'd said he wasn't. Disappointed was closer to the truth. She was so damn dependent on men, the wrong kind, like Pierce and Rakubian. If only she had a little more backbone, a little better judgment.

She said, "Should I tell Ryan you want to see him?"

"No. I'll take care of it."

Kenny was paying no attention to them, sitting cross-legged in front of the television, up close, cartoon images assailing his eyes and cartoon voices assaulting his eardrums. Angela pried him away, brought him over for a quick hug and kiss good-bye. "See you, Granpa," he said, and hurried back to the TV.

"He's a cartoon junkie," Angela said apologetically. "Cartoons and computers, that's all he ever thinks about. But he loves you, Dad. So do I, a lot. Really . . . a lot."

More than Pierce, I hope. Enough to forgive me when all this is over.

Pierce's sister and her family lived on the east side, in one of the endless sprawling tracts that had spread like a blight over what had once been rich agricultural land. Tract houses, tract planning, even the more upscale variety, offended his architect's eye. Bland conventional design, corner-cutting by greedy developers that too often resulted in slipshod construction and serious problems within a few years. Starter homes, some of them; fulfilled aspirations for other suburbanites. Little slices of the downsized American dream. He couldn't fault those who were unable to afford something better; the high cost of living in California had forced many to settle for less. But the majority nowadays had been brainwashed into believing conformity and mediocrity *were* something better, all that they needed or deserved.

The only way to do battle against that kind of mind-set, in his professional view, was to try to educate the people by providing better home design, better overall planning, better construction, even if it meant shaving profits. Not the people like Shelby Chesterton, the affluent minority, who could afford the very best and for whom Hollis could now and then indulge his esthetic vision to the fullest. People like the seniors who would inhabit the Dry Creek Valley development, which was why he felt it was important for Mannix & Hollis to be given the job. And they would be, he was sure. Gabe felt the same way; they had agreed that a good portion of their profit margin should be sacrificed in favor of architectural integrity. Do quality work and you'd continue to get quality jobs, and in some small way maybe you could make a difference in the long run.

He remembered the street Rhona Pierce Collins lived on, but not the number, so he stopped in one of the nearby malls (so insipidly conventional it might have been a shopping center anywhere in the country) and looked it up. When he got to the equally uniform three-bedroom tract he didn't see Pierce's pickup; but he stopped anyway, went up, and rang the bell.

Rhona was a female counterpart of her brother, except that she'd put on at least twenty pounds since Hollis had last seen her, the result of two children, poor diet, and not enough exercise. Yes, she said, Ryan had been there, but he'd left more than an hour ago. No, she didn't know where he'd gone. Then, as Hollis was about to turn away, she beamed at him and said, "Well, I guess congratulations are in order, Mr. Hollis."

"Congratulations?"

"Angela and Ryan getting back together, getting married again." He said nothing, but his expression was enough to turn her smile upside-down. "Gee, I hope I didn't let the cat out of the bag. You did know about it, you and your wife?"

"Yes," he said, "thanks, Rhona," and put his back to her before she could read the full message in his face and eyes.

Sunday Afternoon

He couldn't find Pierce anywhere. He looked for the Dodge downtown, on another pass by Angela's apartment, a few other places, and then drove out Western Avenue Extension to Chileno Valley Road. The Gugliotta ranch was seven miles out, a beef and dairy cattle operation on several thousand acres spread over the rocky foothills. The Dodge wasn't there, either; and old Fred Gugliotta, whom he knew slightly, told him he hadn't seen Pierce since Friday afternoon.

Frustration rode heavily with him on the way back to town. He ached to get this business over and done with; the longer it went on the more stressed he would be, and another of Stan Otaki's warnings had been to avoid stressful situations. For the third time he did a drive-by at Angela's. Still no sign of the pickup.

It was nearly one by then, and he was tired and hungry. He gave up the hunt and headed home. Later he'd call Angela, and if Pierce had returned he'd arrange to meet him somewhere. Just the two of them, alone, with the Colt Woodsman in his pocket as backup.

Cassie was home from church and a lunch date afterward; he parked beside her van in the driveway. As soon as he shut off the engine he could hear Fritz barking his fool head off inside the house. Terrific. While Angela was in Utah, Cassie had worked with the Doberman to control his high-strung nature, the worst part of which was incessant barking. Mostly, now, the dog stayed quiet when they were home or arriving home. Something must have set him off.

Fritz wasn't confined to his usual place on the back porch; Hollis could hear him moving around and making his racket on the other side of the front door. He said loudly, "Shut up, boy, it's me," as he opened it. The Doberman backed off to let him enter the hallway, but then stood quivering with hackles up, a low growl in place of the barks. Hollis frowned. "What's the matter with you? You forget who puts the Alpo in your food dish?" He spoke the words in a quiet voice, but the dog kept right on growling.

"Cass?" he called. "What's got Fritz so stirred up?"

No answer.

The muscles in his back and neck began a slow bunching. He called her name again, louder, and again there was no response. He sidled past the Doberman, went ahead into the living room.

And stopped dead, slam-frozen with shock.

The room was a shambles.

Worse than that . . . it had been systematically, brutally raped.

The fabric on the couches and chairs had been slashed by some sharp object, with such viciousness that there was little left except strips like flayed flesh. Stuffing bulged through the wounds in his armchair, gouts of it like white- and black-streaked blood. End tables were overturned, Cassie's glass-fronted curio cabinet toppled and shattered, the glass top of the coffee table smashed, bar stools savaged and tossed aside, bottles broken on the floor behind the wet bar. And over everything, the furniture and the carpet and the walls, a mad pattern of stripes and swirls of shiny black spray paint. Now that he was in here he could smell both the paint and the spilled liquor. The odors closed his throat, intensified the sudden blood-throb in his temples.

Cassie was there in the midst of the wreckage, slumped against a torn couch armrest. She stared straight ahead, not moving in any way; in profile her face had the splotchy white consistency of buttermilk. One arm was raised in front of her, the fingers extended, and he realized she was pointing.

The wall on the far side of the fireplace. A once-beige wall decorated with two watercolors by local artists, now defaced by the black paint. But the marks there were not meaningless like the rest; they formed crude letters a foot high—

18

HE picked his way across the room, trying to avoid the still-sticky paint, to Cassie's side. Except for lowering her arm, she remained immobile; did not look at him when he bent to grip her shoulders. Her eyes had a moist, glassy shine. Her body seemed to have no softness or resiliency, as if he were touching petrified wood. He tried to turn her against him, but she wouldn't yield—not resisting, just not responding.

"Cass? You all right?"

"I haven't been home long," she said, as if she were answering a different question. "Fritz was barking. I went out to the porch to quiet him, but he broke away and came running in here."

"The rest of the house . . ."

"I don't know. This . . . I couldn't . . ."

"I'll check. You stay here."

"It'll never be the same again," she said as he released her and straightened up. "No matter what we do. Never the same again."

His gaze went again to the spray-painted wall. Rage boiled to the surface, came spilling out before he could stop it. "That son of a bitch. He'll pay for this. I'll make him sorry he was ever born."

Now she was looking at him, with a kind of laser intensity. "Rakubian," she said.

He didn't answer. He stepped away from her, around behind the couch and along the inside wall into the hallway. Fritz was still there, no longer growling, but the muscled body still quivering. Hollis sidestepped him and went upstairs first to look into the master bedroom, then Angela's and Eric's old rooms. None of them had been violated. Downstairs again, he checked the dining room, TV room, his study, the kitchen. Intact, untouched. The Doberman followed him here, toenails clicking loudly on the hardwood floor.

All that barking, he thought. Scared Pierce off before he could do any more damage. Unless the living room was his only intended target. Tear it apart, leave his goddamn message, get out quick. The whole thing could have been done in less than ten minutes. Destroy an entire room . . . less than ten minutes.

The side kitchen window was open a few inches. Left that way after breakfast, carelessly, or left unlatched— Pierce could have gotten in through there. Or he could have come in through the front door. Hollis was sure he'd locked it when he left, but Pierce could have taken Angela's key without her knowing it, walked right up, let himself in.

He quit the house by the patio door, went around to the front and into the Archers' yard. There was no answer when he rang their bell. The Lippmans, their neighbors on the north, weren't home, either. He crossed the street to the

Changs'. They were in, but they had nothing to tell him; they'd been working in their backyard all morning.

Well, it didn't really matter, did it? Pierce . . . who else but Pierce? And he couldn't go to the police anyway. On the way back he had a strong impulse to get into the car, go hunting again. He fought it off. The state he was in now, it would be foolish, even dangerous, to brace Pierce.

Cassie was still in the living room, but she had gotten over the worst of her shock. She stood by the wet bar, color in her cheeks again, sparking anger in place of the glassy shine in her eyes.

She asked, "Did anybody see him?"

"No. Archers and Lippmans aren't home."

"He's lucky as well as crazy. The police . . . maybe they can find something in this mess to prove it was him."

"You didn't phone them?"

"No, I was waiting for you."

He took a breath before he said, "I'm not going to report this."

"Why not? Rakubian—"

"Rakubian didn't do it."

"Of course he did."

Another breath, and then the big plunge because he could not hide the truth any longer. "Rakubian's dead, Cass."

"Dead? You . . . *dead?*"

"For two months."

"How do you know that? My God, you didn't . . ."

"No, I didn't kill him. But I have a pretty good idea who did. The same person who sent those notes, who did this."

She was staring at him as if she had never seen him before. "Who?"

"I'd better tell you the whole story first."

"Yes, you'd damn well better."

"Not in here. In the kitchen."

She led him out there, sat down at the dinette table, and waited for him to do the same before she said, "All right, Jack. The whole story."

He told her. The truth and nothing but the truth, withholding only what he'd kept from Eric. She reacted just twice, first with a pained grimace when he explained his belief in Eric's guilt, then with a jerky nod when he said of his cover-up, "I had to do it to protect him." Otherwise she sat and listened and stared at him in stoic silence.

The silence went on after he was done. And when she finally did say something, it was not at all the reaction he'd expected.

"Goddamn you, Jack Hollis." In a coldly furious voice. "You make me so fucking mad sometimes, I could scream."

"Cass, I'm sorry, but I thought I was doing the right thing—"

"The right thing."

"Yes."

"By lying to me, keeping me in the dark."

"I wanted to protect you, too—"

"There, that's what I mean. That's it exactly. It's not Rakubian or what you did that's got me so upset, it's *you.* You and that Superman compulsion of yours."

"What're you talking about?"

"Superman, Superdad, Superhusband. Protect Eric, Angela, me. Shoulder all the responsibility, make all the decisions, take all the risks. Try to be better than your father in every damn way."

"My father? What does he have to do with this?"

"He has everything to do with it. Your whole life has been one constant struggle to prove to yourself that he was wrong about you, that you're a better man than he was. Smarter, stronger, more capable, more compassionate, more protective, more loving, more nurturing, more everything. But you're not the strong, silent, macho type. You're Jack Hollis, not Bud Hollis, and you try too hard and lose judgment and perspective and make mistakes and shut people out because you can't admit that you need help or advice, that you're even a little bit weaker than hard-as-nails Bud Hollis."

The accusations stung him. Denial surged hot into his throat, but he had no words to express it.

"The cancer, too, that's another thing. You're so full of rage and anxiety at what's happening inside your body that it's clouded your reason."

"That's not true!"

"It is true. You think I don't know, don't understand? You're angry and bitter and afraid, and there's a part of you that needs to lash out at something or somebody . . . Rakubian, for instance. But you can't admit it to yourself, it's not an acceptable attitude, so you've shifted it around to something that is acceptable—protecting your family at all cost, making sure we survive because you're afraid you won't survive yourself."

"My God," he said in a choked voice.

"I'm right, you know I am. Can't you see it? Those are the real reasons you've been trying to deal with all this on your own . . . your father, the cancer. But you can't deal with it alone, you never could, and you don't have to. They're my problems as well as yours. I'm your wife, your partner, your coconspirator if necessary, and whether you like it or not I'm just as angry as you are, just as tough and capable, and more clearheaded in a crisis. I don't deserve to be treated as a weakling or an inferior, because I'm neither one. I don't deserve to be treated the way your father treated you."

He shook his head, more reflex than anything else, and got to his feet. Stood indecisively for a few seconds, then sank back down again. All at once he was very tired; his arms and legs had a boneless feel.

"I know all that hurt you," Cassie said in softer tones, "but it had to be said. You've hurt me, too."

"I . . . never meant to hurt you."

"A sin of omission is still a sin."

"All right. All right. Why the hell have you stayed married to me if you think I'm such a loser, if I offend you so much?"

"For God's sake, don't start pitying yourself. I stay with you because I love you and I need you, flaws and all. I'm not attacking you, Jack, I'm only trying to make you see things the way they are so we can move on."

He saw, he really did see; the denial was no longer hot, not even lukewarm. She was right. Everything she'd said, right on the mark. But all he could make himself say was, "Move on to where?"

"Jack . . . you . . ." Her voice had grown hoarse; she cleared her throat. "My mouth is so dry I can't . . ." He watched her get to her feet, move to the refrigerator. With the door open she said, "Do you want anything?"

"No."

She poured a tumblerful of milk, swallowed half before she sat down again. "Better," she said. Then she said, "You haven't told Angela yet. About Rakubian."

"Not yet."

"Do you intend to?"

"Yes."

"When?"

He shook his head.

"It's cruel to keep it from her. You know how frightened she is. You have to tell her—*we* have to tell her. As soon as possible. Tonight."

"She can't come here. The living room . . ."

"We'll go to her apartment."

"I won't do it in front of Pierce."

"For heaven's sake, why not?"

"Who do you suppose killed Rakubian? Wrote those notes, did all the damage here today?"

"You think it's Ryan?"

"Who the hell else?"

"What possible reason—?"

He told her what possible reason.

"I don't believe it," she said.

"You don't believe it. He's a shining example of manhood in your eyes, is that it? Unlike me. The new, improved Ryan Pierce."

"That's the anger talking again."

"Is it? Not if I'm right about him."

"Do you have any proof?"

"Not yet, but I will."

"Then what's got you so convinced he's guilty?"

He was silent.

"You don't like him and you want him to be the one? You were sure it was Eric and you were wrong. Now you're sure it was Ryan and you can be just as wrong about him."

"Who else could it be? Tell me that."

"I can think of somebody right off the top of my head. You won't like it, but he's got just as much motive as Ryan."

"Who?"

"Gabe Mannix."

"Gabe?" he said incredulously. "That's ridiculous."

"He's in love with Angela, you know that."

"So he's in love with her. From a distance. My God, we've known the man more than twenty years. He's my best friend. You can't honestly believe he's capable of all this lunacy?"

"Of course not. Any more than I believe it's Ryan. That's my point."

"I still think Pierce is the one."

A little silence. Then Cassie said, "You're forgetting something. Angela had a date with him the Saturday Rakubian was murdered. She left the house the same time Eric did, remember?"

"She wasn't with him all afternoon, was she? He could've driven to the city after he left her."

"There wasn't time."

"There *was* time. It was two-thirty or so when you called me, and after four by the time I got to St. Francis Wood. If Pierce left town right after he left her, he had nearly two hours to get down there, kill Rakubian, and disappear before I showed up."

"I suppose so," she admitted. "But that's cutting it pretty close."

"Not if he went there planning to kill him."

"So what do you want to do? Confront him, accuse him?"

He hesitated. "It seemed like the best way to handle it."

"But now you're not so sure."

"No." Because she had put doubts in him, not only about Pierce's guilt but about himself, his judgment. "What do you suggest I . . . we do?"

"Talk to Angela before making any decisions," Cassie said. "Right now that's the most important thing."

The aura of violation was strong in the house. They took plastic trash containers, brooms, dustpans, a mop, spray cleaner, and a handful of rags into the living room, and made an attempt to clean up the wreckage. It gave Hollis a sick feeling of déjà vu; he kept having memory blips of Rakubian's library, the blood and gore he'd swabbed off the floor. Futile, wasted effort here. The living room would have to be gutted completely, repainted and recarpeted and refurnished, and even then, as Cassie had said, it would never be or feel the same—the house itself might never be the same comfort zone as before. They managed to wipe most of SUFFER! off the one wall, righted some of the chairs and tables, swept up the worst of the breakage. As they worked they talked in fits and starts, the strain still there between them. That, too, was wasted effort.

When they gave it up, finally, Cassie insisted he go upstairs and lie down. He didn't argue; he needed to be alone as well as to rest. He lay in the semidark of their bedroom, his eyes shut, his thoughts jumping here and there until they settled on Cassie's accusations. No, not accusations, not indictments—facts, insights. What he'd been slammed in the face with were harsh truths, and he'd never been one to run from the truth.

Anger and fear at the betrayal of his body. Yes, he had both those feelings. The need to lash out at something or somebody. Oh yes, he had that, too—it had fueled his plot to kill Rakubian. Might be fueling his dislike of Pierce, his desire for Pierce to be guilty. Rage was a powerful motivating force. And a notorious clouder of reason, just as Cassie had said.

And then there was Pop. Tough-as-nails Bud Hollis, the last man he'd ever wanted to be, the man he'd fought so hard *not* to be . . . the man he'd turned into in spite of himself. It explained a lot of things. Why he and Eric had never been as close as they should have been, Eric's teenage rebellion. At crucial moments he'd treated his son the way Pop had treated him, with an iron fist instead of a gentle hand, blunt censure instead of sensitivity and love, a closed mind instead of an open one; and Eric had gradually drawn away from him, as he'd drawn away from the old man. Angela's dependence . . . his fault, too. Daddy's little girl, run to Daddy every time there was a problem and he'd make it all right. Same thing with the other men in her life, weak men like the younger Pierce, dominant men like Rakubian. One or the other, the weak or the controlling, or both together like her father. And Cassie . . . shutting her out, pushing her away, when he should have utilized her strength and trusted her intelligence and her wisdom. *I'm just as angry as you are, just as tough and capable, and more clearheaded in a crisis.* If he'd confided in her from the beginning, some or all of this crisis could have been avoided.

His fault, his weakness, his mistakes. His failures. Admit it, Hollis. You're not much better than Bud Hollis, as a father, a spouse, or a human being.

The thoughts had become too painful; he made an effort to shut them off, succeeded, and then slept fitfully. When he awoke Cassie was in the room, standing near the bed. She saw that his eyes were open, came over to sit beside him.

"I just spoke to Angela," she said. "We're seeing her at five. Ryan won't be there—he's taking Kenny to a movie."

"Okay.

"I called Eric, too. I thought it was a good idea."

"What'd he say?"

"He's worried, of course. Mostly about you."

"What did you tell him?"

"That we're dealing with the situation. Both of us. He wants us to call him if there's anything he can do."

"He's a good kid. No, hell, a good man. Better man than I am, as young as he is."

"That's not true and you know it." She stroked his forehead, pushing damp strands of hair out of his eyes. "I've been thinking," she said. "I'm sorry I said all those ugly things to you. It wasn't fair—it was cruel and selfish."

"You were right," he said.

"Yes, but it was the wrong time, the wrong words. I was too upset. I should've waited."

"Better it's out in the open." His mouth quirked. The

whole truth and nothing but the truth, he thought.

"Still," she said. Then, "I can't imagine what it must've been like for you, finding Rakubian, all the rest of that day."

"I don't remember most of it," he lied.

"It took more courage than I'll ever have."

He didn't answer. What was there to say? She was only trying to make him feel better, make amends where none were needed.

She kissed him. "I don't want you to think I've stopped loving you."

"I don't. Not for a minute."

And he hadn't, even when she was berating him in the kitchen. It was the one thing he'd never doubted, the one constant he had to cling to.

Sunday Evening

Telling Angela was not quite the ordeal he'd feared. She took it well enough, crying a little with relief and a measure of sorrow. She was nothing if not compassionate, his daughter; she'd cried once as a child, he remembered, over a dead mouse she'd found partially mummified in the garage. Even after all that Rakubian had done to her, there was a small part of her that was able to grieve for the man she'd once loved or tried to love.

If she blamed Hollis for covering up or withholding the truth, she didn't express it. She seemed to understand why he'd done it, to sympathize with what he'd been through. Would she have felt the same if he'd followed through with his original plan, if it were his hands stained with Rakubian's blood? Probably not. It would've been a betrayal of her trust, and what he'd be facing now was disillusionment, censure, even horror. All death diminished her;

she'd told him that once. Anyone who committed murder, no matter what the motivation, was automatically diminished in her eyes.

They told her about the vandalism, too, minimizing the extent of the damage, but he said nothing of his suspicions of Pierce. They let her believe, for now, that they had no inkling of who the new stalker was, what his motives might be, or even if he was the same person who had killed Rakubian. If Pierce *was* responsible, they'd know it soon enough—and with any luck they'd be able to spare her the truth of that until after he was long gone.

Sunday Night

Cold and wide awake, he moved restlessly to fit his body against the curve of Cassie's back. When her warmth seeped into him he thought he'd be able to sleep. But the gentle pressure of her buttocks, the pliant mound of her hip beneath his hand, had a different effect. To his surprise he felt a stirring in his loins, then a gradual hardening and lengthening. For the first time since that Saturday in May, and after another darkly eventful day—as if through some weird physiological reaction, his body was now able to respond sexually only in a time of great stress.

Cassie was awake; she reached a hand around between them. "Well," she said, "what have we here."

"I may not be able to sustain it."

"Let's find out."

He managed. Better than he could have anticipated. Their coupling was a little too fast, but because it had been so long for both of them, he didn't disappoint Cassie. After twenty-six years he knew well enough when her orgasms were genuine.

Afterward, resting with their bodies still joined, he heard himself say, "I am still a man," without any conscious thought or intent.

"Of course you are," she said drowsily. "Mm, yes."

But sexual potency was only part of what the words meant. A small part, and not the most important at all.

19

Monday Morning

THE weather changed overnight. Instead of blue sky and sunlight, he woke to low-hanging gray clouds and a raw wind. Gloomy Monday.

Cassie left early to take Kenny to day care; Pierce had to be at work at eight and Angela had a nine o'clock meeting. Hollis toasted two pieces of bread, soft-boiled two eggs, then found he had little appetite and left most of the food untouched. He'd planned to go to the office this morning, but he didn't feel up to it. Things to do here today, anyhow. Call a couple of small contractors he knew, get estimates on gutting and remodeling the living room. Whatever the cost, it would have to come out of their savings: useless to file an insurance claim because the company would refuse to honor it without a police report. Contact one of the home security outfits, too. He had always resisted an alarm system, giving in to homeowners' fear and paranoia, but now he wished he hadn't been so stubborn on that point (and so many others). If they'd had a security alarm and it had been switched on yesterday, the vandalism would not have happened. Putting one in now would at least ensure that there would never be another break-in.

His first call was to Gloria, to tell her he wouldn't be in but that he'd be available at home if needed. She said, "How'd the submission package look?"

"What submission package?"

"Dry Creek Valley. We worked all day Saturday to get it ready, Gabe and me. Didn't he tell you?"

"I haven't heard from him."

"Ah, *todo esta jodido*. He said he'd give you a call. That's why I just dropped the envelope off yesterday. I thought you'd be expecting it."

"Where'd you put it?"

"In your mailbox. Yesterday morning, on my way home from church. I rang the bell but nobody answered. I wonder why Gabe didn't call you?"

"He'll have some excuse. He always does."

"Envelope must still be in the box. . . ."

"I'll go over the package right away."

"You're gonna be pleased," she said. "If we don't get this job, I'll swim naked all the way down to Black Point."

"That I'd like to see. Tell Gabe to call me when he gets in."

He fetched the envelope, took it into his study, and spread the contents out on his desk. Mannix and Gloria had done a fine job. The fee schedule had been pared to the bone, the schematic site plan and conceptual designs—as much Gabe's in their final form as his—were clean and environmentally sound.

Gabe, he thought, you're a hell of an architect when you set your mind to it. If you'd just stay focused, put a curb on the booze and the woman-chasing. Just had a little more ambition. I wish I could figure out exactly what makes you tick. . . .

I can think of somebody right off the top of my head. You won't like it, but he's got just as much motive as Ryan.

For Christ's sake, he thought. Don't start suspecting Mannix now. Cassie wasn't serious. Gabe, of all people.

Gabe?

The phone rang at a quarter of ten, just after he finished making an appointment with the Santa Rosa rep for Camden Home Security Systems. Mannix. Sounding lugubrious and hungover.

"I screwed up," he said. "Other things on my mind yesterday . . . I just plain forgot to call."

"A woman, I suppose."

"Cute little piece from Paloma Valley. Her only fault is she drinks too damn much."

"And you don't?"

"Weak and easily led, that's me."

"That where you were yesterday, Paloma Valley?"

"Nope. My place."

"All day?"

"We didn't get out of the sack until dinnertime. Why?"

"No reason. Listen, the proposal looks fine. You nailed everything down just right."

"*We* nailed it down, all three of us. So we go with it as is? Or do you want to make any changes?"

"As is. I'll bring it down this afternoon."

"I don't mind swinging by to pick it up."

"I'm not an invalid, Gabe."

"Did I say you were? You sound the way I feel."

"I'm a little pressured right now."

"Reason?"

"Some work that needs to be done on the house."

"What kind of work?"

"Repairs. Living room remodel."

"Kind of a sudden decision, isn't it?"

"Very sudden," he said. "We don't have much choice."

"Meaning?"

"Never mind. Tell you about it later."

He hung up feeling ashamed of himself. There'd been nothing in Mannix's voice except polite interest—of course there hadn't. Why couldn't he get rid of that nagging little worm of suspicion? It was ludicrous to think of Gabe sneaking into the house, slashing the furniture with a knife, wielding a can of spray paint like some drugged-up teenage tagger. It was an act of betrayal to give the notion even a second's serious consideration.

Buy a gun and use it. That's what I'd do in your place.

Oh, hell. Talk, false bravado.

Suppose I do it for you.

No way.

I wouldn't have any qualms about it, moral or otherwise. Same as shooting a rabid dog.

Rakubian wasn't shot, was he? Bludgeoned to death.

I'd do it. No lie and no bull.

Yes, bull. Mannix crushing a man's skull with a statuette? Another ludicrous image.

People like Rakubian don't deserve to live. Do the world a favor, take him right out of the gene pool.

Cut it out, Hollis!

But now he was remembering last week, their lunch at the Thai restaurant. He'd taken Mannix's comment about doing the right thing to mean that Gabe thought he'd killed Rakubian, but it could have meant something else. Could've been an allusion to the cleanup, the body being taken away and disposed of. Guessed he was responsible for that and was thanking him in an oblique way

No, that didn't make any sense. Why thank him on the

one hand, devil him on the other? Those notes, the vandalism . . . what possible reason could Mannix have for turning on Angela, Cassie, himself after committing murder to protect them?

Crazy thoughts, crazy suspicions. It's not Gabe, it couldn't possibly be Gabe, it's Pierce.

Pierce, Pierce, Pierce!

Monday Afternoon

It wasn't Pierce.

By five o'clock Hollis had that proven to him beyond any reasonable doubt.

The day had been busy, and a good thing, because the activity kept him from thinking too much. He dropped off the proposal at the office, met with the Camden Home Security rep, met with the two contractors (explaining briefly to each of them that the damage was a case of vandalism, but offering no details). He was finishing up with Tom Finchley, the contractor he was probably going to use, when Cassie called at 4:10.

"Jack," she said, "I need you to come pick me up."

An edge in her voice put him on alert. "Why? What's the matter with the van?"

"We'll talk when you get here. I'm at the clinic."

"On my way."

Animal Care Clinic was in the narrow part of Los Alegres east of the river that longtime residents called "the DMZ"—a section of older, lower-middle-class homes, small businesses, and light industry that lay between the long-established west side and the newer east-side tracts and malls. It was an old wood-and-brick building, once an irrigation supply company's office and warehouse, with a customer parking lot on the near side and a tiny lot for employees tucked away behind the kennels at the rear.

When Hollis arrived he found Cassie in the employee lot, in conversation with the bearded driver of a tow truck that was drawn up behind her van. All four of the van's tires were flat, so that it seemed to be resting on the ground itself; he couldn't tell from a distance if anything else was wrong with it. There was no room in the lot for the Lexus; he left it outside and walked in with his body bent against the cold wind.

The tow-truck driver was saying, "It's sugar, all right, Mrs. Hollis. No point in trying to fix the flats here, either. All I can do is tow it in."

"Yes, thanks. Go ahead."

She came over to where Hollis waited. He said thinly, "More vandalism."

"Sugar in the gas tank—the empty sack was lying right there in plain sight. One tire punctured with a sharp object, the other three with the air let out and the valve caps taken away."

"What about the interior?"

"I always lock the doors, fortunately." She had one hand in her jacket pocket; she took it out with a sheet of paper in it. "This was under the windshield wiper."

He did not have to look at it to know what it said. He looked anyway. SUFFER! Printed in capital letters with a black marking pen this time. Sloppy, back-slanted printing, possibly in an attempt to disguise the person's hand. Nothing about it struck him as familiar.

"Twice in two days," Cassie said. "It's so damn childish, as if . . ."

"As if what?"

"I don't know," she said, shaking her head. "All I know right now is that I'm scared. Where does it go from here? And how soon?"

Hollis made no reply. He watched the bearded driver begin to work the winch on his truck.

"Nobody saw anything. I asked in the neighboring places after I phoned you. Whoever it is is careful, sly. And lucky."

"Yeah. Whoever it is."

"Not Ryan, if that's what you're thinking."

"Just what I'm thinking."

"No," she said. "When I took Kenny to day care this morning I asked him about that Saturday in May, his lunch with Mommy and Daddy. We thought it was just the three of them, but it wasn't. Rhona was there, too."

"So what?"

"Ryan went home with her afterward."

"Kenny told you that? He's six years old, Cass. You can't trust a six-year-old's memory."

"Let me finish. I called Rhona after I dropped Kenny off. She confirmed it. Ryan spent the rest of that day with her and her family. Had dinner with them, didn't leave their house until after eight o'clock."

"And you believed her. How do you know she wasn't lying?"

"Would her husband lie, her kids? They were there, too. Why would Ryan ask them to lie for him? There isn't anything to connect him to Rakubian's death, no reason for him to prepare an alibi for himself."

He couldn't argue with the logic of that, and he didn't try. But he remained unconvinced until after they got home and he talked to Fred Gugliotta on the phone. Pierce had spent the entire day on the ranch, working with Fred and two others baling hay. From 8 A.M. until 4:30 he hadn't been out of Fred's sight for more than a few minutes.

20

Tuesday Morning

EVEN with the living room closed off, the house had an oppressive feel after Cassie left with one of her co-workers for Animal Care. Yesterday, home alone, he hadn't been so aware of the aura of violation because he'd had ways to keep his mind occupied; there weren't enough distractions today to fill the time until his one o'clock appointment with Stan Otaki. Neither Camden Home Security nor Tom Finchley could get started until later in the week, and sitting around doing nothing, waiting for the mail, waiting for something else to happen, would have him climbing the walls. Work was what he needed. Human contact and the illusion of normalcy.

He let Fritz in from the back porch, giving the Doberman free run of the house. The dog was housebroken and well trained; there wouldn't be any problem unless somebody tried to break in again. Hollis found himself wishing that would happen. That he'd come home later, find Fritz growling over a bloody, chewed-up, half-dead intruder in the front hallway. The image made him smile with his lips flat against his teeth. He'd buy the Doberman a steak a day for the rest of his life if that happened.

He drove to the office at nine-thirty. The morning went well enough except for a call from Pete Dulac about a minor problem with the Chestertons' master bedroom. Every time he had contact with Dulac or Shelby Chesterton these days, he felt twinges of guilt and shame, and it was worse now that he knew how wrong he'd been about Eric; he stayed on the phone just long enough to provide a solution to the problem and to find out that PAD Construction was still on schedule for completion at the end of September.

Mannix arrived shortly after eleven. Late as usual and in one of his uncommunicative moods. With Gabe there, the illusion of normalcy faded and left Hollis tense, unable to concentrate.

Gabe wore a black sweater and black slacks; hunched over his board he seemed almost predatory, like a giant bird of prey. Ridiculous image, but once lodged in Hollis's mind it would not go away. He kept glancing over there, watching Mannix consult spec sheets and code books, the quick jerky movements of his hands as he manipulated T-square and pencil. Big hands, strong hands. *It's not Gabe, it's not Gabe* . . . like song lyrics beating percussively until they lost all sense or meaning. And still, in spite of himself, his eyes kept shifting, watching, as though they were independent organisms no longer under his control.

After a while Mannix sensed it and swiveled his head, scowling. "What?" he said.

"Nothing. Sorry."

"My fly open, piece of snot hanging out of my nose?"

Gloria was listening. She said, "Now, that's disgusting," and laughed appreciatively.

Hollis said, "I'm twitchy today, that's all."

"So am I. You're not making it any better."

"Another hangover?"

"King-size. I collect 'em like bottle caps, didn't you know?"

"Sorry," he said again.

"Don't apologize. Just let me suffer in peace."

Suffer. SUFFER!

Hollis stood and went into his cubicle. Developing a headache now. He opened the blinds, stared out. Downriver, the drawbridge was parted into two upslanted halves; a tall-masted sailboat with its sails furled was gliding in toward the turning basin, its hull and superstructure cream-colored against another overcast sky. Restless, that sky, the clouds being driven inland by high winds. The colors up there were varying shades of gray, with traceries of black like poisonous veins.

Poison, he thought.

An evil time bred that, too, a slow, insidious psychological contamination that changed your outlook, ate away perspective, turned you sick and withered inside. You saw people differently, as if through a dark filter. Everyone seemed to be a potential enemy, or at best a hindrance or an irritant—close friends, even members of your own family. It was happening to him, here and now. He couldn't be in the same room with his partner and best friend without wondering if maybe, just possibly, despite all the arguments against it, the stalker *was* Gabe. The same thing had happened with Ryan Pierce. Hating him, condemning him without any real justification. Who would he start suspecting next? Gloria, who didn't have a mean bone in her body? Pete Dulac? Shelby Chesterton? Eric again? Cassie, for God's sake?

Poison, as virulent as any of the chemical variety. And only one sure antidote: the identity of Rakubian's murderer.

Cassie, last night: "I wish we still had the dossier on

Rakubian. There might have been something in it, a name from his past, some clue. The person doesn't have to be anyone we know, does he?" But Hollis didn't need the actual dossier; he knew it by heart, and it had contained nothing to point to anyone past or present. Besides, what possible motive could a stranger, one of Rakubian's long list of enemies, have for stalking *them*?

"What if it's two people?" she'd said. "The one who killed him a stranger, the one tormenting us someone we know."

He couldn't credit that at all. Too much coincidence, too little motivation. Cassie didn't really believe it any more than he did. The same person was responsible, for whatever reason; and it had to be someone known to them, perhaps not intimately as he'd first believed, but well enough to have formed and nurtured an irrational hatred.

Not Gabe. Definitely not Gabe.

But the poisonous seed of doubt was still there.

Goddamn it, he thought, I *can* get rid of it. I don't need the antidote for that. Just suck it up and spit it out.

He went back out front. Mannix was on the phone; he waited until the conversation ended and then said, "Let's take a walk."

"Walk? What for?"

"I need to talk to you."

"So talk. It's cold outside and I've got a lunch in fifteen minutes—"

"This won't take long. And it's important."

He pulled his overcoat off the rack, slipped it on as he pushed through the door. Mannix followed him, scowling, a few seconds later. They walked across the grass strip that separated their building from the River House, down past the restaurant's outdoor patio and along the seawall toward the turning basin. The wind was sharp enough so that they had to hunch their bodies against it.

"Freeze our asses off out here," Mannix grumbled. "What's so important?"

"David Rakubian.

"What about him?"

"What do you think happened to him?"

"We know what happened. He disappeared."

"How? Why?"

"What the hell is this, Bernard?"

"Is he dead? What's your take on that?"

"Sure he's dead. If he wasn't, he'd've shown up by now and started making everybody's life miserable again."

"How do you suppose he died?"

"Somebody killed him. A hero, in my book."

"Who?"

"Listen," Gabe began, and stopped, and then said, "Oh, for Christ's sake, let's quit all this pussyfooting around. What're you trying to get me to say, that I think you bumped the son of a bitch off?"

"*Is* that what you think?"

"Come on, man. It doesn't make a damn bit of difference who killed him, just so long as he's dead."

"It makes a difference to me."

"All right, then. Yes, I think you did the deed. I also think you deserve a medal for it. Satisfied?"

"I didn't kill him," Hollis said. "I planned to, I even convinced myself I had the guts to go through with it—not once but twice. Somebody beat me to it."

"No shit?"

"You, Gabe?"

". . . What?"

"Was it you?"

Mannix stopped walking, turned to gape at him. Then he threw his head back, let loose a bray of laughter that swiveled heads on the sailboat that had just tied up at one of the floats. He kept right on chuckling, his eyes wind-reddened slits in the rough plane of his face.

"What's so funny?"

"You. Me. A couple of big clowns."

"You didn't answer my question."

"Sure I did—you weren't listening. That's what's so funny, Bernard. I thought you offed Rakubian, you've been thinking I did it, and we both kept our suspicions to ourselves and we're both dead wrong."

"Are we?"

"*Dead* wrong." Mannix laughed again. "You want me to swear my innocence on a Bible?"

Hollis blew out his breath; it made a gusty sound, like the wind. He didn't say anything.

"There was a time," Gabe said, "a week or so before he disappeared, that I considered it. I mean really considered it. I didn't think you were capable of it, not then, and I couldn't stand the thought of that bastard hurting Angela. I guess you know how I feel about her."

"Well enough."

"Pathetically obvious, right? My best friend's daughter, and half my age to boot. But I've never done anything about it and I never will. You believe that?"

"I believe it."

"Good. It's the truth. Okay, so I had a little scenario all worked out. But when push came to shove I couldn't go through with it. Bullshitted you that I could, bullshitted myself, but I don't have the balls for a thing like that. I could probably blow somebody like Rakubian away in self-defense, if I had enough Dutch courage in me, but in cold blood, eye-to-eye? No way."

"No way," Hollis echoed.

"Like that for you, too?"

"Pretty much. I got closer than you, right up to a time

and place, waiting for him with a loaded gun, but even if he'd shown up I doubt now that I'd've been able to go through with it. Enough nerve to reach that point but no more. Not even to save my daughter's life."

"Clowns and gutless wonders, a pair."

"No. A couple of average guys incapable of crossing the line."

"Maybe so," Mannix admitted. "So who did have the guts to cross it? Any idea?"

"Not anymore."

"Well, we were wrong about each other. Could be we're wrong about him being dead."

"He's dead, all right."

"That sounds definite."

"It is. I found his body, at his house two days before Angela went away. Head smashed in. At the time I believed Eric did it, so I erased the evidence and took the body away and buried it."

"Jesus," Gabe said softly.

"I won't tell you where. That's between me and my conscience."

"I don't want to know. It wasn't Eric? You're sure of that now?"

"Positive. But that's not all. It isn't over yet—I didn't get away with what I did. Things are almost as bad as they were when Rakubian was alive."

And he told his partner, his friend the rest of it. Sucking up and spitting out the last of the poisonous seed. One long look into Mannix's eyes when he was done, and even the bitter aftertaste disappeared.

Tuesday Afternoon

Stan Otaki said, "It's too early to tell yet if the antiandrogens are shrinking the tumor. There's still plenty of room for optimism."

"But," Hollis said.

"There's always a 'but' in prostate cases. As we've discussed before, no two are exactly alike—it's a predictable disease in some respects, unpredictable in others. In case the hormone treatments don't do the job, I think you need to start considering the remaining options."

"Surgery and what else? Or is there anything else?"

"A clinical trial of new techniques in radiation therapy. Other clinical trials."

"Such as?"

"Hormonal ablation, for one. Chemical castration."

Terrific. Chemical castration translated to mean radical hormone-block treatments that deprive the tumor of the testosterone it needed to grow. Reversible if the patient stops the treatment, but stopping it meant that the cancer was likely to recur . . . if the growth process were arrested in the first place. Catch-22. The best-case scenario was a permanently limp dick. Along with the usual splendid array of potential side effects, such as weakened bones, loss of muscle, and personality changes.

"Normally," Otaki was saying, "that's a radical procedure implemented after the prostate has been surgically removed and there are indications that the cancer is still metastasizing. In such cases the patient is five times more likely to survive."

"And without surgery?"

"The jury's still out."

"Uh-huh. Would you recommend that option?"

"Not before a prostatectomy, no."

"What are my chances with surgery? Survival, and the ability to function sexually?"

"At this stage, assuming the absence of complications,

the survival rate is very good. The impotence factor is prob-
lematical no matter what we do."

"How soon before we know about the hormone treatments?"

"A few weeks at the outside."

"And if they're not working, I'd need to go under the
knife right away?"

Otaki raised an eyebrow. "Does that mean you may be
changing your mind?".

Did it? Maybe so. Funny, but the prospect of submitting
his body to a surgeon's scalpel did not seem quite so terri-
fying now as it had for so long. If there was a chance, even a
small one, that surgery would keep him alive, make him
whole again, didn't he owe it to Cassie as well as to himself?
Pigheaded, selfish, angry, closed off . . . he'd been all of that
and more. Chained to Pop all these years. And chained to
Mom, too, by the way she'd died. It didn't have to be that
way. Cassie had opened up his mind for the better. Why not
let a frigging scalpel open up his body toward the same result?

"Let's say I'll be in a more receptive frame of mind," he
said, "if and when the time comes."

Tuesday Evening

Cassie said, "I think we may have been looking at the stalker
from the wrong perspective."

"I don't follow."

"It's been nagging at me all day. We keep assuming it
must be a man. Eric, Ryan, Gabe . . . all men. But the more I
think about it, the more it feels to me like a woman."

"A woman smashed in Rakubian's skull?"

"Why not? Women can be just as violent in the right, or
wrong, circumstances. You know that. And the weapon . . . a

statuette, heavy but not too heavy . . . it's the sort of object a woman would grab in self-defense or the heat of anger."

He was silent, weighing the possibility.

"Then there's what's been done to us so far," Cassie said. "Written threats, poison pen notes . . . woman's methods more than a man's. The phrasing in the notes, too. 'What did you do with his body?' 'You'll suffer for what you did.' Wouldn't a man be more likely to say, 'Where'd you hide the body?' 'You'll pay for what you did' or 'I'll fix you for what you did'?"

"Maybe," he said slowly. "Maybe."

"And the vandalism. Everything breakable in the living room smashed, couches and chairs slashed to ribbons, all that spray paint . . . it had a tantrumy look, didn't it? Not that a man is above throwing a tantrum, God knows, but the way the room looked . . . it just didn't feel like a man's work. Neither does sugar in the van's gas tank. It's the first trick I'd think of if I wanted to sabotage someone's car. One tire punctured, three tires flat—that's another thing."

He knew what she meant by that. "Takes strength to jab a sharp object deep enough into hard rubber to bleed the air out. Try it once, find that out, and then you start unscrewing the valve caps."

"Exactly. None of this is conclusive, but when you take it all together . . . I think I'm right, Jack."

"Who, then? I can't think of any woman we know who'd have it in for us."

"Someone Rakubian was seeing after Angela left him, or even before she left him."

He shook his head. "Not as obsessed with her as he was."

"A woman from his past, then. Didn't he tell Angela he had one serious relationship before he met her?"

"That's right, he did. He wouldn't say when, or who the woman was. He kept his private life too damn private."

"The police might've found out."

"I can check with Macatee. But it still doesn't add up, Cass. Why would a woman, anybody from Rakubian's past, be stalking *us*? Angela, yes, that's conceivable—some sort of crazy jealousy thing—but why would you and I be targets?"

"I can't imagine. If we just knew who she is . . ."

"I'll call Macatee first thing in the morning. But if he can't point us in the right direction—"

"Then we'll think of something else."

21

Wednesday Morning

MACATEE couldn't help them.

"I talked to at least two dozen people acquainted with David Rakubian," he said. "They told me pretty much anything I wanted to know about his professional practice, background, ethics or lack of 'em. But none of those people, his office staff included, had anything but a superficial knowledge of his private life. He guarded that like a miser. All we really know about it came from your daughter, Mr. Hollis, and she couldn't give me any idea who he was involved with before he met her."

"Wasn't there anything in his house—old letters, photographs . . ."

"Not a thing," Macatee said with weary patience. "My advice is the same as the last time we talked—quit worrying about David Rakubian. Quit wondering what happened to him or who might've had something to do with the disappearance. Count your blessings and let it be."

After he put the phone down, Hollis rubbed his eyes with

the heels of his hands. Tired, logy today. Stress, not enough sleep . . . oh, he was in fine shape. He stood and slogged out of the study, into the kitchen to talk to Cassie. She had gone there to listen to the conversation with Macatee on the extension.

Now she was at the catchall desk in one corner, rummaging intently through the drawers. "I know I put them in here somewhere," she said when she heard him come in.

"What're you looking for?"

No response. Then, "There they are!" She straightened and turned, holding up what she'd found.

"Keys?"

"Angela's. To Rakubian's house and alarm system. The night she left him and came home, she swore she'd never go back and threw them on the floor. Remember? I put them in the desk and forgot all about them until just now."

"What're you thinking?"

"Well, even though she waived community property she's still entitled to claim her personal possessions. Technically, anyway. And we're her parents, we have a right to go there on her behalf."

"Are you serious?"

"Of course I'm serious."

"You heard what Macatee said. He searched the house, probably more than once, and didn't find a thing."

"It's possible he overlooked something. Why not go down there and see?"

She had a point. He didn't much care for the idea of prowling again through those dark, oppressive rooms, but the prospect of more passive waiting had no appeal at all. "It's worth a try," he said.

"We can leave right away. I'll call the clinic, tell them I won't be in today."

"If that's going to leave them shorthanded, I don't mind going by myself."

"Uh-uh. It's a long drive to the city and back."

"I feel strong enough today."

"Don't try to be Superman again, okay? It's all right to lean on me a little sometimes, you know."

"I know."

"Besides, I want to go. And two can search more thoroughly than one."

"Call the clinic," he said. "I'll get our jackets."

It was one of those inverse-weather-pattern days, overcast in the North Bay but mostly clear in San Francisco. The sunlight hurt his eyes as they started through the park to Nineteenth Avenue; he put on dark glasses to shield them. When Cassie turned her van—she'd picked it up at the repair shop the night before—onto Sloat Boulevard and they entered St. Francis Wood, he felt a curl of tension forming. Criminal returns to scene of his crime, he thought, and then realized he'd spoken the phrase aloud.

"Don't, Jack."

"I'm not looking forward to this."

"You think I am?"

Quiet summer morning in the Wood: dog walkers in the park, mailman making his deliveries, sun-hatted woman working in her garden in the block below Rakubian's. Cassie parked directly in front of the Spanish stucco, no reason not to. The property seemed subtly different to him dappled in sunlight and shadow, less imposing, less bleak. Just another expensive home in one of the city's best neighborhoods. Yet the tension remained as they got out, walked up onto the porch.

The alarm system was on; he shut it off with Angela's key. Cassie was looking in the mailbox. "Empty," she said, "but he must still be getting mail. I wonder what's happened to it."

"Police made arrangements for a temporary hold, probably."

"I don't suppose there'd be anything in it anyway."

"Doubtful."

When he opened the door he expected a heavy, closed-up feel and smell, but that wasn't the case. Cold air, faintly damp, faintly musty. Cassie noticed it as well. "Feels as though the place was aired out not long ago," she said.

He didn't answer. His memory had begun to flare open, to disgorge images from that nightmare Saturday. Ghosts, baby phantoms. In his mind, and in the cold stillness and shadowy corners in here. But they couldn't hurt him unless he permitted it to happen, and he would not.

He located the light switch, flicked it. The electricity was still on; a pale amber glow chased away some of the gloom in the foyer and hallway.

"That's a relief," Cassie said. "I thought we might have to do this by flashlight. Who do you suppose is paying the bill?"

"May have paid it himself a month or two in advance. Even if he didn't, it hasn't been long enough for PG&E to shut the power off."

"Where should we start?"

"Library, I guess."

"Is that where—?"

"Where I found him. It's also where he kept most of his papers."

They moved ahead, their shoes clicking on the terra-cotta tiles. At the library arch he hesitated, but only for an instant before he stepped through. Cassie was a pace behind him, so that when he stopped abruptly, staring at the floor in front of Rakubian's desk, she bumped into him.

"What's the matter?"

"The carpet," he said. "It's gone."

"What carpet?"

Memory flash: The tiles so bare after he dragged the body out and wiped up the blood; didn't look right, so he'd rolled up the smaller but similar Sarouk in the formal living room and spread it out in here. Now the tiles were bare again. He pivoted around past Cassie, hurried up the hall.

The three-by-five Sarouk had been put back in its original spot in front of the fireplace. And the furniture . . . all of it was placed as it had been before he'd shifted it around, back to Rakubian's original arrangement.

"My God," he said.

"Jack?"

He explained as they returned to the library. She said, "The police wouldn't do a thing like that."

"No. They'd have no way of knowing the original placement anyhow."

"Why would somebody else . . . ?"

His gaze roved the dark room. The wall hangings, the screaming souls in the Goya "black" seemed to stare back at him. And on the fireplace mantel—

Black statuette.

A bird, a raven—Poe's Raven.

Dry-mouthed, he stepped over for a closer look. Replica of the murder weapon and the statuette in Rakubian's office, except that this one was slightly larger and more ornate. It even had a *Nevermore!* plaque.

"It's as if somebody is trying to erase what happened," he told Cassie. "Not for the reason I did, to cover up . . . By putting everything back as it was, as though the murder never happened at all."

"His killer?"

"Nobody else would have a reason."

"Then it has to be a woman," she said. "Somebody full of guilt and remorse . . . somebody who loved and hated him both. The hate killed him, the love drove her back here. To the scene of *her* crime."

They hunted through Rakubian's desk, the rest of the library. Paper files, computer disks—all neatly arranged. The woman again: the police would not have left everything in such pristine order. There were a few obvious gaps, items taken away by Macatee for one reason or another and still in his possession. None of the paper files revealed anything. The disks were all labeled with year and month and content—bills, business expenses, charitable donations. Any that might have contained personal references were missing, appropriated by either Macatee or the woman. There didn't seem to be much point in going through the remainder, here or later at home.

There was nothing else to find in the living room. The guest bathroom seemed the same as he'd left it two months ago; the spare bedroom and small sitting room next to it were dusty, musty, and empty of anything revealing. They went across the hall to the master bedroom. The door was shut; Cassie pushed it open.

"Oh!" she said.

Incense. That was the first thing that struck him—the faint but still pungent odor of burnt incense. Then his eyes adjusted to the gloom in there, and he saw what Cassie, with better vision, had seen immediately.

Candles.

Dozens of them, fat and thin, tall and short, in a variety of dishes and holders. On the furniture, on the carpet ringing the bed, on every flat surface in the room.

"Lord," Cassie murmured, "it's like a shrine."

He put the ceiling light on. The big double bed was made, but the counterpane lay crooked and a little wrinkled at the bottom. The doors to the walk-in closet and master bath were closed. That was all there was to see except for the candles; they dominated the room, phallic images in red, white, green, and yellow wax. Even the bowl on the dresser where the incense had been burned had a long taper jutting from its center.

"She's been sleeping in here," he said.

"In his bed. Yes."

"How often, that's the question."

"It's hard to tell. Not every night . . . I don't think she's living here, at least not regularly. The incense odor isn't fresh."

"Sick. Certifiable."

"Unstable to begin with," Cassie said, "and killing him pushed her over the edge. All that love and hate mixed up together."

He crossed to the closet doors, swung them wide. Suits, shirts, ties, a few items of casual wear—all Rakubian's, all carefully arranged on hangers and racks and shelves. Untouched since his death, probably. A small section at the rear contained women's clothes, a rack of women's shoes. Cassie went in to look through them.

"Angela's," she said. "This silk blouse—we gave it to her for Christmas two years ago."

"All of the clothing hers?"

"I think so. Everything she left behind."

They searched the bathroom. The shower stall and circular tub were both dry. The only item that seemed to have been used recently was a toothbrush; its bristles were dry, but it lay beside the sink rather than in the chromium holder with two others. The medicine chest held nothing that could not have belonged to Rakubian or to Angela.

In the bedroom again they opened dresser drawers, nightstand drawers. Same thing: all the contents were his, could have been Angela's.

The incense, a smell he'd never liked, was making his sinuses ache. He left Cassie still poking around the bedroom, went to check the kitchen. The refrigerator was empty; so was the trash container under the sink. The woman was not eating her meals here, or if she was, she brought them in with her and took the remnants away when she left. Cassie joined him and they examined drawers, cupboards, cabinets there and on the rear porch. But they were only going through the motions and they both knew it.

No clue here to the woman's identity.

At least now they had a way to find out who she was. If she came back to spend another night; if she did it soon. Hire a detective, have the house put under surveillance. It might be expensive and time-consuming, it meant more waiting, but it was all they could do. And it was *something*.

In the van they discussed doing the hiring immediately, trying to make arrangements in time for someone to be on watch tonight. Not feasible. He was fading, starting to feel tired and a little shaky—that was one reason. The other was that it took time to choose and hire a detective. You didn't just pick a name out of the phone book and walk into an office unannounced and expect an experienced investigator to be available and willing to drop everything to do a job for you, the way it was done in books and films. You had to select the right person for the job, make an appointment, discuss the matter, settle financial arrangements—the same as with any other professional business dealing.

They drove straight home, to take care of the preliminaries from there.

Wednesday Afternoon

The San Francisco telephone directory contained two full pages of listings for private investigators—large and small agencies, individuals, numerous boxed ads outlining ser-

224 ◆ BILL PRONZINI

vices. The first six they tried, picked at random, were wasted calls. Four said they didn't do that sort of surveillance work; one told them he could handle it but not until next week, he was booked solid until then; the sixth was an answering service. Then Cassie pointed out that more than a few of the agencies were operated by women and suggested that a woman investigator might be better in their case. Hollis thought so, too.

The seventh call went to McCone Investigations at Pier 24½ on the Embarcadero. They spoke to the owner, Sharon McCone, who seemed both professional and amenable. If she agreed to take their case after meeting them in person and hearing all the particulars, she said, she could have one of her operatives on surveillance by tomorrow night. They set an appointment for one-thirty the next afternoon at her offices.

Wednesday Evening

An early dinner at the Mill with Angela and Kenny and Pierce. Angela's idea; she seemed to need family closeness now more than ever, and for Cassie and him to accept Pierce as part of the unit again. "Drawing us around her like shields," Cassie said. Hollis felt better after a nap, so how could they refuse her?

The dinner went all right, better than he'd expected. Pierce was on his best behavior, polite without being deferential; he actually seemed to be enjoying himself. If Angela had told him anything about Rakubian's death, he didn't let on. It was obvious that he genuinely cared for her and his son; you could see it in the way he looked at them, interacted with them. You could see, too, if you looked closely enough, the difference he'd made in both their lives already. When he and Angela were first together, and especially after Kenny was born, they hadn't seemed quite comfortable with each other, with their roles as husband and wife, father and mother. Too young, too immature. The ease was there now, even after such a short time in this new relationship.

It had been there for a while, Hollis realized. He hadn't seen it before tonight because he hadn't wanted to see it—one of the many things he hadn't seen or wanted to see until Cassie opened his eyes for him.

Thursday Morning

Tom Finchley and his helper were due at eight-thirty and arrived, unlike a lot of contractors, on time—one of the reasons he'd chosen Finchley for the renovation work. Neither he nor Cassie cared to be there while the living room was being shoveled out; they drove downtown separately, had coffee and croissants at a café on Main, and parted there afterward. They'd each work half a day, meet again at noon for the drive to the city and the appointment with Sharon McCone.

When he reached Mannix & Hollis, it was just nine-thirty. Surprise waiting: Gabe was there ahead of him. Talking to Gloria, who seemed a little flustered about something.

"What's this?" he said. "In the office before noon? Don't tell me you've found your work ethic again after all these years?"

Mannix didn't smile. His mouth, Hollis saw then, was pinched at the corners. "Something like that. I was just about to call you."

"Why? What's going on?"

"Tell him what you just told me, Gloria."

She said, "I feel kind of bad about this. I mean, I didn't think you were having any more trouble. . . ."

Hollis glanced at his partner, who shook his head. Mannix's eyes said: *I didn't break your confidence. That's not what this is about.*

"Go ahead," he told Gloria.

"Well, I went to the River House for lunch yesterday. You know how cold it was, right? That's how come I noticed her, this woman. Sitting out on the patio all by herself, bundled up in a parka, drinking coffee and staring over here. Like she was watching this building, our office. There's nothing else to see in this direction, not from where she was sitting—no other windows."

Hollis felt himself tightening inside. "You get a good look at her?"

"Good enough to recognize her."

"Somebody you know?"

"No, but I've seen her before. Twice."

"Where?"

"Once last week, on the River House patio again. Sitting at the same table, looking over this way. I didn't think anything about it then. Sunny that day, lots of folks having lunch outside."

"The other time?"

"Sunday morning. At your house."

"At my—"

"She was coming down the front steps when I drove up," Gloria said. "About eleven-fifteen, when I dropped off the Dry Creek package. I thought maybe she was a friend of Cassie's. She wasn't doing anything, just walking down the steps—going away because nobody was home. That's why I didn't mention it before. But then there she was again yesterday, three times in less than a week, and the way she was sitting there in the cold staring . . . it just seemed funny, the more I thought about it. So I told Gabe when he came in and he said we'd better tell you right away."

"What did this woman look like? Describe her."

"Thirty-five or so. Skinny, not much in the titty department. Dark hair like mine, but cut short. Narrow face, big beak nose. Wears glasses with gold rims."

"Christ!"

Mannix said, "You know her?"

"Yeah," he said. "Yeah, I know her."

Rakubian's paralegal, Valerie Burke.

22

JUST like that.

You stumble around, speculate, make a glut of false assumptions, exist in a constant state of confusion and frustration—and the answer is right there all the time, obvious and yet not obvious at all until it's dumped in your lap. Valerie Burke. Close to Rakubian, worked with him for five years, but you never considered her because he seemed always to keep his private life separate from his professional one; because she was older than he and unattractive compared to Angela. What you overlooked is that neither youth nor beauty was what attracted a man like Rakubian. It was vulnerability. He wanted a woman he could dominate, mold like warm plastic into his ideal mate. Only Valerie Burke hadn't quite fit the bill, for whatever reason, and he dropped her in favor of Angela, and she'd never gotten over it. . . .

Mannix was saying something to him. He blinked, focused again. "What'd you say?"

"I asked you who she is."

"Paralegal who worked in Rakubian's office. Valerie Burke."

"So that's it. The connection to Angela."

"Yes."

"But why would she have it in for you and Cassie?"

He thought he knew the answer to that, too, now, but he did not want to talk about it in front of Gloria. Or with Gabe, for that matter.

He wagged his head, turned to ask Gloria, "Where're the San Francisco phone directories?"

"Same place they've always been, on the bottom shelf with the other directories. Jack, what's this all about?"

"I'll explain later. Gabe can tell you some of it."

"But if I see that woman again, what should I do? Call the cops?"

"No. No police. Don't do anything." He started across to the row of wall shelves, stopped and swung around again. "You didn't happen to see what kind of car she's driving? On Sunday?"

"No, I didn't pay any attention."

"Well, if she shows up around here again, try to find out. The license number, too."

Mannix asked, "What're you going to do?"

"I'm not sure yet. Something."

"You want my help?"

"Thanks, but no. We have to handle this ourselves, Cassie and me."

He shut himself inside his cubicle, opened the San Francisco white pages to the Bs. No residence listing for Valerie Burke, but there was one for a V. Burke: 9871 Parnassus. That *had* to be her. Make sure, though. Call Macatee, give him an excuse, ask him to check his files.

He put through a call to the Hall of Justice, spoke to a man in Missing Persons whose name didn't register.

Macatee wasn't in. Wouldn't be until later in the day. He tried to talk the phone voice into giving him the information about Burke, but all it got him was a refusal and a hang-up.

Hollis put the receiver down, jerked it up again, and rang Animal Care. The first thing Cassie said when he finished relating the news was "We can't keep this from Angela. Not now."

"I know it. You'd better be the one to tell her. I'm too wound up. Ask her if she's had any personal contact, any trouble with Valerie Burke. And what she knows about the woman."

"Then what do we do?"

"Try to find Burke. There's one listing in the S.F. phone book that may be her. I tried to get hold of Macatee to confirm, but he's not on duty."

"Confront her, try to frighten her off?"

"Yes."

"If she's as far gone as we think, it won't do any good."

"We have to try. We don't have any other choice."

"The police."

"No, not yet. Not without some kind of proof. The cops are our last resort."

"I guess you're right."

"Call Angela," he said. "I'll pick you up in ten minutes."

Cassie was pale and tense when she got into the Lexus. He tried to find reassuring words; his mind was blank. At length he said, "Angela?"

"I talked to her. Now all three of us are shook up."

"What did she say about Burke?"

"Not much. She hardly knows her—saw her a few times at Rakubian's office, never socially. But she had the feeling the woman didn't like her, resented her for some reason."

"They have words or anything like that?"

"No."

"Does she know anything about Burke's personal life?"

"Nothing at all, and no idea where she lives."

Dead air hung thick in the car until they were on 101 headed south. Traffic was moderately heavy; it became a constant struggle not to keep changing lanes, to stay within the speed limit.

When the silence grew oppressive, he broke it by voicing his earlier thoughts—that Valerie Burke was someone Rakubian felt he could dominate. Cassie had been staring straight ahead; she roused herself, shifted position so that she was facing him.

"Vulnerable and unstable," she said. "Love can turn to hate pretty quickly in that kind of personality."

"He was so arrogant and self-involved, he probably didn't even notice."

"Or care if he did. I wonder what put her over the edge that afternoon at his house. Did she go there to kill him? Plead with him to take her back? Or did it have something to do with Angela?"

Something to do with Angela. Hollis remembered his visit to Rakubian's law offices the day before, Friday. It was possible Burke had eavesdropped, heard some or all of what was said, the lie that Angela was ready to reconcile with Rakubian. Brooded about it that night, and showed up at his home on Saturday in a desperate attempt to talk him out of keeping the appointment in Tomales Bay. He wouldn't have liked that; he'd have berated her, scorned her, maybe threatened to force her out of his life entirely by firing her. And when she couldn't stand any more abuse, up went the statuette and down went Rakubian.

It could have happened that way. If so, would Burke say something about Tomales Bay in front of Cassie? He'd have to lie again then, much as he'd hate doing it—pass it off as the ravings of a deranged mind. Cassie must never know how close he'd come to committing murder.

He changed the subject. "Must've been a terrific shock for her when she found out his body was gone."

"Yes, but how did she guess you were responsible?"

She'd eavesdropped, all right: Knew about the appointment, guessed that Hollis must have gone to the house to find out why Rakubian didn't keep it, and worked out his motive for the cleanup and removal of the corpse.

"Whatever the explanation," he said, "she knows it was me and she hates me for it. First Angela took him away from her—her interpretation—and then I took away and hid what was left of him. She couldn't bury him herself, tell him she was sorry, say good-bye."

"She might even blame us for his murder. You know, 'I didn't want to hurt him, I loved him, they made me do it and it's all their fault.' But why did she wait so long? Two months is a long time to be plotting revenge."

"Has to be another reason, something specific to explain the timing."

After a pause Cassie said, "Angela."

"What about Angela?"

"*She's* the reason. She took Kenny to Utah two days after the murder. Burke didn't know where she'd gone, had no way of finding out."

"That must be it. She was waiting for Angela to resurface, come back home. The first note arrived less than a week after the kids returned. If she'd begun stalking us before then, we might've told Angela to stay where she was. Burke wanted us to think we were safe—and for all of us to be together again where she could get at us."

"It wouldn't have been hard for her to monitor the situation," Cassie said. "Drive to Los Alegres once or twice a week, check our house, your workplace and mine, ask discreet questions here and there. She'd've known within a few days that they were home."

She shivered as if with a sudden chill. "It gives me the creeps, thinking of her spying on us, stalking us all that time."

"She's gotten bolder, too. As if . . ."

He let the rest of it slide, but Cassie was thinking along the same lines. She said, "As if she doesn't care anymore if we know it's her. That really scares me. That, and what we found at Rakubian's house yesterday. God only knows what she'll do next if we don't find a way to stop her."

The Parnassus Street address was a four-story brick-and-stone- faced apartment building two blocks from the University of California Medical Center. A bank of mailboxes climbed one wall of the entranceway, each labeled with the tenants' names. Neither Valerie Burke nor V. Burke was among them.

Hollis rang the bell on the box that bore the words "Bldg Mgr." A young woman cradling an infant told them that yes, Valerie Burke had been a resident here, but she'd given up her apartment and moved out at the end of June. No, she hadn't left a forwarding address or said where she was going. No, the woman had no idea where Burke worked or anything else about her; she'd kept to herself and besides, people in this building minded their own business. That last with an edge to it, as if she were making an accusation.

In the car Cassie said, "Now what?"

"I don't know, let me think. . . . South Beach. The converted warehouse where Rakubian had his offices. Maybe somebody there knows where we can find her."

✦

Another dead end.

There were half a dozen small law firms in the building on Harrison Street; they asked in all of them, and the answer in each was the same. No one knew what had happened to Valerie Burke—or to the secretary, Janet Yee, after Rakubian's offices were vacated. The building manager there couldn't tell them anything, either.

Frustration ate at Hollis like acid. "We could try to find Janet Yee," he said, "but there's not much chance she'd know Burke's current address."

"Is there a professional organization for paralegals? If there is and she's a member, they might know."

"They might, but I doubt it. The state she's been in the past two months, the trips to Los Alegres . . . I don't see her notifying a professional organization of her whereabouts or even holding down another job."

"Then what has she been living on?"

"I don't know—savings, a loan from somebody."

"We're just running around in circles," Cassie said, "asking a lot of questions we can't answer. We can't do this by ourselves. Like it or not, we need help. Professional help."

"You think we should keep the appointment at McCone Investigations?"

"It's less than an hour from now. And we're practically within walking distance of the pier. A private investigator has the resources to find someone much faster than amateurs like us."

"Okay," he said. "We'll talk to her, see what she has to say."

Thursday Afternoon

Pier 24½ was next door to the SFFD fireboat station, its cavernous interior renovated into office space for a variety of different businesses. Hollis wasn't sure what to expect of a detective agency located in such surroundings, though McCone Investigations had to be reasonably successful; a prime waterfront location would not come cheap. Their suite of offices impressed him, and so did Sharon McCone. She kept them waiting less than five minutes, and when she appeared she was as crisply businesslike as she'd been on the phone. She was about forty, dark-haired, attractive in a striking way. More than that, she radiated competence and inspired confidence in return.

The private office she ushered them into had windows that extended to the pier's sloping roofline, providing a broad view of the bay and the East Bay hills. The only negative thing about it was that it was noisy; the span of the Bay Bridge was directly overhead, the throb and hum of traffic muted but constant. When the fire sirens went off next door, he thought, it would probably make people here jump out of their seats.

They sat in comfortable chairs arranged before a functional desk. McCone asked if they minded having their conversation taped; Hollis gave permission. With a small recorder whirring, she asked a few preliminary questions and then requested that they outline their problem in detail. Hollis told most of it, as much as he felt she needed to know. They had no clear idea, he said, of why Burke was stalking them, unless it was because she blamed them somehow for Rakubian's disappearance.

McCone didn't interrupt, also took a few written notes. When he was finished she said, "One stalker in a lifetime is bad enough, but two within a few months is as bad as it gets. I sympathize, believe me. And I understand why you're reluctant to involve the police. There isn't much that can be done officially based on what's happened so far."

Cassie said, "It sounds as though you've had experience with stalking cases."

"Oh, yes." At least one unpleasant experience, judging from the faintly rueful quirking of McCone's mouth. "I won't pretend they're not hard to handle for all concerned, because they are. There're as many different breeds of stalker as there are people, each one predictable in some ways, unpredictable in others. On the surface it seems David Rakubian was the more dangerous of your two. What Valerie Burke has done to you so far—the anonymous notes, the vandalism—are childishly vicious acts. She may intend to continue in that vein, but she may also be planning something more overt. We don't know enough about her yet to make an accurate assessment."

"You're not telling us anything we don't already know," Hollis said.

"I realize that, Mr. Hollis. But I believe in maximum communication with my clients, in making sure we understand each other and the situation we're dealing with. Sometimes that requires stating the obvious, covering familiar ground."

"Yes, of course. I'm sorry."

"Don't be. I'd be pretty distraught myself in your position. Another thing. Most of Valerie Burke's actions so far have been directed at the two of you, but that doesn't necessarily mean you'll remain her primary targets. The note to your daughter indicates she could also be in danger."

He nodded. "What can you do to help us?"

"The most important thing right now," McCone said, "is to locate Burke. If she has a fixed new residence in or out of the city, we ought to be able to find it pretty quickly. If she's living with a friend or in a hotel or motel somewhere, that'll take longer. I'll put David Rakubian's home under immediate surveillance; if she shows up there, the operative will be instructed to follow her wherever she goes when she leaves. We'll run a DMV check to determine what kind of car she's driving and the license number—assuming she has and is using a legitimately registered vehicle. We'll also make a thorough background check on her—build a personal, professional, and psychological profile. The more you know about any individual, a stalker in particular, the better your chances of gauging what they might do next."

"How long will that take?"

"The background check? It depends on how much of Burke's life is a matter of public record. We ought to have some information for you—the DMV material, at the very least— by close of business today. Additional information, possibly a useful profile, by close of business tomorrow. Of course, I can't make any definite promises, but what I will do is to mark your case priority with my staff."

It sounded straightforward enough to Hollis. He asked, "What do you advise we do in the meantime?"

"Be cautious and vigilant," McCone said. "Specifically, convince your daughter to move herself and your grandson back in with you until the matter is resolved. Don't go anywhere alone after dark if you can avoid it. Alert your friends and neighbors and ask them to contact you immediately if they see a woman answering Burke's description. Make certain your property is as secure as possible night and day. That includes your cars—parking facilities at home, at work, in public places."

Cassie asked, "Would you recommend putting one of your people on watch at our home?"

"No, I wouldn't. It isn't likely Burke will try to break in again or even turn up in your neighborhood. She knows you'll be wary, and stalkers are nothing if not sly. Whatever she intends to do next, it probably won't be either repetitive or obvious. There's another reason I wouldn't recommend home surveillance at this point. One operative couldn't stand a twenty-four-hour watch; it would take a team of three. And a much larger team to maintain regular surveillance on your entire family, day and night. The cost would be prohibitive over a period of time, and there's no telling how long it will be before Burke is located. Also, there'd be no guarantee my people would be able to catch her at anything overt enough to put her in jail. We may believe she's a dangerous stalker, but there's no proof of it, remember."

There was more give-and-take before they moved on to financial matters. The fees McCone quoted were about what Hollis had expected—substantial, in keeping with the size and location of her operation, but a long way from exorbitant. They signed a standard contract and he wrote a check to cover the retainer fee; five minutes later they were on their way out of the pier building with McCone's assurance that she would contact them as soon as there was anything definite to report.

Outside, Cassie said, "I feel a little better now. I think we did the right thing."

"So do I."

She smiled up at him; he answered with a smile of his own. Thin mouth-stretchings, both, meant to be bolstering but gone in an instant, like scraps whipped away by the chill Bay wind.

23

ON the drive to Los Alegres, Cassie phoned Angela again and spent fifteen minutes trying to convince her to move back home. Angela kept saying she didn't think it was necessary. Stubborn, prone to wearing blinders—just like her old man. She finally agreed to talk it over with Pierce. If he thought it was a good idea, she said, then maybe she'd change her mind.

Tom Finchley and his helper were just finishing up when they reached the house. The living room had been emptied completely, the one wall painted over to erase the remains of Burke's message. It was just a room now, like any other empty room awaiting a personal stamp. Yet the aura of violation still lingered.

Hollis called the office, spoke briefly to Gloria and then to Mannix. There had been no sign of Burke at River House or anywhere else in the vicinity today.

Shortly before five, Sharon McCone called to report that the vehicle registered in Burke's name was a 1992 Nissan

Sentra, four-door, white, with the personalized license plate VALBLAW. The woman's current residence hadn't been found yet, but McCone had two of her staff working on that and on the background profile.

He and Cassie made the rounds of their neighbors, explaining the situation in terse terms and supplying Burke's description and the information about her car. The response, as it had been with Rakubian, was strongly supportive.

At five-forty the phone rang again. Pierce. And what he had to say put him solidly in Hollis's favor. He agreed that Angela and Kenny would be safer living at the Hollises and had talked her into a temporary move. He'd stay in her apartment and keep an eye on things there, he said.

"Angela's packing right now. Soon as she's ready, she'll drive over with Kenny."

"Follow her in your truck. You're welcome to stay for dinner."

"Thanks, Mr. Hollis. I'd like that."

"And I'd like you to use my first name. Mr. Hollis makes me sound as old as I feel."

Thursday Evening

Angela wore a smiley face, but her reluctance was plain—she really didn't want to be dependent any longer, at least not on Cassie and him. Kenny was too quiet, always a sure sign that he was troubled. Hollis scooped him up, took him into the study, and installed him in front of the computer. But the boy's interest in video games was less avid than usual tonight.

He said as Hollis started to leave, "Granpa? Is David coming back to hurt us?"

My God. "No way. What gave you that idea?"

"I heard Mama and Daddy talking. She's scared, like she was before."

"It's not David Rakubian she's scared of."

"Then how come we're gonna live with you and Granma again?"

"What did your mom tell you?"

"She said it's just for a little while. She said we never have to be afraid of David again, but I didn't believe her. Who's she scared of if it's not that asshole?"

"Not a nice word, kiddo."

"Mama says it sometimes. Lots of people say it."

"Well, they shouldn't and neither should you."

"Who're we afraid of now, Granpa?"

"A bad lady. But it won't be for long."

"What bad lady?"

"You don't know her. Don't worry, she won't hurt your mom. As long as I'm around, nobody's going to hurt anyone in this family ever again."

Eric called just before dinner. Hollis filled him in on the most recent developments, then turned him over to his sister.

The after-dinner conversation, with Kenny out of earshot in the study, was all about Valerie Burke. Angela said, "I had no idea she was so deeply involved with David, or that she was capable of so much hate. She always seemed . . . I guess the word I want is passionless. Colorless, too."

"She kept her feelings well hidden," Cassie said. "People like her often do."

Pierce asked, "Did Rakubian ever mention her?"

"Once or twice, but always professionally. I still can't imagine him with her. She isn't very attractive, and David was handsome if nothing else . . . they just don't seem to fit together."

"Physical attraction isn't everything."

"No, but still. What would make him want a woman like her?"

Hollis steered her away from that by asking, "You don't know anything at all about her? Where she was born, where she went to school, how she got into paralegal work?"

Angela shook her head. "The whole time I was with David, I barely knew she was alive. I mean, I saw her at his office two or three times but I didn't really pay attention to her. He never seemed to, either, unless she spoke to him directly. It was as if she was . . . I don't know . . ."

"A piece of furniture?" Cassie supplied.

"No. As if she was hardly even there."

"Like a shadow," Pierce said.

Like a phantom, Hollis thought.

Friday

A day like any other recently, except that he felt as though he were living it on the edge of a precipice: moving forward at a retarded pace, watching carefully where he walked, trying not to look down.

Cassie went to work at Animal Care because they were short-handed and needed her. Angela stayed home with Hollis and Kenny. Tom Finchley and his helper arrived to finish repainting the living room. The computer, the TV, and his mother kept Kenny out of mischief while Hollis tried to do a little work in his study. At eleven the Camden Home Security rep arrived with catalogs and a practiced sales pitch, and when he left forty minutes later he had a check for a thousand dollars and Hollis had a receipt for Camden's top-of-the-line security system and a promise that it would be installed the first of next week.

The phone rang twice: Mannix wondering if there was any news, Gloria with a question about one of their jobs. The silence from McCone Investigations must mean that Burke hadn't shown up at Rakubian's house last night.

Twelve-thirty. He bundled his daughter and grandson into the Lexus and drove downtown to the Mill, where Cassie met them for lunch. No one had much appetite, not even Kenny. Hollis felt exposed sitting there in the crowded restaurant, as if he were a character in an action film—one of those loud, messy flicks where somebody in a ski mask suddenly bursts in and opens fire with an automatic weapon. Nothing happened, of course, but by the time he pulled into the driveway at home he had developed a tension headache.

An abortive try at a nap, design work that went badly, a couple of mindless computer games with Kenny . . . the afternoon crawled away. The phone rang at 3:10: somebody wanting to sell him aluminum siding. Cassie came home at 3:50; Pierce showed up at 4:20. And just as Hollis was about to put in a call to McCone Investigations, the phone rang again and it was McCone herself on the other end.

Some news, but not the news he wanted to hear. Burke still hadn't been located. No-show at Rakubian's house, no fixed address after the one on Parnassus, no listing with any of the paralegal services or the American Society of Paralegals, no apparent affiliation with any legal firm in the Bay Area. The background check had produced a still-sketchy but emerging profile of an unstable woman: born in Chico, raised by a single father who ruled her upbringing with an iron hand until he died suddenly of a heart attack when she was eighteen. Married and pregnant at nineteen, to another dominant male who physically abused her and caused her child to be stillborn. Divorce, a mental breakdown that put her in a sanitorium for three months. Moved to San Francisco after her discharge in an effort to turn her life around. Studied law at Heald College, graduated, became an accredited paralegal, worked for one of the larger paralegal firms and a private law firm before joining

244 ◆ BILL PRONZINI

Rakubian's operation five years ago. No significant male presence in her life after her divorce and before or since her evident relationship with Rakubian.

Not a good profile, McCone said, but not necessarily an alarming one, either. The only documented violence in her background had been directed at her, not by her toward someone else. Even as unstable as she apparently was, she might not be capable of an act of overt violence against another person. Putting the best possible spin on it for their benefit, Hollis thought bleakly.

Drinks. Dinner. Talk. Two games of Monopoly that they all played more or less by rote. Early to bed and eyes wide open in the dark as usual. Long, dull, stressful day. Good because nothing had happened, bad because it meant they would have to do it all over again tomorrow and God knew how many days after that.

Saturday Morning

The weather turned clear again, windy but warmish. Kenny was in a tantrumy mood, and the combination of that and the paint smell from the living room drove Hollis outside shortly after breakfast. He didn't feel much like puttering in the garden. Or doing anything else, for that matter, but busy work would keep his body if not his mind occupied. The garden shed drew him. Its door had warped and needed planing and weather-stripping; he'd meant to do the repairs in the spring, hadn't gotten around to it with all the upheaval since then. This seemed as good a time as any for the task.

He got his tools, removed the door, set about shaving the bottom. The effort tired him more quickly than he cared to admit. He kept at it at a dogged but slower pace until the door fit the frame without sticking when he rehung it. He took it down again to add the weather stripping.

Cassie came out a few minutes past ten, saw the sweat

on his face—he was working in the direct sun now—and warned him against overdoing it. He grumbled a reply; he was not up to being mothered this morning.

She said, "We need some things from Safeway. Angela and Kenny are going with me."

"All right."

"After lunch I thought we could all drive to Santa Rosa, look at furniture and carpeting for the living room. It'll give us something to do."

"All right."

He finished the door, rehung it again, and decided he'd done a decent job. He still wasn't ready to go in and rest; he fiddled around inside the shed, rearranging things. He was done with that and on his way to the garage, to see what kind of chore he could find to do in there, when he heard the phone ring.

His first thought was that it might be Sharon McCone with news. He hurried inside, snagged the receiver on the kitchen extension on the fifth or sixth ring.

"Jack!" Cassie, her voice octaves higher than normal. Calling on her cell phone: the background was staticky. And there were other sounds, too . . . sobbing? "Oh, God, something terrible . . . Safeway, the parking lot . . ."

The sweat on him had turned icy; nerve endings contracted and wired him so tight his body thrummed. "What happened? Burke?"

"She was right there, but we never saw her until it was too late. She had a gun, it all happened so fast, I couldn't . . . We tried to catch her, but she's gone, I don't know where. The police . . . we're on our way there now. . . ."

"For God's sake, slow down, you're not making sense. What did Burke do?"

Ragged, hissing breath.

"Kenny . . . she took Kenny!"

24

THE police station was on North Main, not far from the Safeway where they regularly shopped. He reached it in less than ten minutes, driving as fast as he dared on city streets. The waiting room was empty; he rushed ahead to the bulletproof Plexiglas wall that bisected most of the ante-room, gripped the edge of the counter in front of the speaker opening.

"My name is Hollis, Jack Hollis," he said to the uni-formed cop on the desk. "My wife and daughter—"

"Yes, right, they're here. Mrs. Hollis is with Lieutenant Davidson, your daughter's resting in the women's lounge."

"My grandson . . . any word?"

"Not yet." The cop's tone was sympathetic. He was a few years older than Hollis, probably had grandchildren of his own. "We've got an APB out on the car—not just Paloma County, all of northern California. We'll find them."

When? How soon?

"I'd like to see my daughter."

"Right away. She's been asking for you."

The cop buzzed him in, led him back to the women's lounge. Angela was lying on a couch in there, a policewoman watching over her. She said, "Oh, Daddy!" when she saw him, and struggled to a sitting position. Tear tracks, stained black with mascara, covered her face; her eyes were enormous, too much white showing, not quite focused. The sick, impotent rage in him was close to unbearable now. She was trying to get up; he went to her, kissed her, murmured words that even to him sounded empty, and made her lie back again. When he glanced at the policewoman, she mouthed the words "Paramedics are on the way."

"Why?" Angela said in a choked voice. "Why would she kidnap Kenny?"

"I don't know, baby."

"What if she hurts him? He's so little. . . ."

"She won't hurt him." Wanting to believe it so desperately, he repeated the words. "She won't hurt him."

"They have to bring him back safe. They have to!"

"They will."

She made a little sobbing, hiccuping sound. "Ryan," she said. "Does he know?"

"Not yet. I'll call him right away."

"Tell him to hurry. Tell him . . . Kenny . . ."

It was too painful being in there with her. He felt awkward and helpless, not worth a damn to her or to himself. He left her with the policewoman, asked the desk cop for the use of a phone, called the Gugliotta ranch, and broke the news to Pierce. The kid wasted no time with questions; he said, "I'll be there as fast as I can," and broke the connection.

The paramedics had arrived; he saw them go into the women's lounge. A few seconds after that a gray-haired cop in uniform appeared. Lieutenant Max Davidson—Hollis knew him slightly from Rotary meetings. Davidson shook his hand with professional gravity, reiterated that everything possible was being done to find Hollis's grandson, and then ushered him down a hallway to a private office where Cassie was waiting. He let Hollis go in alone, shut the door after him to give them privacy.

When he embraced her she clung to him fiercely, with such strength he felt her fingers digging deep into his flesh. Gently he stood her off at arm's length so he could look at her. Pale, shaken, but in rigid control.

"I'm okay," she said. "But Angela . . ."

"I know, I just saw her. Shock. Paramedics are here, they'll give her something."

"She won't go to the hospital."

"No. And they won't force her to."

Cassie pulled on her lower lip, pinching it hard enough to turn it white. "It's our fault, Jack. We should've known that crazy bitch would go after Kenny."

"How could we know?"

"We should've been more careful, taken better precautions."

Hindsight, the great teacher. Nobody's ever completely safe. You can't live in a vacuum. Hollow clichés. He said, "Yes," and nodded like a ventriloquist's dummy.

"She won't hurt him. I keep telling myself she wouldn't go that far."

"No." *She might. We both know she might.* "Hold him for a day or two, then let him go."

"Angela won't be able to stand that kind of waiting."

"She won't have to. They'll find him."

"The FBI? Have they been notified yet?"

"I don't know, I'll ask Davidson. How much did you tell him about Burke?"

"Everything we know."

"Give him McCone's name?"

"Yes."

"She may have found out by now where Burke's been living. That has to be where she's taking Kenny."

"If she harms him, I swear to God I'll kill her."

"Don't talk like that."

"I mean it. I'll rip her fucking eyes out." She pinched her lip again; her eyes were haunted. "I should have *seen* her there. But I didn't, I just didn't."

"Seen her where?"

"Safeway lot. I looked around when we came out . . . so did Angela, but she had Kenny to contend with. It was my responsibility."

"Don't keep beating yourself up," he said. "If you'd been able to stop her, you would have."

"You weren't there, you don't know."

"Tell me what happened."

Cassie squeezed her eyes shut; shuddered and popped them open. "Everything seemed all right in the lot," she said. "The van was in the end row, on the Main Street side. When we got to it I unlocked the side door. . . . Angela was taking one of the bags out of the cart, Kenny right there beside her. All of a sudden she cried out, 'No, don't!' Burke . . . it was as though she materialized out of nowhere. Except she'd been there all along. She had hold of Kenny's arm, he was squirming and trying to pull free. In her other hand . . . a gun, a little automatic. She said something like, 'Don't either of you move or yell, I'll shoot the kid if you do.' Then she told me to put my car keys into her coat pocket. I had to do it, the gun was only a few inches from Kenny's head. Then she dragged him to her car, shoved him inside—the door was wide open—and slid in after him and I heard the door locks click. The engine must've been running, as fast as she drove away, but I don't remember hearing that. Just the door locks clicking. Kenny's face . . . I'll never forget the way he looked.

Pressed to the window glass, his mouth open as if he was screaming . . ."

"Easy."

"It all happened so fast. Just a few seconds. And then she was gone onto North Main. Angela was yelling, people were staring, but not one of them came over to try to help. I ran and got the spare key out of the bumper case, but I was so wild I dropped it and had trouble picking it up. By the time we were in the van and moving, there was no sign of them. I thought we might be able to catch up at one of the stoplights . . . my Lord, I must've driven like a maniac all the way to Corona Road. She must've turned off somewhere . . . I don't know. Angela was hysterical. Screaming at me to keep going to the freeway interchange. But it was too late, we were just wasting time. She tried to grab the wheel when I turned around at Corona and I had to slap her to get her off me."

"You said Burke was there all along in the lot. Where?"

"In the space next to the van. Not when we arrived, when we came out with the groceries. Either she followed us from home, or found out somehow Saturday morning is when I shop and was waiting there for us."

"Cass, how could she've been parked next to the van and you didn't notice? A white Nissan—"

"That's just it. We were looking for a white Nissan, but she was driving a silver BMW."

"A silver—"

"Rakubian's car. Her Nissan must be in his garage."

Saturday Noon

Pierce got there just as the paramedics were about to leave. As upset as he was, he handled the situation far better than he would have when he was younger. Took charge of Angela, and as soon as he'd been briefed, bundled her into his pickup and drove her home.

Hollis met with Lieutenant Davidson, Police Chief Reese, who'd been summoned from home, and two ranking county cops from Santa Rosa. The FBI hadn't been called in yet and he wanted them to do it right away. Premature, they said. But the plain truth was, local law didn't like federal law; they intimated that the feds took over, pushed everyone around, and exacerbated the jurisdictional problems that already existed between city and county law enforcement. Angrily he insisted on the family's behalf, and because he was considered a prominent citizen and they were all scared to death of adverse publicity, they gave in. If Burke and Kenny weren't found by one o'clock, the FBI office in San Francisco would be notified. The one issue they all agreed on was that a media lid should be kept on the kidnapping as long as possible. Reporters, TV remote crews, crowds of sensation seekers would make matters even more difficult for everybody.

When the meeting broke up, he and Cassie drove home separately. To be with Angela. To wait.

Saturday Afternoon

One o'clock.

Neither the phone nor the doorbell had rung.

At 1:10 Hollis called Chief Reese. Yes, the FBI had been informed on schedule. Agents were on their way from the city; they'd be by to talk to the family within a couple of hours if the status remained unchanged. Reese tried to sound confident; he succeeded only in sounding grim.

Time, accelerated at first, ground down until each minute was like a slow-forming, slow-falling droplet of water. The four of them waited in the house, in the backyard, in the house again. Even after the effects of the sedative began to wear off, Angela stayed more or less calm. Pierce's presence, even more than his and Cassie's, seemed to have a soothing effect on her; she sat clinging to his hand and staring at the phone as if willing it to ring. Hollis had called Eric shortly after their return, gotten his answering machine, left a message to call his father's cell number; that phone, too, remained silent. They drank too much coffee, talked little because the only things left to say were too painful to express. Hollis's prostate started to bother him; he kept going in to stand at the toilet and dribbling as slowly as the time was passing, unable to relieve much of the pressure.

Two o'clock. 2:15. 2:30. And the phone didn't sound and no one came and the minutes continued to drip, drip, drip away.

3:05. Doorbell. They all jumped and Hollis hurried to open the door. The FBI, but not to tell them what they needed to hear. One sixtyish Jewish male, one fortyish black female: the Hoover days of young, crew-cut, blank-faced, Anglo-Saxon clones were long gone. Special Agents Feldman and Lincoln. No-bullshit types—polite, businesslike, efficient. Half an hour's worth of detailed Q & A, all of it recorded. The only information they had to impart was that they'd been in touch with McCone Investigations; there were still no leads as to Burke's whereabouts, but the profile that had been compiled might prove helpful. Exit Feldman and Lincoln, leaving cold comfort behind.

Four o'clock.

Four-thirty.

Five o'clock.

No word from anybody, including Eric.

Five-thirty. Cassie heated soup, set out a plate of sliced

bread. None of them ate more than a few mouthfuls, Angela nothing at all.

Six o'clock.

And Pierce said abruptly, "I can't take any more of this sitting around, it's driving me nuts. I've got to *do* something. Drive out by Corona Road, check some of the back roads . . . maybe the cops missed seeing that BMW. For all we know, Burke's holding Kenny somewhere around here."

Hollis thought it was a good idea. "We'll both go," he said.

"Together or separately?"

"Two cars cover twice as much territory."

Angela didn't want them to leave; the cocooning was what had been getting her through this. Pierce soft-talked her into accepting it. All Cassie said was, "Don't stay out past dark unless there's a good reason," and they both agreed to that.

She gave Ryan her cell phone and Hollis wrote down the number of his so they'd all be connected. Then he and Pierce divided the ground to be covered—Ryan the east side from North Main to the Paloma Mountains, Hollis the west side as far out as Two Rock Valley. They were in their cars and rolling by 6:15.

Saturday Evening

Driving aimlessly was only a little more endurable than the passive waiting. At home there'd been a few distractions; in the Lexus there were none. Drive a random route, stare around at too-familiar sights, think too much. Worry too much. Imagine and fear too much.

Back roads, side roads, motels, campgrounds, even a couple of abandoned farms. Seeing nothing out of the ordinary. Waiting for his cell phone to ring. Praying it would and dreading what he might hear if it did.

Time passed less slowly when you were on the move. Seven o'clock, 7:30. He came back into town to fill the gas tank, headed west again. Eight o'clock. 8:15.

8:20. He was on Roblar Road, west of the Washoe House bar and restaurant, when the phone went off.

The unit was on the seat beside him, the sudden sound like a blade slicing into a nerve. He snatched it up, flicked it on. "Cass? Is there any—"

"How does it feel, Hollis? How does it feel to really suffer?"

His heart lurched. In reflex his foot jabbed the brake and he twisted the wheel. The Lexus slid to a rocking stop at the side of the road.

"Now you know what it's been like for me," the voice said in his ear. Calm, steady, no hint of mania—except that the mania was there, hidden but palpable, like laughter behind the walls of an asylum. "Hurt, hurt, hurt all the time. Burning in the fires of hell."

"Let me—" The words caught; he cleared his throat. "Let me talk to my grandson."

"No."

"Is he all right? You haven't . . ."

"Not yet. Not *yet*."

Hate and fury boiled in him. *Don't provoke her!* He forced a plea through the dry cavern of his mouth. "Please don't hurt him. He's just a little boy."

"I had a little boy once. He died before he was even born."

"Do you want me to beg, Valerie?"

"Oh, so you do know who this is. Good. I want you to know."

"All right, then I'll beg—"

"Because it doesn't matter anymore," she said. "You'll never never find me in time. No one will."

"What're you going to do?"

"You'll find out." In the brief pause between those words and the next, he heard a background noise. It was quiet on the road, quiet in the car except for the purr of the engine, and the connection was clear. So was the sound—a kind of whistling. "Soon, Hollis. Very soon."

"I'll do anything you want," he said. "Trade myself for the boy. You can kill me if that's what you—"

"No. That would be too easy."

"Tell me what isn't too easy. Tell me what it'll take for you not to harm my grandson."

"You don't understand, do you? I already have what I want and I'm going to do the only thing that's left to do." Another pause, and he heard the background noise again. Louder, even more distinct: a whistling and then a shrill howling. "I told your wife and now I'm telling you. You took David away from me, you and that bitch daughter of yours. You made me kill him. You destroyed my life. Well, now I'm going to take someone you love away from you. Now I'm going to destroy all *your* lives."

"Wait, listen to me

"Suffer like I'm suffering!" And the line went dead.

She means it, she'll kill Kenny, and she won't take long to do it. Tonight, after it gets dark. . . . Evil needs the dark.

The phone rang in his hand.

Cassie, he thought, to report Burke's call to her. Instead of answering he turned off the unit, threw it on the other seat. He could not talk to her now; couldn't talk to anyone now. He put the car in gear, came down hard on the accelerator, the tires squealing as he pulled away. Driving this time with urgency and purpose. Praying he'd get there in time.

He knew where they were, Kenny and that crazy woman.

The freakish whistling and howling had told him; they were sounds like no other he'd ever heard, sounds high winds made in an old, warped chimney flue.

She'd taken the boy to the one place no one had thought to look: the cottage at Tomales Bay.

25

Saturday Night

FIFTEEN miles.

So close, so far away. Driving too fast and not fast enough on the two-lane country roads, doing all the road-rage things—tailgating, flashing his lights and sounding his horn—that he despised in other drivers. Kenny's image luminous in his mind: pocket-sized, defenseless, so full of laughter and innocent mischief, saying, "I love you, Granpa," saying, "Who're we afraid of now?" And himself looking down into that shining little face and vowing, not once but twice, with stupid, hollow arrogance, that he wouldn't let him or anyone else in the family be hurt.

Fifteen miles.

Valerie Burke. He hated her intensely, yet it was a different kind of hatred than he'd felt—still felt—for Rakubian. Tempered with grains of pity. She was another of that bastard's victims, an instrument of his vengeance as well as her own—as if he really were reaching out from the grave. Sick, shattered woman, but cunning. As cunning as

Rakubian. She'd picked the perfect spot to take the boy. Knew about the cottage from his conversation with Rakubian . . . found out exactly where it was located from public records, the same way she'd gotten his cell phone number . . . found out it was seldom used anymore by going there, looking around. For all he knew she'd been squatting there off and on since giving up her apartment in the city.

Fifteen miles.

A small, insistent voice kept urging him to call the FBI, the county police, or to call Cassie and have her do it. He didn't listen, could not obey. Explanations, the grinding of official wheels—he'd be out to Tomales Bay himself before deputies or Agents Feldman and Lincoln had time to respond. And the law would go in announcing their presence, with bullhorns and drawn weapons, or else take too much time to mobilize a more stealthy approach. There was so little time. And he knew the property, the whole area, far better than anyone else.

Fifteen miles.

Time, time, time . . .

Two Rock Valley, the Coast Guard training station, Tomales, the narrow coiling stretch of Highway 1 leading to the bay—the last few miles a fragmented blur like the drive across San Francisco with Rakubian's body in the trunk. Almost dusk when he saw the gleam of water off to his right, gunmetal gray flecked with gold from the last rays of the sun, the trees and rocks of Hog Island bathed in the same golden glow. Fantasy, illusion: darkness waited, eating away at the light.

He was focused again, intently aware of his surroundings, when he passed Nick's Cove. The cottage was a half-mile beyond there. He made himself slow down, take the sharp curves along this stretch without having to brake hard and fight the wheel. Time, time! The bay was dark gray now, all the gold bled away, the sky over the hills above Inverness a fading salmon pink. Full dark in fifteen or twenty minutes.

Ahead, at long last, he saw the trees that separated the highway from the cottage. He was alone here, no other cars; he slowed even more, hunching sideways to peer through the screen of pines. First glimpse of the cottage: no lights showing, no sign of the silver BMW. But that meant nothing one way or another. There was only one window on this side, and from the highway you couldn't tell if the shutter louvers were open or not. And the BMW could be hidden inside the garage. Burke would not have had much difficulty getting into either building. The locks on both were flimsy; there had never been a break-in here and he'd seen no reason to replace them. A kid could have smashed them open with a rock or a tire iron.

He fought off the impulse to turn into the access lane. He'd be too exposed approaching the cottage from this direction; she might be at the kitchen table, the louvers open so she could look out toward the highway. When he rolled on past he had one last, partial view of the place. Still nothing to see.

He accelerated through the two short uphill turns beyond, the longer one downhill through a patch of thick woods. At the bottom was a grassy verge broken by deep grooves that led in to a closed gate. Past the gate and below the woods was a peninsula, short and humped in the middle—land that belonged to a dairy rancher and that was used for cattle graze. He stopped crosswise on the ruts, leaned over to unlock the glove compartment. He tore the chamois cloth off the Colt Woodsman and jammed the gun into his jacket pocket.

The wind was strong here, whipping in off the bay with enough force to billow his coat and bend him at the middle as he hurried to the gate. The highway was deserted; he climbed over quickly, ran along the overgrown ruts until they petered out into a single-groove cow track near the top of the hump. Prostate pain and back pain surged with every step; he blocked his mind against it, against the fatigue he felt. Functioning now on urgency and adrenaline.

On the far side, short-cropped grass and clumps of gorse sloped down to the water's edge. Earthquake fissures showed like dark scars among the green. He followed the longest of them, still bent by the thrust of the wind, the smells of salt water and tide flats sharp in his nostrils. Halfway down he veered away at an angle to an inlet on the north side. The mudflats there had once been the property of a long-defunct oyster company; decaying bed stakes jutted out of the mud at oblique angles like rotting teeth. He skirted a strip of beach and a fan of discarded oyster shells, followed the outward curve of the shoreline.

It was almost dark now, only a faint band of light showing along the horizon, the rest of the sky a velvety purple. He had to slow down, because he could no longer see more than a few yards in front of him. The flash from the car would have helped, but he hadn't brought it because he could not afford to risk showing light. It wasn't far now anyway to where he'd be in sight of the cottage—just around a gorse-covered neck of land ahead.

A gull came swooping in over the tide flats as he cleared the neck; its thin shrieking made him grit his teeth. The only other sound was the beating of the wind. The cold had numbed him, raised gooseflesh on his arms. He kept his hands in his coat pockets, his fingers loose and restless around the handle of the .22.

Now he could make out the cottage, sixty yards away, dark and squatty between the pines and the faintly gleaming surface of the bay. It was directly in front of him and there were no windows in the south-side wall; even if Burke were looking out toward the bay, she wouldn't be able to spot him in the darkness at this angle. He expected to see light glowing behind the deck doors—the drapes were old and a bad fit, leaving gaps at the edges and in the middle—but there was none. A hollow churning started under his breastbone as he slogged ahead. Wrong about the whistling and howling, and she hadn't brought Kenny here after all? Or had she been here and gone because she'd already carried out her threat? Both possibilities were intolerable; he blocked them out as he blocked out the pain and fatigue.

The shoreline became a wide stretch of gravel and mud, and he cut inland onto firmer ground. An unseen rock caught the toe of his shoe and he stumbled, nearly fell. It was like moving in a dream, the darkness closing down, objects losing definition, shadows gathering into grotesque shapes. Sweat flowed and chilled on his body. The cottage seemed no closer, no larger, as if he were stepping in place instead of progressing forward—a delusion that lasted until he could make out the dock, the attached float where Pop had died. Then it was as if the building were too close, too large, a hulking presence in the night.

A faint petroleum smell came to him as he reached the dock. He glanced out over the water; there were no powerboats in the vicinity, no running lights anywhere. The old wood landing at the foot of the stairs creaked when he climbed onto it, but the gusty wind was loud enough to hide the sounds he made from anyone other than himself. He paused halfway up the stairs to listen. Just the wind. Even the gulls were quiet now.

When he reached the top he detoured away from the cottage, around behind the sagging garage. In the wallboards back there were gaps where they'd buckled and separated; he bent to peer through the largest of them. All he could see were layers of black. He took out his key ring, poked its

mini-flashlight through the gap, and flicked it on just long
enough for a quick look.

The BMW was parked inside.

Burke was here, Kenny must be here too.

But why hadn't she put the lights on? Holed up in the
cottage in the dark . . . he didn't like that. Nerving herself?
That must be it. She wouldn't still be here if she'd already
harmed the boy, would she?

Quickly he went back the way he'd come, approaching
the cottage at a diagonal, his footfalls on the dry pine needles muffled by the wind. The shutters were closed over the
kitchen window; he couldn't see in, she couldn't see out. He
edged up to the door. His breathing came short and ragged;
he sucked air in openmouthed drags as he unpocketed the
Woodsman. The wind shifted, moaning, and then gusted as
if it, too, were having trouble with oxygen. He caught another brief whiff of petroleum.

He could not just stand out here and wait for something
to happen. Get inside fast and as quietly as he could, put a
light on right away, do whatever the situation dictated. Point
and shoot, Hollis—literally, if that's what it takes. He knew
he could pull the trigger this time, without hesitation or
compunction.

He laid his left hand on the doorknob. If the lock was on,
he'd use his key.

The lock wasn't on.

He turned the knob, heard the latch click, eased the door
inward. And the petroleum smell came rolling out at him as
if released, strong and pungent, flaring his nostrils, closing
his throat.

Gasoline.

A lot of it, spilled around inside.

Oh God, no!

He let the wind take the door, blow it inward until it

bound up tight halfway on the uneven floor. He stepped in past it, fighting panic. The gasoline stink was everywhere in the clotted darkness, overpowering, nauseating.

There was no wall switch; the nearest light source was the pullstring to the globe over the kitchen table. Every inch of the interior was burned into his memory—the table three steps to his left, no obstructions in between. He took one step, two—

A snick, a rasp, and a small flame bloomed suddenly in the black. The yellow flare chased shadows, showed him pieces of a nightmare scene out of one of Rakubian's Goya paintings.

Burke was sitting in Pop's old Morris chair, turned so that she was facing toward him. Sitting there almost primly, knees together, the flame jutting from a cigarette lighter held up in front of her and steady now because her hand was steady. It threw off enough light so that he could make out the horsehair sofa nearby, distinguish the small, unmoving, blanket-covered mound on the cushions. He saw something more, too, that froze his blood and brought a stillborn cry into his throat.

In the flickery glow, everything gleamed wetly: the floor, the window drapes, the chair, the sofa, the blanketed mound, her upraised arm and high-necked blouse and composed face and white-rimmed eyes staring out of shadowed black. She'd soaked it all, soaked Kenny, soaked herself with the gasoline.

Not just murder, suicide too.

Burning in the fires of hell.

She said in a clear, calm voice, "So you found me after all. But not in time, Hollis."

"For God's sake, don't—"

"Too late. Too late."

"No!"

She said, "Suffer!" with a kind of fierce joy, and flung the lighter at the sofa.

Hollis lunged that way in the same instant, dropping the .22. The lighter struck the backrest, bounced onto the blanket covering the boy, and then, still lit, skittered to the floor. Flame spurted, surged, whooshed up and out at him. Frantically he tore the burning blanket off and hurled it aside. *Kenny, Kenny!* Hollis grabbed him and swung him up—his small body wasn't wet, she'd only doused the blanket—a moment before the cushions became a nest of fire.

The woman screamed.

He spun around, crouching, cradling Kenny's limp form against his chest, covering the child's head and face with his free arm. The racing flames had swept back and up, consuming Pop's chair, consuming Valerie Burke. She came out of the chair as if propelled, sheeted with fire, shrieking her torment. He twisted aside as she lurched toward him, saw her whirl the other way and carom off the fireplace bricks with her arms spread wide—demon's dance, blazing vision from the pit.

The fire was all around him now, spreading with incredible speed. He staggered in the direction of the door, gagging on oily smoke and the stink of cooking flesh, the heat singeing his hair and eyebrows, his body hunched and both arms wrapped protectively around the child. His shoes felt as though the soles were burning; sparks stung his face, his neck above the coat collar. He couldn't see. He bumped into something—the door!—and groped around it, tasting the cold breath of the night outside, the crackle-thrum of the flames and Burke's banshee screams swelling in his ears. Then he was through, out, running and gasping into the night.

The wind cooled his feet, his face; he could no longer

feel the fire at his back. Or hear the shrieks. He began to shiver. He slowed then, stopped, and for the first time glanced back. He'd covered more than fifty yards, uphill into the trees—a safe enough distance.

Kenny.

He lifted the boy, turning his head so he could look closely at his face in the reflected glow.

Alive . . . thank God!

Breathing more or less normally except for little whimpers and coughs. The fire hadn't touched him—no burn marks, not even his hair singed. Didn't look as though Burke had harmed him in any other way. His features had a scrunched look, eyes squeezed shut in fitful sleep. She must have given him a drug of some kind that was now beginning to wear off.

Relief had weakened Hollis's knees. He wobbled a couple of paces to his left, hugging his grandson close, close, and leaned heavily against the bole of a pine. Through wet and stinging eyes he stared at the cottage. It was an inferno now, all roiling smoke and high-licking flames that stained the night sky ocher and blood-red. Before long there would be nothing left but blackened bones and ash. He felt no sense of loss or regret. *Yours in every way, Pop, never really mine.*

Yellow-red blossomed in the dry needles that had collected on the garage roof. Pretty soon wind-flung sparks would ignite the crowns of the closest pines and this whole section would burn. For that he did feel regret. Over the beat of the conflagration he was aware of sounds behind him, cars stopping on the highway, voices shouting. He stayed where he was a few moments longer. Afterimages of the horror he'd just witnessed and lived through lingered in his mind, yet he was filled with a strange kind of peace.

Survival. Everything else stemmed from it, depended on

it. Love, hate, all the emotions; the lives we lead, who we are. He'd given it to Kenny tonight, to Cassie and Angela and Eric in other ways. God willing, Stan Otaki would give it to him and he'd have plenty of time to atone for all the mistakes he'd made.

He turned his back on the burning past, on the death throes of their evil time, and moved on to what lay ahead.